Dog Have

Mercy

A Golden Retriever
Mystery
by Neil S. Plakcy

Neil S. Plakcy

Copyright 2015 Neil S. Plakcy. All rights reserved, including the right of reproduction in whole or in part in any form.

This book is a work of fiction. Names, characters, places, and incidents either are products of the author's imagination or are used fictitiously. Any resemblance to actual events or locales or persons, living or dead, is entirely coincidental.

Reviews for the Golden Retriever Mysteries:

Mr. Plakcy did a terrific job in this cozy mystery. He had a smooth writing style that kept the story flowing evenly. The dialogue and descriptions were right on target.
--Red Adept

Steve and Rochester become quite a team and Neil Plakcy is the kind of writer that I want to tell me this story. It's a fun read which will keep you turning pages very quickly.
--Amos Lassen – Amazon top 100 reviewer

We who love our dogs know that they are wiser than we are, and Plakcy captures that feeling perfectly with the relationship between Steve and Rochester.
-- Christine Kling, author of *Circle of Bones*

In Dog We Trust is a very well-crafted mystery that kept me guessing up until Steve figured out where things were going.
--E-book addict reviews

1 – Pet Therapy

I DIDN'T THINK THAT MY GOLDEN RETRIEVER Rochester would be calm enough to visit nursing home patients, because he was always eager to pull me down the street, jump up on strangers and lick effusively. But he surprised me when we went to visit Edith Passis at Crossing Manor, the nursing and rehab center where she had gone to recuperate from a broken hip.

Edith was my childhood piano teacher, and she'd been one of the first people I reconnected with when I returned home to Stewart's Crossing, a small town along the Delaware River in scenic Bucks County, Pennsylvania. With both my parents gone, I'd enjoyed keeping in touch with her as a reminder of my childhood.

She loved Rochester, the big, goofy golden I had adopted two years before, and when I called to check on her, she'd asked if he could come by to say hello. "People bring dogs in all the time," she said. "Those tiny ones. I'd love to see Rochester."

I called the Manor to be sure he'd be welcome, and the administrator said that as long as he could behave I could bring him. So one Saturday morning in mid-December, when the roads were clear of snow and the sun was shining brilliantly, my girlfriend Lili and I loaded him into my ancient BMW sedan for a visit.

It seemed strange to call Lili my girlfriend when we were both in our forties, and had already been living together for a couple of months, but the English language hasn't caught up with modern-day dating practices. She was a professor of visual art and chair of the fine arts department at Eastern College, where I also worked, and sometimes I looked at her, her auburn curls cascading around her heart-shaped face, so beautiful and smart and funny, and marveled at

Neil S. Plakcy

my luck in finding her.

A block before we reached the rehab center we passed a man wrapped in ragged layers pushing a rickety shopping cart piled with cans and newspapers and other unidentified packages. A brown teddy bear with a missing arm was strapped to the front.

"That's so sad," Lili said. "Every time I see someone who looks like they live on the streets I wonder how our society can consider itself progressive when we don't take care of all our citizens."

"Some of us are lucky," I said.

Crossing Manor was a low-slung building down by the Delaware River at the edge of town. A couple of tall pines stood sentinel by the front doors, but the rest of the landscaping was brown, from the grass to the leafless maples and oaks. Shortly before he passed away, my father had spent some time there, recovering from a stroke, and my inability to visit him then still haunted me.

I signaled to turn into the driveway, but had to wait for a hearse from the local funeral home to pull in first. I felt a chill and remembered that many of the patients at Crossing Manor might be leaving like that.

But at least they'd have died of natural causes, unlike those whose deaths Rochester and I had investigated. My neighbor Caroline, who had originally adopted Rochester as a rescue; my old friend and mentor Joe Dagorian; and others Rochester and I had met, known, and lost. I reached over and squeezed Lili's hand, glad that she was by my side, and that my happy dog was behind me.

Once the hearse had turned in and driven around to the back of the property, I parked and we went inside, to a cheery, clean lobby festooned with photos of staff and patients and posters about bingo night, exercise groups and what to do if someone was choking. Signage indicated that Crossing Manor was home to both short-term rehab patients, and those who needed long-term care. One poster had a photo of a woman whose lip was curled oddly, and the legend "This woman is having a stroke. Get help immediately."

"You be good, Rochester," I said, holding my dog on a tight leash. He walked proudly, his head up and his plumy tail waving from side to side.

A plump thirty-something whose name tag read Cindee sat behind the reception desk, a wooden semi-circle stacked with Crossing Manor brochures. A teenaged girl in scrubs decorated with cartoon animals stood beside her. The girl had shoulder-length blonde hair and her right eyebrow was pierced with a small gold ring. "What a beautiful boy," she said. "Can I pet him?"

When she spoke I saw that her tongue had been pierced as well, and repressed a grimace. "Sure," I said. "Rochester, sit."

He plopped his furry butt on the ground and looked up at the girl, who offered him her palm to sniff. "I have a teacup Yorkie at home," she said.

He didn't lean forward the way he usually did with new friends, but I assumed that was because he was trying to be quiet and gentle, or perhaps because he could smell the Yorkie on her.

I signed the visitor's book. "My name is Steve Levitan," I said to the receptionist. "We're here to see Edith Passis."

Cindee looked at me. "Any relation to Dave Levitan?" she asked. "He was a patient here a couple of years ago. Very sweet man."

"That was my dad," I said.

She nodded. "He came in right after I started, which is why I remember him so well. He used to come out to the desk and talk to me. I think he was lonely, poor thing."

A pain rose from the pit of my chest. He was lonely because his only child was in prison in California and couldn't come to see him.

Lili must have sensed my unhappiness because she took my hand. Her right arm was stacked with silver bangles that tinkled softly as she raised it. She'd worn an old pair of LL Bean duck boots that morning, and they gave her an extra inch in height, so she was almost at my six-one. "Where can we find Edith?" she asked.

"She's in the lounge. I can take you down there," the girl said. "I'm Allison." Rochester ignored her hand, instead rearing up to sniff her pants pocket, then going back to the floor. Allison suddenly reached down to pat her pocket.

"Oh, no, did he take something from you?" I asked. "He likes to grab tissues."

Rochester lay down on the floor and I could see he had spit whatever was in his mouth out between his paws. It was the shape of a tube of lipstick, but I couldn't see anything more because Allison quickly reached down and grabbed it from him.

She slipped the tube back into her pocket. "The dining room, exercise rooms and offices are to the right," she said as she led us through a door to the left. "There are twenty-four rooms with capacity for fifty patients, though some of the triple rooms have only two patients in them right now."

Most of the rooms we passed were empty, and when I asked, Allison said, "The nurses like to get the patients up and out of bed whenever they can. And it gives the staff a chance to clean the rooms."

Rochester was behaving very well, walking by my side, not pulling or stopping to sniff anywhere. I was impressed.

"Are you a nurse?" Lili asked Allison.

"Oh, no, I'm still in high school. I'm really interested in science, so I'm a volunteer here. Kind of like a candy striper. I was one of those at the hospital until they told me I had to leave."

I'd never heard of someone being kicked out of a candy striper program – usually the kids either got bored, or finished their required hours of community service. I had a couple of friends in high school who volunteered that way, and all they ever did was push people around in wheelchairs, fill water pitchers and fetch magazines.

Crossing Manor seemed like the kind of place few teenagers would be willing to volunteer, so perhaps the administrators had been willing to overlook whatever Allison had done wrong at the hospital.

She stopped at the doorway to a large room where a documentary about the clubbing of baby seals was playing. Patients sat in chairs and lay on gurneys positioned around the room, some watching the TV, others looking out the large windows to the parking lot. A few just stared into space.

Edith sat in a large armchair with her feet planted on the floor. Her normally puffy white hair was flat against her head, and her salmon-pink skin had faded, but her eyes were still fierce and blue, and she smiled when she saw us. "You came!" she said.

Rochester gently tugged me toward Edith, as if he knew what his purpose was. He sat obediently by her side, sniffing, and she reached down to scratch behind his ears. "Oh, this is such a treat!" she said.

Lili pulled over a couple of chairs for herself and me, and we sat. "How are you doing, Edith?" she asked.

"I'm getting stronger," she said. "I can't wait to get back to my own house, so I'm working extra hard at my therapy. You get so weak so quickly when they have you lying in bed, you know. But I can stand on my own now, and put weight on my new hip. So I should be going home in a few days."

An emaciated elderly woman on a gurney beside Edith extended her hand toward Rochester, and he turned in her direction, allowing her hand to rest on his head. "That's Mrs. Tuttle," Edith said. "Poor thing has dementia. She doesn't usually respond to any of the staff. I'm surprised she reached out to Rochester."

"He has that effect on people." I watched as Mrs. Tuttle caressed Rochester's head for a moment, then brought her hand back up and smiled a gap-toothed grin. A bag of fluid hung on a movable stanchion beside her, with a tube running into her arm. "They must have a nursing staff here, if they give IV fluids," I said to Edith.

"They can give us basic care," Edith said. "I read about it in their brochure before I agreed to come here. Some of the patients have PICC lines – you know, those long-term catheters—and the nurses can use those to dispense medications. They also give insulin shots, clean wounds and change tubes and so on."

She looked over at the woman beside her. "Mrs. Tuttle is my roommate. She was throwing up this morning and when the doctor stopped by to see her he said she was badly dehydrated. He's the one who ordered the IV, but he said that if she didn't respond to the fluids they'd have to send her to the hospital."

She shook her head. "Poor thing. I pray I don't end up like that. When God is ready for me, I hope he takes me quickly."

"Let's hope he won't be ready for you for quite a while," Lili said.

From across the room, an elderly black man called, "Can I pet your dog?"

I looked at Edith for permission. "You go on, I don't want to be greedy," she said.

While Lili sat with Edith and chatted, I took Rochester on a circuit of the room. The old man, Mr. MacRae, had a smooth, ebony face with a bit of grizzle at his chin, and short, nappy iron-gray hair. He had been a janitor at Crossing Elementary when I was a kid, and he remembered a couple of the teachers who'd made an impression on me.

"How long have you been here?" I asked.

"Going on five years now," he said. "My kidneys ain't no good anymore, and they take me for the dialysis. My kids done grown up and moved on, and I can't live on my own, so I thank God and

Franklin Roosevelt for the Social Security and the Medicaid."

A very short, skinny man in his fifties walked into the lounge leaning heavily on a cane. His face lit up when he saw Rochester, and once he was settled in a chair Rochester went over to be petted. "I could never have a dog when I was a kid," the man said. "Too sick to take care of one. But I always wanted one."

He looked down at Rochester. "What's your name, handsome?"

"He's Rochester," I said. "I'm Steve. Levitan."

"Mark Pappas." He looked at me. "You grow up around here?"

"I did. In the Lakes. You?"

"I thought you looked familiar. I live on Lakefront Drive."

Though he was a few years older than I was, the Lakes was a compact neighborhood centered around two lakes – Mirror Lake and Reading Lake – and most of the kids knew each other. I vaguely remembered Mark as a sickly kid who often missed school. It was a shame that he was still so sick as an adult.

As we moved around I learned that Mrs. Curry, a quadriplegic woman in her sixties, had been at the Manor for nearly twenty years, while Mr. Bodnar, who was about my age, had been there for fifteen. "Got hit by a car when I was walking down State Street in Trenton," he said. "Cut my lumbar spine like that. If it wasn't for these people here, I'd have been dead long ago."

It was awfully sad. I was glad when we finally made our way back to Edith; at least she had a chance to go home soon. Not that the place was terrible; the certified nursing assistants who moved around the room seemed genuinely caring, and the patients were clean, their sheets and bandages white and fresh. Posters advertised bingo nights, card games and knitting circles, and relatively new movies were shown on Tuesday afternoons. Motivational posters of beautiful landscapes urged patients to soar, believe and achieve.

"Now, no more walking on ice," Lili said to Edith as we prepared to leave. "If you ever need anything, you call us, all right? One of us can bring you groceries or clear your walk for you."

Edith had no children of her own, though I knew that many of her former piano students considered her part of their families. "I hate to impose," Edith said.

"It's not an imposition. Do you have someone to take you care of you at home when you're ready?"

Edith nodded. "I have a long-term care policy, so as soon as I'm

Dog Have Mercy

ready I can go home and have an aide live with me for a few weeks until I can get around easily."

We both kissed her goodbye and Rochester led the way back out to the front door. Allison was chatting with an older woman I thought might be a doctor. "That's Rochester," Allison said to the woman. "He's a sweetheart."

"I'm Marilyn Joiner," the woman said, walking over to us. She wore a pink wool turtleneck under her lab coat, with an intricate gold chain around her neck. Her straight brown hair was flecked with gray. "I'm the administrator here. I happened to look into the lounge when you were visiting. Thank you so much for coming. I'm a big proponent of pet therapy, and so many of our patients respond very well to dogs and cats."

"We're happy to be of help," I said.

"Do you think you might come back sometime? I know you came to visit Edith, but she'll be going home soon. As you may have seen, we have a mix of long-term and short-term patients—it's something that Manor Associates does with facilities in small towns, to keep people close to family and friends. But some of our long-term residents have no one to visit them, and I'm sure they'd appreciate seeing your handsome boy."

"We'd be happy to," Lili said. We waved goodbye to Allison as we walked outside. As soon as the door was closed, Rochester nearly pulled my arm off tugging me over to the base of a pine tree, where he lifted his leg.

"Good boy," I said when he was finished. I reached down to scratch around the scruff of his neck. "You were very well-behaved in there. I'm proud of you."

He nodded his head and woofed once.

"Sometimes I think that dog really understands you," Lili said.

"I know he does."

On the ride home, I wondered how my father had done at Crossing Manor. Because I was in prison at the time, I couldn't fly back to visit him. Had anyone else? He could be a prickly guy, and I could remember many times when he'd yelled at me as a kid, usually because I mouthed off to him. But he also had a lot of friends from work and from our old neighborhood. I hoped he'd had good care and the love of those around him.

9

Neil S. Plakcy

2 – Final Papers

ON THE WAY HOME, we stopped at the supermarket so Lili could run in and pick up a few things she needed for the dinner she was preparing that night for my friend Rick and Tamsen, the woman he was dating. Rick and I hadn't seen each other for a while; I'd been nesting with Lili after she moved into the townhouse with me and Rochester, and he'd been spending time with Tamsen and her young son.

Rick and I were the same age, though he was graying faster than I was – probably all the stress of police work. He was a couple of inches shorter than I was, and more muscular, from running and regular gym workouts. We'd first met in high school chemistry class, becoming pals over fumbled experiments. When I returned to Stewart's Crossing we'd met up again at the Chocolate Ear café, and bonded once more over bad divorces. He was a detective with the Stewart's Crossing police department, and occasionally Rochester and I had been able to help him with investigations, often against his will.

As soon as Lili got out of the car at the grocery, Rochester tried to squirm his way between the seats to the front. At eighty-plus pounds, though, he was having trouble, and I pushed gently on his chest to reinforce that he belonged in the back. "You stay there, puppy." I turned in my seat to face him. "Did you have a good time today? Did you like having all those people pay attention to you?"

I already knew the answer was yes. Rochester was true to his breed – a happy dog who loved attention, was gentle with kids and was always ready to play. I had worried a bit about how he'd react to having Lili move in, when he wouldn't be the center of my life any more. But instead, he'd been delighted to have another human around for tummy rubs and treats. Lili and I often walked him together after dinner and talked about our days as he sniffed and

Dog Have Mercy

peed. I called Rochester my Velcro dog, because he always wanted to be around me, curled around behind my office chair or lying on the floor beside my bed. It was nice to have another person in the house he could pay attention to sometimes.

As the time Lili was in the grocery stretched out, I took Rochester for a walk around the parking lot. It was cold and dry but he had his own fur coat, and he happily chased a squirrel up a tree, then sniffed the wheels of a couple of cars.

When Lili finally reappeared she was pushing a cart full of groceries. "All this for Rick and Tamsen?" I asked when I met her at the car.

"I figured as long as I was here I'd do a big shop."

I started loading the bags into the Beemer's trunk, where they'd be safe from Rochester's inquisitive nose and tongue. Though it was chilly and gray, felt happy to have Lili and Rochester there in my world.

Once we got home and unloaded the groceries, Lili and I went into the kitchen and started to prepare dinner, and Rochester lay down flat on the kitchen tile, his front paws outstretched, his head resting between them. His eyebrows twitched as he watched me sprinkle the baking potatoes with kosher salt, then wrap them in aluminum foil.

I gave in to the pleading in his eyes and handed him a doggie treat. I'd had to stop buying the little ones in the shape of T-bone steaks, because they were made in China, and I had read a couple of horror stories online about dogs getting poisoned. The new treats weren't as cute, but they were made in the US with all natural ingredients. Rochester didn't mind; he gobbled them all.

"I have some final papers to grade," Lili said, once the roast and potatoes were in the oven. "I'm going upstairs to try and knock them all out."

"This is one of those times when I don't miss teaching." I had taught as an adjunct at Eastern for a couple of semesters, but since becoming the administrator of the college's Friar Lake conference center, I'd stopped. "When are grades due?"

"Tuesday. So I have time. But I hate to let things slide until the last minute. And I'll be busy policing the rest of the department."

In addition to teaching classes in photography, Lili was the chair of the fine arts department, which involved a great deal of

Neil S. Plakcy

administrative work. She went to the small bedroom we shared as an office, and I relaxed on the sofa downstairs, with Rochester sprawled on his side next to me.

Lili had given me an early Hanukkah present, an iPad, and I was still setting it up. I'd always considered myself a PC guy and resisted Apple products, but once I'd bought my first iPhone I had gotten hooked. I wasn't going to give up my Windows-based laptops, though – partly because the tools I used for my occasional illicit forays online were there.

I had spent a year in a California prison for computer hacking, and only recently finished my two-year parole. Mine wasn't a malicious crime; I had hacked into the databases of the three major credit bureaus and placed a red flag on my then-wife's credit cards, so that she couldn't drive us into bankruptcy in a flurry of retail therapy after suffering her second miscarriage.

Though the state of California had tried, I hadn't been rehabilitated, and I had continued to use my hacking skills to help Rick, though he frequently told me not to. But that summer, after he and Lili had staged an intervention, I had acknowledged that my itchy fingers and my arrogance could get me into trouble again if I wasn't careful.

I had joined an online support group for ex-hackers and promised that I would talk to either Lili or Rick before I tried anything stupid again. I'd only screwed up once so far, but I knew how slippery that slope was. I was sure that part of Lili's incentive to buy me the iPad was to remove some of the temptation, because the hacking tools I had required a PC's operating system to work.

I played around at the Apple store for a while, looking for interesting apps I could download, and eventually the smell of the rib roast in the oven brought Lili back downstairs. I set the table with my mother's Lenox china and the Baccarat crystal tumblers Lili had collected on duty-free shopping sprees, and by the time the food was ready, the house was glowing with candles and filled with delicious scents.

Rochester heard Rick's truck pull up in the driveway, and answered the joyful barks of Rick's bristly-haired black, white and brown Australian shepherd, Rascal, with a few of his own. It was a canine cacophony that didn't stop until both dogs were in the house, chasing each other up and down the stairs.

Dog Have Mercy

Tamsen was a beautiful blonde who had also grown up in Stewart's Crossing, but she was a few years younger than Rick and I were. She had a natural grace that made me think she might have been a fashion model at some point. She certainly had the figure for it, with a shapely bust and long legs. There was also a gravity to her, perhaps the result of losing her husband when she was young and having to raise her son Justin on her own.

After all the kisses and handshakes, Tamsen said, "Something smells yummy."

"Standing rib roast with baked potatoes," Lili said.

"That was Kyle's favorite," Tamsen said. "I haven't had it in years." Kyle Morgan, Tamsen's first husband, had been an Army lieutenant and had been killed in Iraq a few years before. "I'm sure it's going to be delicious. My mouth is watering already."

Lili took her arm and the two of them walked into the kitchen. Rick and I went into the living room. "How's it going?" I asked.

"In general, or with Tamsen?"

"Whichever."

"Tamsen is great. We really connect. A couple of weeks ago, before it got cold, Justin went to her sister's for the weekend, and we went up to a country inn in the Poconos with Rascal. We hiked during the day and played pool in the evening and had a great time."

"And the whole Kyle thing?" I knew Rick had been reluctant to date Tamsen because he'd be competing with a dead war hero.

"He's a part of her life, the way Tiffany will always be a part of mine." Tiffany was Rick's ex, who had left him shortly before I returned to Stewart's Crossing. "He sounds like he was a great guy, but Tamsen has made it clear he wasn't a saint. And Justin was still so little when Kyle left for Iraq that he doesn't remember his dad much."

"Okay, boys, dinner is served," Tamsen called from the dining room, and Rick and I joined her and Lili there. The dogs were right on our heels, and settled beside us on the floor, waiting for tidbits.

"How's the crime beat in Stewart's Crossing?" Lili asked Rick over salad. "Nothing new for the Hardy Boys?"

When Rochester and I first began helping Rick, he'd referred to me as either Nancy Drew or Miss Marple, but eventually I'd graduated in his eyes to Joe Hardy, the younger of the two investigative brothers.

"Only ordinary drama," Rick said. "A couple of break-ins out at Crossing Estates, though we pulled in a guy for that, an ex-con with a long record for burglary. A shoplifter at the hardware store and a couple of domestic disturbances. And it looks like we've got a growing homelessness problem."

I remembered the man we'd seen outside the nursing home and realized I'd seen a few other homeless people around town.

"The economy is taking its toll," Rick said. "Lots of people are upside down on their mortgages, and those layoffs in New York and Philly are reverberating here. I know a guy who used to be a greenhouse assistant at Teacups and Tulips until they had to cut back because the rich folks weren't buying fresh flowers. Now he sleeps in the woods behind their parking lot."

"Hannah says that the Friends are getting involved," Tamsen said. Hannah was her older sister, the Clerk of the Meeting in Stewart's Crossing. "We're going to serve dinner to the poor and the homeless on Christmas day."

"That's a lovely gesture," Lili said. "There's a problem in Leighville, too. People gravitate there because students can be so wasteful, so the dumpsters are full."

"You haven't been dumpster-diving, have you?" Rick asked.

She shook her head. "But I'm putting together lesson plans for the course I'm teaching this winter on photojournalism, and I'm including a unit on homelessness."

"What does that involve?" Tamsen asked. "When I think of photojournalism I think of those pictures in the newspaper of wars and natural disasters."

"That's the way things used to be," Lili said. "But with the budget cuts in print media, that career is going the way of buggy-whip makers. Today's photojournalists are more likely to focus on issues and use their pictures as a way of pushing social change."

Lili and Tamsen took away the salad plates and brought out the rib roast and potatoes. We talked more about photojournalism and life in Stewart's Crossing as we ate, and the dogs nosed us for handouts. By the time we had demolished slices of the awesome carrot cake that Tamsen had baked, the dogs had slumped into post-beef comas and the humans were lounging in back in their chairs.

After Rick, Rascal and Tamsen left, Lili and I took Rochester for a quick late-night walk. "Do you ever stop to think how fortunate we

Dog Have Mercy

are?" Lili asked. "We both have our health, we have jobs, and we have a roof over our heads. So many people aren't as lucky." She turned her head and pretended to spit three times. "*Keyn ahora.*"

I remembered my father using that same expression after mentioning anything good in our lives, an imprecation against the evil eye. "We've both been hit with life events," I said. "But we've been resilient."

Lili had bounced back after two divorces and an abortion, and though I knew she still suffered from some of the things she had seen as a photojournalist, she was at heart an optimistic person. I had suffered the loss of two unborn children, the destruction of my marriage and my career in IT, as well as my year's incarceration.

"It's not just the ability to be resilient," Lili said. "Some people don't have the emotional and financial resources we do. I read somewhere that a huge percentage of people on the streets have psychological problems."

"I consider myself very fortunate," I said, taking Lili's hand. "I had a home to come back to and a dog to teach me how to love again. And then I met you, which was the luckiest thing yet."

I hoped that my luck would hold, and that I wouldn't do something to screw up my relationship with Lili. Even after less than a year together, my heart told me that what Lili and I had was so much stronger than what I'd had with Mary. Sure, Lili and I had small problems, but at heart I knew we were well-suited to each other, and she seemed to agree.

* * *

Sunday morning Rochester didn't want to walk very far, which was unusual for my happy-go-lucky dog, and he seemed to be favoring his back right leg. I was attuned to his moods and I'd learned that he could be very skilled at hiding pain. When we got home, I sat down on the tile floor and pulled him over to me. "Let's see what you've got going on, puppy," I said.

He squirmed and wiggled but I immobilized him and shifted so I could see check each of his paws. He had torn a toenail on one of his back paws, and the nail bed was red and swollen. "What did you do? I trimmed your toenails last week."

He looked up at me with a woeful face. We had a regular grooming routine. I cleaned his teeth every couple of days with turkey-flavored toothpaste; I groomed him with a special brush that pulled dead fur from his undercoat; I swabbed his ears with medicated pads and whenever his toenails got too long I trimmed them with an electric gadget.

"What's up?" Lili asked as she walked downstairs.

"We're going to have to go see Dr. Horz first thing tomorrow morning," I said. "Rochester has an infected toenail." I cleaned the wound and squeezed some antibiotic ointment onto it, and then sat on the floor scratching Rochester's belly.

Edith called later that day to thank us for our visit. "It was so wonderful to see you," she said. "I admit, I get a little depressed here. Sometimes it feels like God's waiting room, that people come here to die. My roommate, that poor Mrs. Tuttle? She passed away right after you came to see us."

"I'm sorry, Edith," I said.

"I'm sure it was her time, dear," Edith said. "It was very sweet that she reached out to Rochester just before she died. He might have been the last being who touched her."

I shuddered. Rick had occasionally referred to Rochester as "the death dog," because he had a knack for finding dead bodies, or clues in the solution of who killed them. I didn't want to believe that he'd moved on to initiating the deaths of people who petted him.

I chatted with Edith for a few minutes and promised to bring Rochester for another visit soon. Lili went out to take some photographs around River Bend, our townhome community, and I went up to the office. Rochester followed me, and once I was in my chair, he slumped down at my feet.

I opened the desk drawer and pulled out the laptop I had inherited, along with Rochester, from my late next-door-neighbor Caroline Kelly. It was close to four years old, at least, and didn't have as much power as my desktop computer, but I kept my hacking tools on it. I didn't have any plans to break in anywhere I didn't belong, but I did want to keep my software updated.

The online hacker support group I had joined would have called that a red flag – simply thinking about hacking was enough to trigger an alert. But I was trying to channel my impulses to snoop in protected places—recognizing that I'd always have those urges, and that if I tried to ignore them completely I'd only get myself in trouble.

Hackers are an elusive bunch, and the sites where people

Dog Have Mercy

uploaded new and improved tools were always changing, so I had to keep up. As it was, several of the sites I'd bookmarked had been shut down, and I spent an hour following coded messages and encrypted links before I could find where my tribe was hiding.

I read blogs and posts about updated port sniffers and password-breaking programs, and downloaded a couple of programs. While I waited for the last of them to come through, I remembered our conversation with Rick and Tamsen the night before, that an ex-con with a long record had been arrested for the break-ins at Crossing Estates.

There but for the grace of God go I, I thought. I had been incredibly lucky in my online forays. I had only made one major mistake, and I had paid for that. But I had done many other things, almost all with good intentions, and hadn't been caught.

I had to keep reminding myself that I wasn't as smart as I thought I was, that if I got too cocky I could end up in trouble again. And this time I had so much more to lose. Lili knew about the laptop, and my struggles to keep from hacking, but what if I got caught again? Would she see my actions as a betrayal of her trust, and be terribly hurt? Would she stand by me, or would she dump me the way Mary had?

I had to be strong enough to resist temptation. But just updating my tools wasn't illegal – or at least that's what I told myself.

Rochester sat up and sniffed me, and when my download finished I shut down the laptop and lowered myself to the floor to rub his belly.

Rochester was a constant reminder of what was important in my life. His love and devotion had helped me climb out of the despair I had felt after I left prison, and I was determined to do everything I could to take good care of him.

I checked his nail and dabbed more antibiotic cream on it, and when he dozed off I Googled as many sites as I could find about what might have happened and how I could help him heal. One site scared me – a vet blogged about a dog whose owner had ignored an infection, which had then spread to the dog's vital organs, eventually causing its death. That was not going to happen to Rochester.

Neil S. Plakcy

3 – Nail Bed

MONDAY MORNING AFTER BREAKFAST I kissed Lili goodbye and bundled Rochester into the car. The vet's office was on the other side of Stewart's Crossing and we drove through downtown to get there, beneath illuminated snowflakes hanging from light stanchions along Main Street. Storefronts were decorated with multi-colored lights, and Santa and his sleigh rested on the lawn in front of the hardware store, each reindeer wearing a tool belt.

I parked in the vet's lot and took Rochester for a quick pee before going inside. He was still limping, but that didn't stop his enthusiasm for sniffing every possible smell. The vet had put up a new sign out front, with room for custom messages, and that morning it read "Live Nude Dogs. Free Lap Dances."

I was surprised to see Rick's truck in the parking lot. I hoped that Rascal hadn't gotten sick or hurt himself running around the house with Rochester. I didn't see Rick or his dog in the waiting room, though it was crowded with people and pets. A yappy Yorkie in one corner kept up a barking and snarling match with a persnickety Pekingese. There were cats in crates and dogs big and small on leashes, mostly sitting beside their owners.

I walked up to the receptionist's desk with Rochester by my side. She was a young Indian woman I'd never seen before, with red dot in the middle of her forehead. Maybe it was the influence of the spy movie I'd seen a while before, but I couldn't help seeing that dot as the target from a laser rifle.

"We have a small emergency," I said to her. "Can Dr. Horz squeeze in a quick look at Rochester's toenail? I'm afraid it's infected."

"Dr. Horz is running behind," she said. "We've had some trouble this morning. But things should start moving again soon and

Dog Have Mercy

I can squeeze you in."

The tag on her blouse read "Sahima." I signed in with my name, Rochester's, and my phone number, and took Rochester to a chair by her window. He slumped by my feet and watched with interest the parade of pets. He tried to make friends with an elegant Lhasa Apso beside us, but she kept her queenly distance from the hoi polloi.

A big sign beside the receptionist's desk announced that the clinic would be closed for two weeks over Christmas, and that all pets who had been left for boarding had to be picked up by 6 PM Monday, December 22. At the bottom was the name and address of another office that would be open during the holidays.

A twenty-something guy with bristly short hair and arms covered in tattoos stepped out of the door to the examining area. He called the Yorkie and his dad, a huge bald guy in a Harley Davidson T-shirt and as they went in, Rick came out, alone, to another cascade of barking from the Peke.

Rick walked toward me, but stopped at the receptionist's desk. While he waited for Sahima to get off the phone, I asked, "Nothing wrong with Rascal, is there?"

He shook his head. "Business visit," he said.

"Really? What happened? Someone got bit?"

Sahima ended her call as Rick pulled on his sheepskin-lined leather jacket. "Tell Dr. Horz I'll call her later today," he said.

"Rick--" I began.

He held up his hand. "Lousy day. I'll talk to you later."

He didn't stop to pet Rochester on his way out the door, which was unusual for him. Even when he'd been mad at me in the past, he'd always made time for my dog.

I figured he wasn't mad, just busy. The Peke went in next and calm fell over the room. I turned to the receptionist. "What happened?" I asked.

She leaned forward and spoke in a low voice. "There are drugs missing from Dr. Horz's cabinet." I could tell from her eagerness this was the most exciting thing that had happened in her life for a while.

"What kind of drugs? Like a junkie would steal?" I asked.

She shook her head. "Not pain meds. We keep those double-locked. And not the Euthasol, either, for putting dogs to sleep. That's locked up, too."

I was intrigued. "Then what?"

Neil S. Plakcy

She almost whispered, "Potassium."

"Really? What do you use that for?"

She shrugged. "I don't know. I'm just the receptionist. But I figure it must be something important because Dr. Horz got into a real state. This morning, after she discovered that there were five of these little vials missing, she pulled each of us into an examining room. It was crazy. We had dogs and cats all over the place, and she was freaking out over this stuff."

Her phone rang and I sat back down with Rochester. I sent a couple of texts and checked my email, and the waiting room began to clear. After an hour, Rochester was getting restless, and I was glad when the tattooed guy appeared and called, "Here with Rochester?"

My big golden boy bounded up at the sound of his name, and I had to hold tight to his leash to keep him from tackling the guy.

"I'm Felix," he said. "Follow me, please." He had the mumbling and flat vowels of a real Philly accent—my favorite example was the way the city's football team had become the Fluffyah Iggles.

As we walked down the antiseptic corridor, I asked, "Where's Elysia?" Rochester liked our regular vet tech.

"She went to take care of her sick mom. I usually take care of the dogs and cats we got staying with us, but the doc asked me to fill in out front until Elysia gets back."

We stopped at the digital scale in the hallway, and Rochester, usually so reluctant to step onto it, followed Felix's instructions easily. "Eighty-five point two," he said, then led us into an exam room. Rochester circled twice and then flopped down on the floor. Felix picked up a clipboard with a series of questions printed on it and asked, murdering the r's in the statement, "What's the reason faw yaw visit today?"

I told him about the toenail, and he sat down on the floor with Rochester and very gently examined his paw. "He probably tore this when he was playing," he said to me. "Goldens are such big happy dogs."

"We had a dog come over Saturday night and they played a lot," I said. "Could it have been then?"

"Nah, maw like a few days before that," Felix said. "These infections, they don't come up overnight. But yeah, he probably screwed with it Saturday night."

As I heard him speak, I wondered why I didn't say things like

Dog Have Mercy

"Satiday," when I'd grown up so close to Philadelphia. Was it a socio-economic thing? Because I'd had excellent teachers? Because my parents were first-generation Americans who had impressed on me the importance of speaking clearly? I remembered Lili's comment about how fortunate she and I had been to have the backgrounds we did.

Felix labored over the clipboard, gripping his pen like it was a spear ready to stab at the paper. When I was a grad student at Columbia I had done some student teaching in city schools, and I remembered seeing kids hold their pens that way, as if they were determined to beat the words into submission.

Dr. Horz's office was gradually becoming computerized, but she and her vet techs still wrote out case notes by hand, and Felix looked relieved when he put down the pen and took Rochester's temperature and a fecal sample. I was pleased to see that my dog had taken a liking to him and let him do whatever he needed without complaint. Not that he was a fussy puppy, but who wants to let a stranger mess around with your butt?

Felix went back to the clipboard and his face darkened. He chewed on the end of his pen. "Can I give you a hand with anything?" I asked. "I've taught writing in the past."

"My writing sucks," Felix said. "I can never make the words say what I want."

He shifted the clipboard so I could see it. Under "History" he had written "owner founded redness and swelling on golden retriever's right hind paw yesterday PM," and I pointed out that it should be "found" rather than "founded." I corrected a couple of other mistakes I recognized as second-language ones, including a lot of missing articles.

Then we talked through the notes he wanted to make. He knew all the right terms, but his writing was very rough. "Let me guess, your first language isn't English, is it?"

He shook his head. "Spanish. I was born in Puerto Rico. Didn't move to Philly until I was ten, and they dumped me right into regular English classes."

"Yeah, I've seen that in my students," I said.

He was relieved when we finished everything. "Thanks faw yaw help," he said. "Dr. Horz will come see you."

He left us in the examining room with all the diagrams of canine intestinal disorders. "Ingestion of foreign substances is the number one reason for emergency veterinary visits," the first poster read.

Yeah, I'd been through that routine a few times.

I sat on the floor with Rochester and stroked the smooth hair on the back of his head. "You'll be all better soon, puppy." I leaned down to kiss his head. "I promise."

I had plenty of time to read about inflammatory bowel disease, coronavirus, and canine minute virus, which involved diarrhea, difficulty breathing and anorexia. At least Rochester didn't have any of those.

We had to wait quite a while for Dr. Horz. She was a small, slim woman with a great bedside manner. "Sorry, I've been run off my feet this morning." She had a smear I hoped wasn't dog poop on her white coat, and several strands of her graying hair had come loose.

"I heard," I said. "Some potassium was stolen?"

She looked at me. "I guess Rick Stemper was right. When he was here earlier he said you and Rochester are often nosing around in his cases." She smiled. "I'm impressed that you already know what happened."

"I wouldn't call it nosing around in his cases," I said. "Rochester has... some skills. I just follow along."

She picked up the clipboard, then sat on the floor beside the dog. "How's my handsome friend?" she asked, as she looked at the notes Felix had written.

"He's been great, except for this little problem," I said.

She looked up at me. "Felix's writing has improved dramatically here. These notes are pretty good. Did you help him, by chance?"

I shrugged. "Was that wrong?"

"Not at all. He's a smart guy, but he's had some bad luck in life. I'm hoping he can turn things around. One area he's got to improve is his writing skills. When he's working back in the kennel for me, all he has to do is check on the animals and record data. But if he wants to be a vet tech, he has to be able to write notes."

"They have remedial courses at the community college he could take," I said. "I have a friend who teaches over there, and she says that almost three-quarters of the incoming students need help with writing."

"I've been trying to convince him," she said. "He wants to go into a vet tech program at a college in Jenkintown, but they won't

Dog Have Mercy

accept him until he improves his skills. I can't blame him for not wanting to spend three semesters and a thousand dollars to get where high school should have gotten him."

She wrote a couple of notes at the bottom of the form, then looked up at me. "Standard treatment for a bacterial nail bed infection is an oral antibiotic, with antimicrobial foot soaks and a topical ointment. I'll have Felix bring in the prescriptions for you."

She reached down and chucked Rochester under his chin. "You ought to be less rambunctious, mister. You must be at almost three by now." She looked up at me. "I know you don't have his exact birthdate, but he first came to us almost two years ago, and my records say that based on his teeth, we estimated that he was about a year old."

"Was there anything I could have done to prevent this?" I asked.

Dr. Horz shook her head. "You take great care of this dog. I can see that you trim his nails regularly. He just got one caught. Sorry to be so abrupt, but I have a whole raft of animals waiting for care. And I need to reevaluate my security procedures, and talk to my staff. It's going to be a long day." She shook her head. "And I thought Friday was bad."

Though I knew she needed to go, I couldn't resist asking. "What happened Friday?"

"A teenaged girl came in after I'd sent the staff home, as I was about to close. She insisted her dog was deathly ill and I *had* to look at him right away." She smiled. "You know how teenagers are. So I took him back into the examining room, and she texted furiously on her phone all the time I was examining him. Then she had to go the bathroom. There was nothing wrong with that dog and I had to wait in the room with him until she got back."

"Teenagers," I said. "I see the same kind of thing in the classes I teach." I hesitated. "Do you think she could have been the one who took the potassium?"

She cocked her head and for a second I recognized Rochester in her. "What would a teenager want with potassium?"

I shrugged. "For a chemistry class?"

"The science labs at Pennsbury High are well-funded," she said. "I know, because I've been over there to visit. And as far as I know they don't experiment with potassium."

"Just a thought," I said.

"It's more likely that one of my staff either misplaced the missing vials, or that our record-keeping needs to improve and we used the last supply without noticing it. But I still thought I ought to notify the police, in case we find anything else is gone."

I thanked her for looking at Rochester, and a few minutes later Felix came back with a bottle of pills, a tube of ointment, and a bottle with a dropper built into the cap. "This stuff here is organic iodine. You don't gotta worry about it -- it's safe, non-toxic, antifungal, antibacterial, and anti-yeast."

"Do I put it on his nail?"

He shook his head. "Here's what you do. You got some kind a pot, right? You fill it with water, add a couple a drops then swish it around until looks like iced tea." He laughed. "You don't drink it. You dunk Rochester's paw in faw like two to five minutes."

He sat down on the floor beside Rochester and opened the dog's jaws. He dropped one of the pills into his mouth and then shut it and tilted the dog's head back. He massaged Rochester's throat as he spoke. "If he don't like having his foot in the water, you can give him a rawhide to chew."

I expected Rochester to spit the pill out on the tile floor as soon as Felix let go of him, but instead the dog smiled and licked Felix's hand.

"You're good with him," I said, as Felix stood and then put everything into a bag for me. "He can be finicky sometimes."

"He's a pussycat," Felix said. "I've worked with way worse dogs than him. I was with this program when I was in prison--"

He stopped, and I could tell he'd said more than he wanted to.

"I was inside for a year in California," I said. "Finished my two-year probation a couple of months ago."

He relaxed visibly.

"What program?" I asked.

"Called Paws Up. They bring in these shelter dogs that nobody wants because they got problems. This one Staffordshire Terrier mix came to stay with me. He'd been a bait dog and he went between scared and vicious, and you never knew which was gonna come out."

He pushed up the sleeve of his shirt and pointed to a scar in the middle of a tattoo of the island of Puerto Rico with the word "Boricua" in script beneath it. "See this? He bit me real bad. But I got him calmed down and trained so good he got a family in the

Dog Have Mercy

Northeast to take him in."

He was about to leave when I said, "Listen, I hope you don't think I'm meddling in your private business. But Dr. Horz said you need some help with your writing. I'd be happy to give you some tutoring."

He looked suspicious. "Why?"

I shrugged. "Because I've been where you are. When I went to prison, I lost my job, my wife divorced me, and all my friends but one melted away. I got lucky when I moved back here, and a couple of people took chances on me, helped me get my life going again. Just want to pay it forward."

He nodded. "Yeah, I got one friend who stuck by me, Zeno."

I must have misheard him, because I asked, "Zero?"

"Zeno," he said more clearly. "Yunior Zeno. My home boy from Mayaguez. But he speaks as bad as me. At the program, they gave us a lot of help, but they weren't there to teach us to write good. And nobody I know can help me with that."

"You know where Friar Lake is?" I asked. "Up River Road by Leighville?"

He shook his head. "But I can find it. That where you live?"

"It's where I work. It's owned by Eastern College. If you come by I could get you started with some stuff to read, some practice exercises."

"I'm off tomorrow," he said. "That good?"

"Sure. Come by any time in the afternoon." I pulled out a business card and handed it to him, then wrote directions from Stewart's Crossing on the back of a flyer for a new kind of doggie halter. "You have access to a computer somehow?" I asked.

"My buddy Dan has one he lets me use for email and stuff," Felix said. "He's one of my roommates." He took the directions and shook my hand. "I really appreciate this."

I led Rochester to the check-out desk. We stood beside a tall potted plant waiting for a petite black woman to check out ahead of us. Her brindle cat crouched at the rear of a carrier, but Rochester was more interested in nosing behind the plant.

"Rochester, please," I said, tugging on his leash. When I looked at him, he had a torn piece of paper in his mouth. I reached down and pulled it away.

It was sticky with his saliva, and I had to use a wipe from the

Neil S. Plakcy

dispenser on the counter to clean it off. It was the left-hand side of a permission slip from Pennsbury High, where Rick and I had gone. The student's last name was Brezza, but the paper had been torn vertically after that. It didn't seem to be important, so I crumpled it up and tossed it into the trash.

I paid for the visit and we walked outside, where Felix leaned against the building in a sheepskin coat, puffing a cigarette. "Thanks again faw helping me," he said.

"My best friend's always complaining about me being an English teacher," I said. "I guess it's a habit I can't break." At least it was one habit that wasn't likely to get me in trouble, I thought.

4 – Little White Angel

FLURRIES HAD BEGUN TO FLOAT DOWN from the overcast sky. With Rochester beside me, resting his big golden head on his paws, I left the vet's and drove down Ferry Street, busy with last-minute shoppers in big SUVs.

As I turned onto the River Road to head toward my job at Friar Lake, I thought about potassium. Why would someone steal it? Wasn't it one of those vitamins you could buy at the drugstore?

I remembered that when Mary was pregnant for the first time, she'd had malaise and muscle weakness, and been diagnosed with a potassium deficiency. She was a picky eater, and wouldn't eat many of the foods that were high in the vitamin, like tomatoes, potatoes and bananas. Her doctor had given her an injection and prescribed some additional vitamins.

After her miscarriage, that was one of the reasons she had seized on. Had the baby been deprived of some essential nutrient? As soon as she discovered she was pregnant the second time, she had gone on a strict diet and nutritional regimen, but that hadn't helped, and she miscarried in the fourth month of that pregnancy.

I tried to push those memories away and focus on the upcoming Christmas holiday, and the time I'd be able to spend with Rochester and Lili. As I drove up the River Road, I passed white split-rail fences hung with pine boughs and a stately Norway spruce decorated in vertical strings of lights, which glowed even in the gray morning light.

I turned in at the driveway up the hill to Friar Lake, Rochester looking eagerly out the side window. The property's original name was the Abbey of Our Lady of the Waters, and after Eastern purchased it, contractors had begun exterior work on the property: a new, wider access road up the hill, paved sidewalks between buildings, improved water mains and electrical service, roof and gutter repairs.

With the cold weather, the contractors had moved indoors to update the electrical and plumbing systems, refinish wood floors and add new carpet and tile. Eventually the new classroom and dormitory furnishings would arrive.

As the property manager I had a large, airy office with big windows in the abbey's gatehouse, a small stone building at the top of the hilly drive. A second office was being used by Joey Capodilupo, the construction superintendent for the renovation of the property.

From what I could see, Joey was keeping the contractors on schedule and doing good work. His father was the head of physical plant for Eastern College, so I knew Joey had a great background for the job. As I parked, I noticed that Joey had hung a wreath studded with cranberries on the front door of the gatehouse, and a small pine tree at the edge of the property had been decorated with stars and Santa hats made from carpet scraps and bits of lumber. A white angel perched precariously on the top.

A dusting of early snow rested on the high pines beyond the chapel building and the air was cold and damp. When I let Rochester out of the car, he scampered over to a hedge and left his mark, then followed me inside. I spent the morning sending emails, filling out purchase orders and answering phone calls.

Just before noon Joey came in. He was a tall, good-looking guy in his early thirties, wearing neatly pressed jeans and an off-white fisherman's sweater. He had an Eastern College ball cap on his head.

"How's it going?" I asked.

"My dad says because this is Eastern property, I have to shut the site down when the college is closed—something about insurance, I think. And only Christmas and New Years are paid holidays so the crew is bitching about missing so many days. All morning I've been shifting them around to other sites that aren't closing down, and I can't get any of my own work done."

"Anything I can help you with?"

He sat down in the chair beside my desk, stretching out his long legs, and Rochester got up from his place beneath the picture window to rest his head in Joey's lap. "There is something," Joey said, scratching Rochester's ears. The big dog yawned a happy grin.

"What's that?"

"Mark and I are supposed to go off on a cruise this weekend," he said. "Seven day Western Caribbean."

A few months before, I'd introduced Joey to my friend Mark Figueroa, who ran an antique store in Stewart's Crossing, and they had started dating. "What's the problem?"

"Brody." Joey's golden retriever puppy was about six months old. He was almost pure white, with a streak of gold down his back and some gold around the fringes of his ears. "My parents were supposed to take him for the week, but you know my dad fell last week and fractured a couple of ribs."

"Yeah, I heard. How's he doing?"

"Says it hurts to breathe. I tell him not to, but he doesn't listen." I laughed.

Joey leaned forward. "So he can't handle Brody, and my mom says she's done raising kids, and she's not going to be walking a puppy out in the cold and the snow."

"I know what that's like," I said. "I didn't get Rochester until he was already a year old, but he's still a big puppy, and he wears me out sometimes."

"But having a second one isn't so bad," he said. "They play with each other, they keep each other occupied."

I realized where Joey was going. "You want me to take in Brody while you go away?"

"Would you, Steve? I'd owe you one. Mark and I both would."

I'd only met Brody once, at a party during the fall, and I remembered him as a ball of endless energy. "How come you don't just board him somewhere?"

Joey shook his head. "I'll cancel the trip before I leave Brody in a cage."

"I don't know," I said. "I'd have to ask Lili. And I'm not sure Rochester would like having a puppy around. He's kind of spoiled."

"Please? Could you ask Lili? Maybe I could bring Brody over tonight, for a visit, see how he and Rochester get along?"

I looked at my dog. "What do you think, Rochester? You want to have a puppy come to visit?"

He thunked his plumy tail on the carpeted floor, and rested his head in Joey's lap again, looking up at me with those big brown eyes. I sighed. "Come over tonight. You can ask Lili yourself, see if she's as much of a sucker as I am."

Neil S. Plakcy

Joey bounded up out of the chair, and I could see in him the same kind of enthusiasm that Rochester demonstrated.

I still needed to talk to faculty members about programming for the spring, but it was impossible to get hold of any of them during that last week, as they scrambled to finish their grading and then escape for the holidays. So I focused on developing copy for each of the programs I had planned for the spring and the summer and researching what it cost to place ads in selected publications.

I had seminars planned on personal financial planning; the resurgence of interest in Jane Austen; a historical retrospective of the 1960s; and one on the process of new drug approvals, co-facilitated by a member of our science faculty and an alumnus in the field.

But the question of the missing potassium kept floating around the edges of my thoughts, and after I finished the work on my plate I went back online to look for more information. I found an interesting article on the Department of State's website about the use of potassium in processing cocaine. Potassium permanganate could also be combined with pseudoephedrine to produce methcathinone, a synthetic stimulant similar to cocaine. On the street it was called Cat, Jeff or Charlie; it was usually snorted, but could be smoked, injected or eaten. Unlike potassium, it was a Schedule 1 controlled substance. It had been prescribed as an anti-depressant in the Soviet Union for decades, where it was called Ephedrone, and was frequently abused.

I'd read about the inroads the Russian Mafia was making in the US. Could they be bringing methcathinone production to our shores? Would it be the next crystal meth? It was closely related to methamphetamines, according to the bit of chemistry I understood. The article indicated that it was difficult to produce in amateur labs, but suppose someone had perfected a process? And suppose that process needed potassium in its liquid form, rather than the pills you could buy at the drugstore?

By the time I got home that evening, my brain was full of drug-related drama, but I had to switch back into dog daddy mode.

I laid the bag from the vet's down on the counter and told Lili what kind of treatment Rochester needed. "The vet tech taught me a neat trick this morning," I said. "Let's see if I can do it." I took one of the big antibiotic pills and pried open Rochester's mouth.

"I'm not hurting you," I said. "Chill out, dog." I dropped the pill in, closed his jaws and massaged his throat the way I'd seen Felix do it.

Rochester slumped to the floor. I was sure he was going to spit the pill out the moment I turned my back but when I got down and opened his mouth again, the pill was gone. "Amazing," I said. In the past I'd had to trick him by coating the pill with sticky peanut butter or cheese and hoping he wouldn't notice. That had worked about fifty percent of the time.

I ruffled his fur and told him he was a good boy, and then he lay by my feet as Lili and I ate dinner. After we finished, I filled a shallow basin with warm water and poured in a few drops of the iodine, watching as the water turned a reddish brown. I wet half of a clean towel and gathered fresh bandages for Rochester's paw. Then I sat on the floor and called him over.

He approached reluctantly. I told him to sit, and he leaned down to sniff the water in the basin. I had to pull his snout away before he started to drink. "Not for drinking, puppy. Now come on, stop wiggling! I need to get your bandage off."

We began to wrestle. Sure, I was bigger than he was, and stronger, but when an eighty-pound golden doesn't want to do something, it takes more than brute strength. I had to call in reinforcements. "Lili!"

She joined us on the floor, stroking Rochester's head as I unwrapped the bandage and then stuck his paw in the brown water. He didn't like that, but I spoke to him in low, reassuring tones, and Lili continued to pet him. After a couple of minutes, I pulled the paw out and wiped it down, then dried it, Rochester wriggling all the time.

The phone rang, and Lili stood up to answer it. "Sure, send him in," she said, and then turned to me. "Joey Capodilupo is at the gate to see us?"

"Oh crap, I completely forgot." I let go of the dog, and he scampered up to the stair landing. I explained the situation to Lili. "I didn't say yes or no," I said. "It's up to you."

She put her hands on her hips. "So you want to make me the bad guy?"

"Not at all. But I know Rochester can be a handful, and I wouldn't blame you if you said you couldn't cope."

"We'll see how the dogs get along," she said.

I followed Rochester up to the landing and rubbed some

antibiotic ointment into the wound, then wrapped it with a fresh bandage. As soon as I finished, he began to bark like mad and rushed toward the front door.

I flipped on the outside light and opened the door to Joey, Mark and Brody. Mark was at least three inches taller than Joey, about six-six or so, and scarecrow-skinny. Both of them were bundled up with scarves and heavy coats. "Come on in," I said.

The little white puppy needed no invitation. He jumped up over the threshold and sniffed at Rochester. Joey reached down and unclipped his leash, and the two dogs -took off, tearing around like Indy 500 racers.

"I guess Rochester likes him," I said.

"We were just going to have dessert," Lili said, though I had no idea she had anything planned. "Can I offer you some carrot cake? Coffee? Cappuccino?"

There was general agreement, and we walked into the dining room, the guys shedding coats and scarves and the dogs racing up and down the stairs. Lili brought out the leftover cake from Saturday night, and I turned on the cappuccino maker and began brewing. By the time I returned to the dining room, everyone was sitting around the table, and Brody had his paws up on Lili's thigh. "Aren't you a little white angel," she said. She ruffled him behind the ears. "You're adorable."

Rochester snuffled his way in beside the puppy, large and in charge. Mark pulled a couple of dog treats from his pocket and handed one to each dog.

"I thought you were the one who didn't like dogs," I said to him.

"I'm learning," Mark said. "Notice the khaki pants? They don't show the white hair so much."

"So I guess Steve told you," Joey said to Lili, as we started to eat. The dogs slumped on the floor together, chewing their treats. "We're flying to Miami Sunday morning for a seven-day cruise. My dad was supposed to take Brody but he fractured a couple of ribs."

"And you won't consider boarding?" I asked, in a last attempt.

"I wouldn't leave Brody at a kennel," Joey said. "I'd cancel the cruise first."

"Please, Steve?" Mark asked.

I looked at Lili, who was already besotted by the puppy, calling him *shayne punim*, Yiddish for "pretty face." He had finished his treat

Dog Have Mercy

and was begging for cake. She looked at me and we both smiled. Then I looked down at Rochester. "You're sure about this, dog-o? You're going to help look after the puppy?"

He slapped his tail a few times on the floor. "I'll hold you to that," I said.

5 – Light

AFTER JOEY AND MARK LEFT, Lili lay down on the sofa with a book, and I went upstairs to the desktop computer. I was still curious about why someone might have stolen potassium from Dr. Horz's office.

I discovered that it was a very important mineral for the proper function of all cells, organs and tissues in the body, that it was crucial to heart function and important in normal digestive and muscular function. But as I remembered in Mary's case, if someone had a potassium deficiency, a doctor could easily prescribe the remedy. Why steal the stuff? Couldn't you just buy some at the drugstore?

Further snooping revealed that having too much potassium in the blood caused a condition caused hyperkalemia. Older people were particularly at risk for that, because their kidneys often didn't do an adequate job of removing potassium. Having too little potassium was called hypokalemia. But again, if you had that, why not get a doctor's prescription, or buy the pills yourself at the local pharmacy?

I wanted to call Rick and ask him what he thought was going on, but I resisted, because he'd told me many times before that he didn't appreciate my meddling in his cases. And since it wasn't like there was a murderer on the loose, I didn't see the urgency in pushing myself forward.

The next morning I read the Bucks County *Courier-Times* over breakfast while Lili read the Philadelphia *Inquirer*. I'd started getting the *Inquirer* after Lili moved in, because she wanted better coverage of international issues than the local paper provided.

I had an endless appetite, it seemed, for local news; I read about a tow-truck driver who'd been picking up cars at the railroad station and then selling them at a junkyard; a bar robbery that was an inside job; and an arson fire at a dance studio. Then I stopped at the

Dog Have Mercy

obituaries.

When I was a kid, my mother had read the obituaries in the paper first. She had joked that it was so she could be sure her name wasn't there, but she had deep roots in Trenton, across the river from Stewart's Crossing, and she had a morbid interest in noting the deaths of people she knew, even vaguely.

Now that I was in my forties, I had picked up that habit, too. But the world was changing, and few of the people I'd grown up with were still in the area. The older ones had moved to Florida, while the ones my age had settled where they went to college, or wherever they were offered jobs.

I didn't recognize any of the names but I still read the little squibs for the stories they held. I was stunned to realize that Mr. Pappas, the man who'd grown up near me, and whom I'd met at Crossing Manor, had passed away. His obituary read "Michael George Pappas, 52, passed away at Crossing Manor Nursing Home in Stewart's Crossing due to complications from Crohn's Disease. Predeceased by his parents, George and Anastasia Demos Pappas, he is survived by several cousins. Services were held."

I must have shivered visibly, because Lili looked at me. "What's the matter? You look like somebody's walking on your grave."

I showed the obituary to her. "That's so sad," she said.

"And creepy, too," I said. "Edith said that Mrs. Tuttle passed away, too, right after we saw her."

"Mrs. Tuttle had dementia. And Crohn's Disease is serious. Mr. Pappas had to be sick to be at Crossing Manor."

"I know. But he was only a couple of years older than I am. It reminds me how tenuous life is, you know? One day you're fine, the next day you're in the ER after an accident, or worse. And I don't have anyone to survive me beyond a couple of cousins, just like Mark Pappas."

"I'll survive you, sweetheart. Would you like me to be called your girlfriend or your paramour? Companion, perhaps?"

"Go ahead, make fun of me," I grumbled, but I couldn't help smiling. "And you have to remember to put Rochester in the obituary, too."

"Of course. Now go to work, and drive carefully." She kissed my cheek and I left the house, with Rochester by my side. As I drove up to Friar Lake, I kept thinking about those poor people at Crossing

Manor. Maybe it wouldn't be a good idea for us to take Rochester back there again. Not that he was an angel of death or anything, but I'd had enough sadness in my life. I didn't need to look for more.

Since I knew Felix, the kennel assistant, was coming by that day, I looked for materials I could use to help him improve his writing. Eastern had a writing lab, and as a sometime faculty member I had an access code for it that I could give to students. I logged into the site and set him up to take the diagnostic tests for each of the twelve subject areas, from capitalization to comma use. Then I went to the website for the vet tech program he was interested in and printed a couple of the program's informational pages, including one on how students would learn to administer a variety of veterinary medications.

I left them beside the scale model of Friar Lake on the coffee table in the lobby, then went back to work. The next time I walked out of my office, I saw that Rochester had knocked the pile of papers to the floor. I picked them up and wiped some doggy slobber off the page about giving shots. "Yes, you got an antibiotic yesterday," I said. "Are you telling me you didn't like it?"

He shook his big head, then leaned down in his play posture. It was too cold to take him outside for a ball toss, so I played tug-a-rope with him for a couple of minutes, until the front door opened and Felix walked in. Rochester abandoned the rope to romp over and greet him.

Felix took off his parka and knelt down to the ground. "How's your paw doing today?" he asked. He lifted Rochester's back paw. "Looks a lot better."

He stood up and he and I shook hands. I led him toward Joey's office, where I planned to leave him while Joey was out on the property. I sat down behind the computer and logged into the writing lab, then stood up so Felix could take my place.

"I want you to take these diagnostic tests, which will tell me what you need to work on. When you're finished, come back to my office." He looked wary, but he wiggled his fingers, then set them on the keyboard.

I went back to work on the ad copy for the upcoming programs, and didn't look up at the clock until Felix walked back in. It had taken him two hours to complete the diagnostics, which was about average. "Some of that stuff was damn confusing." He ran his hand

Dog Have Mercy

over his short, bristly haircut.

"Yeah, it's not the best test. But it's a start."

He sat down, and Rochester rested his head in Felix's lap. "I'll look over your results and find tutorials you can do online to improve the areas where you're weak."

"I appreciate yaw help. You've given me some light at the end of the tunnel." He started to rise.

"Hold on," I said. "You've got homework."

"For real?"

I laughed. "Get used to it, if you want to go back to school." I handed him the printout about the goals and objectives of the vet tech program. "As you read this, look up any words you aren't familiar with, and write out a brief description, in your own words."

He gave me his email address, felix.logato@gmail.com, and we agreed that I'd send him some tutorial links once I reviewed his test results, and that we'd meet again in about a week. "Next week, can you come to my house in Stewart's Crossing?" I asked. "Eastern will be closed for Christmas vacation."

"Sure." He stood up. "I never knew guys like you when I was inside. Maybe I would have come out better."

We shook again. "I've seen you with Rochester. I think you came out just fine."

The big golden sat on his haunches and watched Felix go, then slumped back to the floor. I logged into the writing lab and looked up Felix's results. From his answers I could tell he had no clue what the rules were for comma usage, so I found a good online tutorial with lots of practice exercises on the subject.

Late that afternoon when Rochester saw me begin putting on my layers—sweater, coat, scarf, gloves and so on, he knew we were ready to head home, and he began jumping around me. "I'm working as fast as I can, puppy," I grumbled.

He helped by retrieving his leash from the desk and bringing it to me in his mouth. "Thank you," I said, taking it from him before it got soaked in saliva. A lesson learned.

We took a brisk walk around the property before getting in the car. It was fully dark by then, and the couple of lights on stanchions cast eerie shadows. I already felt very proprietorial about the complex, and I was looking forward to the time when it would be humming with students and faculty.

When we got home, Lili was lying on the sofa, snoring lightly. Rochester hurried over to her and licked her face, and she awoke. "Tough day at school?" I asked. I sat down beside her and lifted her bare feet into my lap.

"Grades were due at three o'clock. Just like the end of every semester, I spent the whole afternoon going around the department making sure all the faculty there were inputting them, and calling the adjuncts who hadn't put theirs in yet. I swear, I wish there was an obedience school for faculty members."

"I can imagine," I said. "Professor, sit! Stay! Enter your grades!"

I began to massage her feet, and she groaned in pleasure. "That feels so good."

Rochester kept trying to nose his way in, and finally gave up and sprawled beside us. "I couldn't get hold of the woman who taught pottery," Lili said. "I am never hiring her again, even if I have to learn to throw pots myself."

We sat together for a while, talking about our days, and then Lili sat up. "We should light the candles, and then have dinner."

It took me a moment to remember that she wanted to light the menorah for the first night of Hanukkah. Fortunately I'd anticipated the holiday, and had found and wrapped presents for both my sweethearts.

We walked into the kitchen, where Lili had set up an eight-branched brass candelabra, with the Lion of Judah as its base. Rochester followed us, then sat on his haunches on the white tile floor of the kitchen, staring expectantly up at us as if he figured the ceremony we were about to begin had to include a treat for him.

"You're sure Rochester can't get up there and knock it over," I said.

Lili leaned down to pet the golden's square head. "He's a good boy," she said. "He'll leave the candles alone." She grabbed a dog biscuit from the jar and handed it to Rochester, and he slumped to the floor, chewing noisily. "See, he's distracted."

She turned back to the menorah and placed one thin blue candle on the slot on the far right, and another for the *shamash*, or leader candle, in the center. She lit a match and touched it to the shamash, and I joined her in reciting the blessings I had memorized as a boy, honoring God, who had commanded us to kindle the Hanukkah lights.

Dog Have Mercy

Lili had a sweet tenor voice that blended with my baritone as we sang all three of the first night blessings, thanking God for doing wondrous things for our people in times of old, and for sustaining us and bringing us to this joyous season.

"I don't know that I've ever heard you sing before," Lili said when we were finished, and the two candles were glowing softly on the counter.

"I sing in the car with Rochester sometimes," I said. "Sometimes he sings along."

"But not in Hebrew," Lili said. She leaned forward and kissed me on the lips. "Happy Hanukkah, Steve."

After Mary and I married she bought a modern Plexiglas menorah and expensive beeswax candles made at a resettlement kibbutz in Israel. She put a veil over her head and waved her hands over the candles as she said the blessings, in a tradition as old as time. But after she miscarried for the second time, she put aside all celebrations, because they reminded her too much of what we had lost.

By the time I got to prison all my religious feeling was gone, but a volunteer chaplain contacted me soon after my sentence began, and to break the monotony I began attending the services she organized.

She brought me a copy of the Old Testament, and I read bits and pieces. Prison rules allowed me only ten books at a time, and the Bible became something I could dip into when I'd finished everything else and had to wait for new books to arrive.

Sometimes when the chaplain had a few minutes, she and I talked. One day, I asked her, "In Exodus, God says, 'None shall miscarry or be barren in your land; I will fulfill the number of your days.' So how can I believe in a God who would say that, and then take those two innocent babies from Mary and me?"

"We can't know why God does things," she said. "All we can do is believe that He has a plan, and that he loves us." She took my hand and squeezed. "Did the doctor ever tell you the reason for the miscarriages?"

"Chromosomal abnormalities," I said. "That when the egg and the sperm met, there were some problems with one or both of them, and the fetus didn't develop properly."

She nodded. "So God was looking out for those babies, making sure that they were not born into lives of pain and suffering."

"That's one way to think of it," I said.

I remembered something Mary had often said to me – *It's not all about you, Steve,* and I began to accept those miscarriages in my heart. They were not about me, or about Mary. The fetuses had failed to thrive because they could not, and even though my sperm or Mary's egg caused the problem, it was each baby's life, not ours.

From then on, I began to take comfort in what I read. Psalm 34, in particular, resonated with me: "The Lord is near to the brokenhearted and saves the crushed in spirit."

By the time I met Lili, I had returned to some level of belief, and we often shared bits of our Jewish upbringing with each other. "Wherever my family moved, we always had a menorah," she said, as we watched the candles flicker. "Cuba, Mexico, Kansas."

Lili was a descendant of Eastern European Jews, as I was, but her grandparents had been unable to immigrate directly to the United States before World War II, so instead had landed in Havana. Lili had been born there, too, but had moved to Mexico when she was five and then Kansas City at ten, so she was fluent in both Spanish and English and often peppered her language with Yiddish expressions.

"Thank you for my iPad," I said. When it had come in a few days before, I couldn't wait for the actual holiday to open it. "Let me see. I think I have a gift for you somewhere."

I grabbed a wooden chair from the kitchen table and stepped up. "Hmm, what's this? Why, I think it's a chew toy for ... Rochester!" He jumped up and put his paws on my lower legs. "Mama Lili will open it for you."

I handed her the toy, a square rubber thing in the shape of a house, with a chimney stuck to the top. "I'm still not sure about that Mama Lili business," Lili said.

"You want to be Mommy?"

"I'll get back to you on that," she said, as she got the scissors to cut open the plastic shell around the toy. Rochester couldn't control his enthusiasm, dancing around both of us. When she got the toy out and handed it to him, he grabbed it between his jaws and scurried up to the stair landing where he began to chew noisily.

"I was sure there was something here for you, too," I said, as I pretended to rummage. "Oh, here it is."

I handed her the square box, which I'd wrapped in paper festooned with menorahs and dreidels. She carefully slit the seam, and I said, "Go on, rip the paper. You know you want to."

She laughed. "Fine." She ripped it open. "It's a lens for my iPhone!"

"Four lenses in one," I said. "I know you take pictures sometimes with your phone when you don't have a camera with you. This way you'll have a 10x magnifier, a 15x, a fish-eye, and a wide-angle, all in one."

"I love it!" she said. I got down from the chair and we kissed. "Thank you! I can't wait to try it out."

"Well, there's a dog on the stairs who loves to have his picture taken."

She picked up her phone from the counter and began fiddling with the lens. "You go up there with him. I'll take some shots of both of you."

I joined the big golden dog on the landing, sitting down beside him. He ignored me at first, fixated on the rubber house, but I wrapped my arm around him and pulled him close, and he began to lick my ear, then jump on me.

In the background I heard the soft click of Lili's camera phone. I laughed and rolled around with the dog, and I thought it was the best Hanukkah I'd had since I was a kid.

6 – Ghost Town

WEDNESDAY MORNING ROCHESTER AND I went for a walk, and he moved more easily, which meant that the treatment was working on his infected nail bed. I stopped on the way back into the townhouse to pick up the papers from the driveway.

The front page headline in both papers read "Feds Raid Bucks Grow Houses," and it was about a DEA operation in Bucks County. Though the southern end of the county is heavily developed, the north end was primarily rural. According to the article, the DEA had raided several isolated houses about twenty miles north of Stewart's Crossing, where a Philadelphia-based drug operation had been growing marijuana under special lights.

Whenever I see an article like that, with a long list of those arrested, I can't help but look at each name. I couldn't help remembering when my name had appeared in those circumstances. The only one that rang a bell at all, though, was someone named Yunior Zeno, who was among those who had been picked up.

I sat back in my chair and Rochester looked up. Where had I heard that name? Was he someone I'd met in Stewart's Crossing? A student at Eastern? I couldn't remember, but it made me uneasy to think that I might have come in contact with some North Philly drug lord.

I ate breakfast with Lili. "You have any plans for today?" I asked.

"Work on my photojournalism course," she said. "I want to talk to Rick and see if he can introduce me to that homeless man he mentioned who lives behind the florist. I'd like to take some pictures of him and where he lives, maybe get a bit of oral history from him. I think it would be a good model for what I'd like students to do."

"Just be careful," I said. "Don't the statistics say that some big percent of homeless people have mental problems?"

"I've faced down drug dealers in Mexico and armed militias in Lebanon," she said. "I can handle a homeless man in Stewart's Crossing."

That didn't reassure me much, but I knew that I had to trust in Lili's instincts. I spent the morning preparing purchase orders for ads in magazines advertising the programs I was planning at Friar Lake. When I checked my email after lunch, Lili had sent me a shot of the area behind the florist's. "Great photo session. Lots to tell you tonight," she wrote.

At least she was safe, I thought. Her homeless project reminded me of the conversation we'd had with Felix Logato about the time he lived on the streets, and I went back to the results of the grammar tests he'd taken, to see what else he had to work on.

Another common problem I found with Eastern students, and with Felix as well, was a failure to understand tense shifts – jumping from present tense to past and back, sometimes within a single sentence. I thought it came from replicating what they heard, often missing the –ed at the end of words.

I found more exercises for Felix to do in that area, and emailed them to him. I was worried that I hadn't heard back from him about the summary I'd asked him to write, but I hoped that meant he was taking his time and trying to do his best.

It was misty and overcast as Rochester and I drove home that night, and the occasional exterior lights seemed eerie in the darkness. I remembered that article about grow houses and wondered if I was passing any of them as yet undiscovered. Would that mean that Philly criminals were cruising the roads of Bucks County now, armed with all kinds of weapons? What was next? Gang-related shootouts on Main Street? Desperate addicts breaking into pharmacies and doctors' offices? I knew there was drug activity everywhere, but I was surprised that the operation was so organized and well-hidden.

When I got home, Lili and I lit the Hanukkah candles together. "How was your day?" I asked. "You went to see that homeless guy?"

"Rick drove over with me and introduced me. His name is Jerry Cheseboro, and he grew up in Massachusetts. Moved here with his wife about ten years ago because her job transferred her."

She had picked up a rotisserie chicken from the grocery for us, and while she prepared a salad to go with it, I put the chicken on a platter and nuked some frozen potatoes.

"Two years ago, she was diagnosed with breast cancer and she died a year ago," she continued. "He couldn't afford to keep the house on his salary at the florist's so he moved in with a friend. But then the friend kicked him out and he lost his job."

She turned to me. "Life is so tenuous, you know? One day you're happy and then the next everything falls apart."

I took her in my arms. "We've been very fortunate, sweetheart. Not everyone has had the opportunities we have. No one can know what's going to happen, but at least we can be prepared. It'll take a lot of bad luck to knock us down."

She kissed me. "I love you, Steve. I'm so glad we found each other."

"Right back at you," I said, and the microwave timer dinged.

After dinner Lili helped me once again to wash and bandage Rochester's paw. He was almost healed but I wanted to give him one more treatment. When my phone rang, my hands were still wet, so Lili answered for me. "I'm so glad you called, Edith," she said. "And I'm delighted that you're back home. I always feel better around all my own things."

She sat on the couch to talk, and I played with Rochester on the floor. "We'll come over to see you tomorrow night," Lili said into the phone. "I'll make you a lasagna. You'll eat that, won't you?" She laughed in response to something Edith said. "And yes, we'll bring Rochester with us."

As Lili hung up, I sat in the ugly but comfortable recliner that had my dad's butt-print permanently impressed into it. "Edith's back home, with an aide to help her out through the holidays," Lili said. "You don't mind if we go see her tomorrow, do you?"

"Not at all. I'm glad she's feeling better."

Lili patted the couch next to her. "You know how much I hate that recliner," she said. "Don't make me look at you in it."

"Fine. I can take a hint." I moved over to sit beside Lili, and Rochester scrambled up to take my place in the chair. Lili and I scooted around so that we were facing each other, our legs crossed.

"It'll be nice to have a puppy for a few days," she said. "That Brody is adorable."

"Obviously you have never had a puppy around," I said. "They get into everything. They chew things. They pee in the house. They jump on people. And Rochester's never had another dog here for more than a few hours. You watch, this house is going to become a war zone so fast it will make your head spin."

"Come on, it won't be that bad."

"I guarantee you, by the time Joey and Mark get back from their cruise and he goes home, you'll be shouting hosannas of praise and we will be back to a one-dog household."

"You never know," Lili said. "There could be another furry bundle of joy waiting for you on Christmas morning."

I leaned forward and kissed her. "Then it's a good thing we're Jewish," I said. "Any Christmas bundles are undoubtedly at the wrong house."

* * *

By mid-day Thursday, Friar Lake was a ghost town. Only a few cars and trucks remained in the parking lot, and as I walked Rochester around I couldn't hear any of the usual sounds of hammering and clanking. We found Joey Capodilupo in the abbey chapel, sitting on the floor refinishing a wooden pew.

Joey and I had made a deal earlier in the fall. The pews didn't fit into the new design for the chapel, but they were too good to throw away. If Joey would refinish a few for seating around the property, he could have the rest to restore and sell through Mark's antique store. He'd completed three so far, two for us and one for him.

"Where is everybody?" I asked. I was glad that I had my coat on, because it was chilly in the abbey. Rochester didn't seem to mind; he sprawled right down on the cold stone floor at my feet.

"I managed to get all the guys shifted over to jobs that will be working next week, and the week after. Don't worry, they'll be back after New Year's."

He looked up at me. "Say, Mark and I have a crack of dawn flight out of Philly on Sunday morning. Would you mind if we brought Brody over Saturday night? After he's been fed and walked? He usually zonks out by then anyway. And he sleeps through the night."

I'd never imagined that the puppy wouldn't. But then, by the time I got Rochester he was a year old, long since house-broken and leash-trained. "And he's potty-trained, right?" I asked, realizing I should have checked that before I agreed to host him.

Joey looked offended. "He's eight months old," he said. "He used the piddle pads for the first couple of weeks after I got him, but he's been going outside for months now." He laughed. "For a while, I had this sign up in my kitchen, 'this workplace has been accident free for X days,' and I changed the number every day Brody was doing fine. Eventually I was able to dump the sign."

"You expect anybody working here tomorrow?" I asked.

He shook his head. "All the subs will be gone. I might come up for a few hours to keep going on these pews. I can make sure the place is all locked up when I leave."

"Sweet," I said. "I'll have time to puppy-proof the house."

"You don't already have it that way?"

I shook my head. "Rochester's always been pretty well-behaved. If he grabs something, it's because he's trying to send me a message."

I leaned down and scratched behind the dog's ears, and he yawned.

Joey raised an eyebrow. "Yeah, a message like, 'you shouldn't have left that where I can chew it.'"

I wasn't going to explain Rochester's uncanny nose for crime, the way he was able to dig up clues that helped Rick bring bad guys to justice. You either believe in that kind of thing, or you don't. I did, and so did Lili, and Rick was becoming a convert.

I looked around. "Why is it so cold in here? Isn't there heat?"

"The electricians are still installing the HVAC system," Joey said. "Right now we've been making do with salamanders."

That was a gruesome thought. "What do you do, burn them?" I asked. "I hope they're already dead."

"Not the lizards," Joey said. "A salamander is a portable kerosene-fueled heater. We use them a lot on construction sites in the winter, as long as there's good ventilation."

"Well, I'm glad to hear you're not burning lizards. I have enough trouble trying to keep Rochester from eating dead ones."

"Tell me about it," Joey said. "Brody's a canine garbage machine. He picks up rocks, mulch, dead leaves, pretty much anything he can wrap his mouth around."

"You're not making the prospect of dog-sitting him look appealing," I said.

"Rochester will keep him in line, I'm sure," Joey said.

At the sound of his name, my dog scrambled to his feet, his

toenails clicking against the stone, and we walked back to the office. At three-thirty Joey came in and said that he wanted to close up for the holidays, if I didn't mind. I helped him do a walk-through, making sure everything was secured for the two-week break, that all the water lines were shut down and all the buildings were locked up.

When I got home, there were two fragrant trays of lasagna cooling on the counter. "I hope one of those is for us," I said, as I kissed Lili's cheek.

She pushed aside an auburn curl that had come out of her loose ponytail. "You think I would tantalize you like that?" she said, smiling.

"I am sure you are capable of many things." I leaned down and took a deep breath of meat, cheese and mushrooms. "As well as being an awesome cook."

I was trying to stop feeding Rochester people food, though it was an uphill battle. At dinner I ended up giving him a few nibbles of ground beef from my plate. As long as he expressed his appreciation by wagging his tail, Lili didn't mind.

After we finished we set the menorah in the sink so that the candles could continue to burn without danger of falling over and igniting something. Then we drove to Edith's Cape Cod house in the Lakes. We parked in front of the house and Rochester left a message for the neighborhood dogs that he'd passed by.

A skinny, nervous Haitian girl in her late teens or early twenties answered our knock. "Hi," Lili said, and introduced us. "We're here to see Edith."

The girl, whose name was Staylene, was clearly frightened of Rochester. "Don't worry, he doesn't bite," I said. "And Edith specially asked us to bring him."

Edith's house was compact and cozy, with the living room to the right, and where others might have placed a dining room table, she had installed a baby grand piano – the very one where I had endured three years of lessons as a kid. Beyond it was her cheery yellow kitchen, decorated with framed music memorabilia – concert programs, autographed promotional shots of famous pianists, and her own photos of concert halls around the world, where she had traveled with her late husband.

We handed the lasagna and cake to Staylene, who took it toward the kitchen. Lili, Rochester and I turned left, toward Edith's bedroom. We found her sitting propped up in a double bed, surrounded by pink pillows. Opera music was playing softly in the background.

Staylene had teased out Edith's white hair for her and applied a bit of blush to her cheeks, so she looked a lot healthier than she had in the nursing home. Rochester paced over to the bed and lifted his nose to sniff her outstretched hand. "Hello my darling," she said to him. "How nice of you all to come and visit me." She turned to the radio by the bed and shut the music down. "It was so wonderful to see you at Crossing Manor, too."

"It's great to see you looking so well. How's the hip?"

"It's surprisingly good," she said. "I had some arthritis there, and cartilage damage, so it was always painful in cold weather. But with the new hip, that pain is all gone. I'm coping with getting back to my activity level."

Lili sat on the bed beside Edith. "We brought you the lasagna I promised, and some leftover carrot cake that Tamsen Morgan made for us."

"She's such a sweet girl," Edith said. "I remember when she and her sister Hannah were girls, running around the Meeting House. They seemed so full of joy. And then to lose her husband that way...." She shook her head. "Is she still seeing Detective Stemper?"

I sat on the floor beside Rochester, who kept his head near Edith's hand. "She is. They appear to be getting along well."

We talked for a few minutes. "I'm glad you got out of Crossing Manor," I said. "Another one of the people we met when we came to see you passed away."

"I saw that in the paper," she said. "He was an awfully nice fellow, Mr. Pappas. He still lived in his family's house on Lakefront Drive, you know, and sometimes I saw him when I was out walking. I was surprised because his Crohn's seemed to be in remission and he was planning to go home soon."

"Do you think there's anything suspicious about two deaths in such a short time?" I asked.

"Suspicious? Not at all. So many of the people at Crossing Manor were very ill, dear. For most of them, it's the last place they'll live. I was fortunate that I was just there for rehab. They took good care of me, and the social worker helped me arrange to have a physical therapist come to the house for the next few weeks." She paused. "The only person there who disturbed me was that young girl. Allison."

"Really? She seemed very nice," Lili said.

"I've known hundreds of young people over the years," Edith said. "Sweet children like Tamsen and Hannah, curious boys like Steve here. Spoiled brats and prodigies. So believe me when I tell you there's something not quite right about Allison."

"In what way?" I asked.

"It's hard to put a finger on it. On the surface, she's very solicitous. Always has a smile on her face, no matter what anyone asks her to do. But I got the sense that she has a very dark place inside her."

"I thought it was odd that she told us she had to stop being a candy striper at the hospital," Lili asked. "Did she ever tell you why?"

"She said she didn't get along with one of the nurses," Edith said. "And she had this almost morbid fascination with what was wrong with people, which might have upset some of the patients. I remember she talked to Mr. Pappas about his Crohn's Disease several times and it was almost like she relished him having a tough prognosis."

"I admire a teenager who's willing to give up her free time to help others," I said. "Though I did find her tongue piercing creepy and sometimes it was hard to understand her. But you know, teenagers are always trying to find ways to express themselves."

Edith yawned, and Lili stood up. "We'll leave you to get your rest," she said. "I hope you enjoy the lasagna."

"Oh, I'm sure I will, dear," Edith said. She thanked us again for coming, and petted Rochester goodbye.

"Now, you be careful," I said to Edith as I stopped by her bedroom door. "No more accidents, all right?"

"I'll do my best," she said.

7 – My Child

FRIDAY MORNING I TRIED TO SLEEP IN, enjoying the start of a long vacation, but Rochester wanted to go for his walk. I stumbled into my sweat pants, long-sleeved T-shirt, woolen socks and running shoes. Added a sweater, scarf, hat and gloves, and then I was ready to go. I left Lili asleep in bed and followed Rochester downstairs. He leapt the last couple of steps, his toenails scrabbling on the tile floor as he landed. Before we walked out, I peeled back the bandage and checked his paw, and it looked like the nail bed had healed. That meant I could stop the povidone iodine baths, though I knew he had to finish the whole course of antibiotic pills.

It was cold and clear. The deciduous trees of River Bend had long since lost their leaves, though the occasional pine or spruce still displayed coats of rich, dark green branches. I waved at a couple of neighbors who passed us on their way to work, feeling mildly guilty that I wasn't going up to Friar Lake. But Joey had already closed the place up, I reasoned, and either Rochester or I would probably muck something up.

When we returned, I fed Rochester, gave him his pill, and made a pair of cheese and mushroom omelets. Lili came downstairs as I was sliding them onto plates. "Smells delicious," she said.

I ushered her to the table and served her breakfast, accompanied by slices of eggy challah bread and a glass of orange juice. We read the papers, and then I left her to clean up and went back upstairs. I read in bed for a while, Rochester sprawled at the foot of the bed, then slid back beneath the covers for a mid-morning nap.

When I woke to Rochester's hot breath in my face, I took him out for a quick pee, then hurried back inside to the warmth of the house. He and I played, then he napped and I read for the rest of the afternoon. That night Lili and I lit the candles again, and the glow of

Dog Have Mercy

the menorah continued to grow. I was glad that we had resurrected that tradition; it was one of those things that make a house a home, and the townhouse on Sarajevo Court had begun to seem much more like a home since Lili had moved in.

I had been nervous at first, because Lili and I hadn't known each other for long, and because we'd both grown accustomed to living on our own. But aside from disagreements about clutter (Lili was pro, I was con) and other small aggravations, we were getting along very well.

Saturday morning after breakfast, I thought about the lonely people at Crossing Manor who had so appreciated the chance to have a furry, golden visitor. Despite the uneasy feeling the place gave me, I thought I ought to go back at least once more. "I might take Rochester back to the nursing home today for a quick visit," I said to Lili. "With the holidays coming, I'm sure some of those people are feeling lonely."

"I'll let you guys go on your own," Lili said. "I want to work on those photos I took of Jerry Cheseboro and finish the outline for my photojournalism course. I can't enjoy the vacation with that hanging over me."

The same teenager, Allison, was in the lobby when Rochester and I walked in, playing cards with an elderly man. Instead of the scrubs she'd worn before, she was in a turtleneck sweater and torn jeans. "Your friend already went home," she said. "Mrs. Passis."

For a moment I had to concentrate on what she'd said, because her tongue piercing made her mumble on certain words. The more I thought about it, it was probably her piercings that had upset Edith—they bothered me, and I had a lot more experience of people her age through my work at Eastern.

"I know. We saw her the other night. I thought maybe we could say hi to some of the other patients."

Rochester sat beside me, behaving sweetly as he had before, though I noticed he was careful to stay on the other side of me from Allison. I remembered how he'd only been interested in what was in her pocket the last time we'd visited, not in making friends with her, and what Edith had said about her. She seemed like an ordinary teenager to me, but I trusted my dog's instincts.

Allison smiled. "I wish there were more people like you. Some of these patients have nobody else, and they don't have much of a life here." She looked at the old man, so thin I could see his bones through his skin, who had clear tubes running from his nostrils to a portable oxygen tank. "Unlike Mr. Watnik, who's a whiz at gin rummy." She picked a card, and then put down three queens in a lay.

I resisted the urge to suggest she might think differently when she got to be their age. Mr. Watnik had nothing laid out in front of him, but he picked a card and then spread out four twos and three sevens. He smiled a toothless grin and said, "Gin!"

"Oh, you," Allison said to him. Then she looked up at me. "Do you want me to walk you guys down to the lounge?"

"No, we can find our way," I said. I stopped at the reception desk and signed in, and then Rochester tugged me down the hall. Allison might have been somewhat callow, I thought, but she was spending her Saturday morning playing cards with an old man, and that meant she had to have a heart.

Rochester and I walked around the room, talking again with Mr. MacRae, the janitor at my elementary school, and with Mrs. Curry, the paraplegic woman who had been at Crossing Manor for years. We also met Mrs. Vinci, who spoke with the harsh, guttural accent of a lower-income New York upbringing.

"My kids brought me down here," she said. "Me, I woulda stayed in Brooklyn, but they got a fancy house out here and said it ain't right I should be up there." Her hair was a salt-and-pepper gray, cropped short like a boy's, and her face was crisscrossed with deep wrinkles.

The woman beside her, Mrs. Divaram, was a plump, dark-skinned East Indian woman with a lilting accent, wearing an intricate red sari. "I am telling you to be grateful you have your children close by," she said. "My son lives in California with his second wife, who does not like me. So he pays to keep me far away. I have not seen my grandchildren in many years."

All those I spoke with were delighted to let Rochester sniff their fingers, to stroke his soft fur and whisper sweet endearments to him. Allison came in and said, "There's one more patient who would like to see Rochester, but he's in his room. Would you mind?"

"Not at all."

"His name is Mr. Fictura, but I calls him Mr. Fistula because he's a pain in the ass," she said. "Maybe Rochester can sweeten him up."

Mr. Fictura was a wizened old man who reminded me of Gollum

Dog Have Mercy

in *The Hobbit*. "I always had dogs before I got stuck in here," he said, as Rochester walked up to be petted. "Picked up a ton of dogshit. But dogs are like everybody else. They die and leave you."

Well, that was a cheery sentiment, I thought. "But while they're with you, they provide unconditional love," I said.

"For what that's worth." He pulled his hand back. "You can go now."

"He doesn't seem that bad," I said to Allison as she led us back to the front door.

"He yells a lot at the nurses and the aides and he refuses to go for therapy. But I guess they can't kick him out as long as he pays his bills."

"I'm sure it's hard to be in his position," I said. I shook her hand and promised we would come back again another time.

When we got home, Lili was still busy with her course outline, and Rochester and I sat downstairs. "Guess we ought to do some puppy-proofing, boy," I said to him. "What kind of trouble do you think Brody can get into?"

He yawned and sprawled on the floor, clearly not interested in helping. I walked around the house, removing breakables and chewables from lower shelves, coiling up unused electrical cords and the cables for various electronic devices. In the kitchen, I made sure all the food was pushed back on the counter far enough to avoid an inquisitive puppy's nose and tongue. By the time I finished, Lili had given up on her course and joined us in the living room, and we spent the afternoon relaxing and reading.

It was close to eight o'clock that night when the gate guard called to announce Joey and Mark. A few minutes later Rochester began to bark and rushed to the front door.

The puppy led the way into our house – always a bad sign, in my opinion. Dogs are pack animals, and they need to know that their human is their leader. Though I did let Rochester pull sometimes when we walked, he and I had an agreement. He knew that I was in charge in the important ways, that I'd always protect him and feed him and love him, and he could relax and just be a dog. Rick had the same deal with Rascal, but I'd seen a lot of spoiled dogs who thought they were in charge, and who fretted and barked when their humans were out of their sight.

Mark and Joey followed, bearing piles of stuff – Brody's bed, a collection of his favorite toys, water and food bowls, and a bag of the puppy version of the chow Rochester ate. I thought Joey made a good physical match for Mark; he was almost Mark's height of six-six, but broader in the shoulders. I was glad that I'd fixed them up.

"Joey and Mark are like you," Lili said, when she saw all the gear. "Puppy-whipped."

"Ha-ha," I said.

As Rochester and Brody chased each other around the downstairs, Joey handed me a typed sheet of everything I never wanted to know about Brody, including his middle name, Baggins. "Your dog is a hobbit?" I asked, raising an eyebrow.

"He's short and has hairy feet," Joey said.

"Joey didn't want to be too obvious and call him Frodo or Bilbo," Mark added. "He's kind of a stealth Tolkien geek."

"Mark does not appreciate the deep insights of the *Lord of the Rings*," Joey said.

Mark snorted. "Elves and trolls and dwarves. Adolescent trash."

"Hey, those are fighting words in this house," I said. "I've read *The Hobbit* and the trilogy twice, and seen all the movies, even the bad animated one."

"Who's your favorite character?" Joey asked.

Mark groaned and Lili led him into the kitchen. By the time they returned with mugs of hot chocolate, Joey and I had compared notes on characters and scenes. I admitted an adolescent crush on Galadriel, the Lady of Light and wife of Elrond, Lord of Rivendell and master of the Last Lonely House. His was on Aragorn, the human leader of the Fellowship of the Ring, who became the king of the reunited kingdoms of Arnor and Gondor.

I figured we were both pretty geeky to know all that.

The dogs circled around us as we sat at the kitchen table with our mugs of hot chocolate, to which Lili had applied generous helpings of Godiva chocolate liqueur.

"I only give Brody organic treats," Joey said. "There's a bag of them in with his stuff."

"Don't worry, Rochester only eats organic himself," I said.

Joey had given us his and Mark's email addresses, their cell phone numbers, and a detailed itinerary. "I made sure to get an international plan for my phone, so I can use it in every port," Joey said. "You use Dr. Horz too, don't you?"

Dog Have Mercy

I nodded. "Don't worry, we'll take good care of your baby."

"He's going to fuss through the whole cruise," Mark said. "You don't know what I had to do to convince him to go in the first place."

"Brody is my child," Joey said, and I knew exactly what he meant. I also knew that Rochester was a handful, and I was sure Brody would be, too. I hoped Rochester would keep the puppy in line. And with luck, neither dog would dig up any dead bodies while Brody was with us.

8 – Alpha Males

JOEY AND MARK SLIPPED AWAY while Brody and Rochester were roughhousing, and it took the puppy a few minutes to realize that his daddy was gone. He sat by the front door and whimpered.

"I hope this dog is not a crybaby," I said. I walked over and picked him up. He was about thirty pounds of wriggling white fur, so it wasn't that easy, but I brought him over to the sofa and lay down. I set him beside me on his back and stroked his belly. Every time he tried to squirm away I put my hands around his muzzle and said, "No!" Eventually he figured out that the easiest route was submission.

Rochester was jealous, and he kept sniffing at me and the puppy. Lili called him over to her, but after a few minutes I let Brody go, and he and Rochester went at it again, running around the house like maniacs. Rochester tried to mount him, and I had to yell at him. "No humping the puppy!"

Then Brody grabbed Rochester's ear and began chewing. "Brody! Rochester is not an edible!"

"Let them work it out," Lili said. "It's up to Rochester to let Brody know his place."

"But what if one of them hurts the other? Could you imagine if I had to call Joey from the vet's even before he left on his cruise?"

"Rochester's smart. He'll manage."

Eventually the two of them calmed down and sprawled beside each other in a temporary amnesty. When we took them both out late that night, it was funny to watch Brody pee – his tail stood straight up and he leaned forward slightly. "He's like a teapot," I said. "You lift the handle and the water comes out."

Rochester waited until Brody was finished, then sniffed around, despite my efforts to tug him away. Then he lifted his leg.

Dog Have Mercy

"See?" Lili said. "He's letting Brody know he's the alpha."

"I like that," I said. "Rochester's saying 'I piss on you, you little piece of fluff.'"

"Not exactly," Lili said.

Rochester usually spent the night at the foot of our bed, but Brody wasn't going to settle for carpet when there was space on the mattress. He jumped up and scooched himself between me and Lili. Then Rochester had to join us, staking claim to the end of the bed. "There's no room for humans here," I grumbled.

"Get used to it." Lili yawned, then leaned over and kissed me goodnight. "This is our new family, at least for the next week."

Sunday morning, Brody gulped down his food as if he was the star of a speed-eating contest, and then tried to nose his way into Rochester's bowl. My big dog barked at him once, sharply, and Brody backed away. But a moment later he was back, and it took three barks and some bared teeth before he got the message.

I watched the whole episode, worrying at any moment that there would be bloodshed. But Rochester's instincts had taken over, and he and the puppy worked out an arrangement. Rochester stepped away from his bowl, leaving behind a few pellets, as if to say "You can have my leftovers, but only after I've finished."

When I checked my email later that morning, there was a message from Felix, Dr. Horz's kennel assistant, asking if he could come over that afternoon to show me his progress and ask some questions. He left his cell number, and I called him back and told him we'd be home.

It was a gray, wintery day, shreds of clouds scudding across the horizon, a cold wind rattling the tree branches. Felix arrived around two, wearing his plaid-lined parka and puffy gloves. Rochester and Brody both tackled him, and he said, "Down!" in a commanding voice, pointing to the floor.

Rochester obeyed immediately. Brody hesitated for a second then followed my dog's lead. "How'd you do that?" I asked, as I took his parka and gloves from him.

He leaned down to pet both dogs and tell them they were good boys. "It's all in the tone of voice, along with the hand gesture," he said when he straightened up. "I didn't realize you had a puppy, too."

"He's just visiting." Brody grabbed the end of the comforter over the sofa in his mouth and began tugging. "And not for very long, unless he behaves."

"I'm going upstairs," Lili said. "I'm finished with the homelessness module in my photojournalism course, and I want to crank out the rest of the lessons."

"It's not pretty," Felix said. "I was homeless for a while, before I went to prison."

Felix had a day's beard on his chin, and between his close-cropped hair and his tattooed arms, I thought he must have been a formidable presence on the streets.

Lili stopped at the foot of the stairs. "Here in Stewart's Crossing?" she asked.

He shook his head. "Nah, in the Badlands of North Philly, where I come from."

"Would you mind if I asked you some questions? Once you're done with Steve?"

He shrugged. "Yeah, I got nothing to hide anymore."

Lili climbed the stairs, and I led Felix to the kitchen table, the dogs following eagerly. I gave them each a rawhide bone to chew and they settled beside us as Felix and I went over his progress. I answered some questions about commas, and it appeared that he was beginning to understand the rules.

He pulled out a page of dictionary definitions that he'd copied out, and I gave him a quick quiz on those words. "You're picking this up fast," I said. "Whoever told you you're not a good student wasn't paying attention."

"In prison, I had to learn fast," he said. "But I guess you know that yourself."

"You bet. I had to figure out who the big dogs were, and stay out of their way. I had an advantage, because I had an education, and I could help them with their appeals paperwork. It was interesting for me, and I got to know a lot of different guys I never would have met in my regular life."

"I didn't have it so easy. I had to fight for my place." He rolled up his left sleeve. "See this tattoo?" It was the word R E S P E C T in rough gothic lettering. "I had one of the guys do it for me, so people would know not to mess with me."

I looked at him. He was shorter than I was, about five-nine, and wiry. It looked like he could take care of himself in a prison fight.

To shift the conversation, I asked, "You want anything to drink?

Dog Have Mercy

I could use a glass of water."

He accepted a glass, then handed me the paper on which he'd hand-written his summary of the vet tech program's website. "It's not very good," he said. "I still got a lot of problems with writing."

"I still *have* a lot of problems with writing," I said. "Using 'got' that way is street language. You can use 'got' with 'have' if you want – I have got a lot of problems. But it's an extra word you don't need."

"And it makes me sound dumb," he said.

"Well, I wouldn't say dumb. But yeah, it's less proper."

I went over his summary with him. He had the main ideas down correctly, but he'd written it all as one big paragraph, and I showed him where he was moving from point to point, and where he'd have to break up into new paragraphs.

By the time we were finished, Lili had joined us again. The dogs were still involved with their rawhides. "Where you want me to start?" Felix asked Lili.

"How'd you end up homeless?"

"You got to understand," he began. "No, you *have* to understand, the Badlands is a tough neighborhood. I grew up near Broad Street and Hunting Park, drug deals going down all around. It's mostly all old rowhouses and abandoned warehouses, all poor people, black, Irish, Puerto Rican. Some of those warehouses, they made them into shooting galleries. I think every junkie in Philly ended up there some time or other."

He took a sip of his water. "By the time I was twelve I was working a corner as a lookout for a dealer. When he went to prison, the Owner got me to take over selling."

"Owner?" I asked.

"That's what you call the boss man. Every dope block in the Badlands is run by one of 'em. He's the one got the dope in bulk from Puerto Ricans or Dominicans. Every couple of days he'd bring me more to sell, these bags of drugs in rubber-banded stacks that we called bundles."

"Must have been a lot of money in that," I said.

He nodded. "Yeah, but most of it went to the Owner, and what I got, I pissed away fast. My moms didn't like me working the streets, but she sure liked me giving her money for food and rent, and buying shit for my sisters and brothers."

"Where were the cops?" Lili asked.

"Shit, they were outmanned and outgunned," Felix said. "There were some decent blocks where families lived, and the cops kept to those places, left the bad zones alone."

He picked up his water glass again, and I noticed his hand shook a bit. "You don't have to talk about this if you don't want to," I said.

"No sweat. I started to get a big head, you know, mouthing off to my moms, and she kicked me out. I lived high for a while, but then I OD'd on some bad shit and ended up in the hospital. Time I got out, I had no money and no place to go. That's how I ended up homeless."

He took a deep breath. "I got stupid, let the cops catch me with a big pile of bundles. Couldn't pay back the Owner, so I fessed up and went to prison. Soon after I got there I got hooked into Paws Up. It was the dogs that helped me turn around."

Rochester got up from the floor and snuffled Felix's hand. "Say, how's Rochester's paw?" he asked.

"Looks like it's healed," I said.

Felix got down on the floor to look at it, but bossy little Brody kept trying to stick his nose in. Felix gently elbowed the puppy out of the way and picked up Rochester's paw. "Yeah, looks good. But you should still have a follow-up with Dr. Horz to be sure. We're closing early on Wednesday for Christmas Eve, so come in before that."

"I will, thanks," I said. "You've made great progress so far, but I want you to practice some more writing, trying to incorporate the grammar you've been learning. I'll send you some more stuff to read and summarize, all right? And there are a couple of other little grammar things you need to work on, too."

Felix reached out to shake my hand. "This is really solid, what you're doing, taking time with me, inviting me to your home and all. I've been blessed lately – getting into Paws Up and working with the dogs, then Dr. Horz taking a chance on me and giving me a job. I feel like I'm finally getting my shit together."

He looked embarrassed. "My act together, I mean."

Lili and I both laughed. I remembered Mr. Fictura's comment. "Hey, you deal with dogs, you've got to deal with shit," I said, and shook Felix's hand.

9 – Cabin Fever

"HOW'S MY BOY DOING?" the voice on the phone asked, and it took me a second to recognize it was Joey Capodilupo.

"Rochester has him in training," I said, as I watched the two dogs tug a rope between them. Brody braced his front paws on the floor and lowered his head, growling.

"He's not crying too much, is he?" Joey asked.

"He cried some last night. But then he and Rochester started to play. Both dogs slept with me and Lili."

"Yeah, Mark hates the way Brody gets in between us. I haven't been able to cure him of that yet."

"My great-aunt Ida used to have a saying. 'When you go to bed with dogs you wake up with fleas.' I've adjusted that, though. 'When you kiss a dog, you get a mouthful of fur.'"

Joey laughed. "I'm sure he's in good hands. But you have my number, if you need anything."

"Relax and enjoy yourselves. How's the weather there?"

"Seventy-eight and sunny," Joey said. "We haven't left Miami yet. Mark and I are out on the deck with a couple of fruity cocktails, looking at the rich people's houses and all the sailboats and powerboats cruising past us."

"I'm jealous."

"Any time you want me to return the favor and watch Rochester, you let me know."

I told him I would, and he promised to call again on Tuesday from Cozumel. After we hung up I looked back at the dogs. Rochester was using his big paw to press down on the rope, giving him extra leverage in his battle with Brody. "Don't cheat, Rochester!" I said. "He's a little puppy." I reached over and lifted Rochester's paw from the rope, and Brody twisted around onto his side, keeping a death grip on it.

Lili had been reading on the sofa in the living room. "Was that Joey?" she asked.

"Yup. Wanted to check on his little boy. And he offered to babysit Rochester sometime if you and I want to go away."

"You'd leave him with Joey over Rick?"

I shrugged. "Rick works all the time, and Rascal spends more time with that old guy who looks after him than he does with Rick. I can tell Joey's kind of obsessed."

"The way you are," she said.

"I guess. I wouldn't leave Rochester in a kennel either. But now Joey will owe us a favor, so maybe the hound can stay with him if we go away. Do you see a cruise in our future? Or some other kind of trip?"

Though Lili had traveled a lot in her work, she'd never hit many of the hot vacation locations.

"I was thinking of that," she said, sitting back in her chair. "Maybe spring break? If you haven't started programming at Friar Lake by then."

"Right now, my first program is a two-day retreat for senior staff at the college, at the beginning of April," I said. "When does spring break come this year?"

"The second full week in March," she said. "You ever been on a cruise?"

I nodded. "Years ago. Mary and I took one of these short cruises from L.A., down to Ensenada and back. We always argued so much about what to do on vacation that we thought the cruise would force us to chill out and do things together."

"Did it work?"

"Our first port was Catalina Island, and she was on her cell phone most of the time we were there, doing business stuff. Then we had a day at sea, and she had a whole raft of spa treatments lined up. We did walk around in Ensenada together for a while, but Mary thought it was dirty and very Third World. I seem to remember she went back to the ship and I drank a whole lot of margaritas."

"So maybe a cruise isn't the right choice for us," Lili said.

"What kind of trip would you want to go on?" I asked. "If you had a week in March, and you could go anywhere or do anything."

"Honestly? I'd like to fly to an island where it's hot and sunny.

Dog Have Mercy

Lay by the beach, wander around taking photographs, eat great meals. I'd lay over a day or two in Miami and see my brother and his family. It's been a long time. And I'd like you to meet Fedi."

"That's an idea I could get behind," I said. "How about if I do some research and see where we could go?"

"Sounds like a plan, man," she said, and leaned over and kissed me.

That evening, I looked for some material I could send to Felix to summarize. I had accumulated quite a shelf of dog books, from Cesar Millan to The Monks of New Skete to Barbara Woodhouse. One of my favorite recent reads was *Until Tuesday*, about a wounded vet and the service dog who bonded with him, and I picked out a couple of pages from that to scan for Felix.

I found him an additional tutorial and exercises, and I emailed him the link, as well as the scanned pages, and told him to let me know when he was ready to meet again.

Then I spent some quality time on the living room floor with both dogs. Rochester was busy with a rawhide, so I pulled Brody over to me and began to stroke his back, where the hair was wavier and coarser than Rochester's. I wondered if that was because his coat was so light, almost white, while Rochester's was a rich gold.

Brody rolled onto his back, holding his paws curled up above him, and I stroked the soft down of his belly. As I moved the hairs around I revealed patches of skin. "This dog is purple!" I said to Lili.

"Excuse me?"

"Come here and see. His skin is purple."

"Steve. There are no purple puppies."

"Not his hair. His skin." She leaned down and I showed her. "See? This is purple. Rochester's skin is pink. Joey got some defective puppy."

"It does look purple," Lili said. "Maybe it's the light, or just a darker shade of pink."

I grabbed Rochester and tugged him over to us, then rolled him over to expose his belly. "See? Rochester's skin is normal. Brody is a mutant."

"Maybe he has special powers," she said. "Like in those X-Men movies. He can shoot lasers out of his eyes, change the weather or create magnetic fields."

"His fur could change into feathers and he could fly," I said, ruffling the fur on the puppy's back.

"Maybe he's a telepath," Lili said.

"Nope, that one's Rochester's special power." I leaned down and rubbed my face against Rochester's. "Isn't that right, my sweetie?"

Lili laughed. I loved it that she could join me on my flights of fancy. Whenever I'd started one of those around Mary, riffing about something that had happened at work, or a T-shirt slogan or a bumper sticker I saw on a car, she'd shut me down, telling me I was stupid, that a man with an Ivy League graduate degree shouldn't sound so foolish.

Lili went back to her book and Rochester to his rawhide. I rolled over and looked at Brody's face. Brown streaks came down from his eyes, making him look doleful. His paws were too large for his body, an indication that he'd be getting bigger. He had lost his sharp puppy teeth, and his regular ones were in. I could tell that like me, Joey must be brushing his dog's teeth, because they were clean and tartar-free.

Brody stood up and then stepped right over my head on his way to reach Rochester. "I am not some obstruction in your path, puppy," I said.

As I watched him try to get the rawhide from Rochester, I wondered what my dog had been like at Brody's age. Caroline had adopted Rochester at about six months, and he'd come to me a few months after that, already full grown. I'd never gone through that adorable little fluff ball stage with him, or the awkward months as he transitioned from puppy to full-grown.

Had he always had a knack for detection, perhaps something Caroline hadn't recognized? We hadn't talked much about him while she was alive. Mostly I'd complained about him jumping on me, and Caroline had apologized, and rhapsodized about what an adorable dog he was. I hadn't agreed until, after her death, I had agreed to take him in temporarily, and we had bonded.

Was that when his ability to sniff out criminal activity had come up, when he helped me figure out who had killed Caroline, and why? Was it some connection between us?

That night, as I walked them, Brody dawdled and Rochester pulled. "Yo, dogs, I'm not Gumby!" I said. I realized that the trick was to loop the two leashes together, so that if Brody balked, Rochester would tug him, and I wouldn't be in the middle.

Dog Have Mercy

It was biting cold, and I tried to hurry them along, but they both seemed oblivious to the temperature, focused on the sights, sounds and smells of Sarajevo Court.

We continued the previous night's pattern, with Brody and Rochester in bed with Lili and me. She had a hard time getting comfortable with so much of the bed's real estate given up to canine contortions, including Rochester stretching out all four legs in one corner.

When we woke Monday morning Lili had trouble stretching. "I slept funny," she said. "My back hurts."

"Want me to rub it?"

"I'll be all right once I get moving." She got up and went to the bathroom, and I used the one downstairs before bundling up to take the dogs. It was so cold that all the smaller dogs we saw were wearing sweaters, and I was grateful for Rochester's double-coat, which kept him warm in winter and cool in summer.

By the time we got back home, I was chilled through and my lips were dry and chapped. I used a tube of lip balm and then fixed breakfast for Lili and me, and poured out kibble for the two dogs. Lili and I shared the morning paper as we ate.

"I want to work on the rest of my photojournalism course this morning," Lili said, as she cleaned up the dishes. "All right if I use the office?"

"Sure. If I need to do anything online I have my laptop or my new iPad."

It was funny to be able to speak so openly about the laptop to Lili, since I kept my hacking tools on it. But I was trying not to keep secrets from her, at least not big ones.

Lili went upstairs and I tried to concentrate on my iPad, but Brody kept grabbing Rochester's leash from the table by the door and dragging it around the floor. "You can't need to go out again," I said to him the third time he did it. "I just took you."

He tried to play with Rochester, but my big dog resisted. Rochester looked up at me as if to say, "This puppy was all right for a while, but he can go home now."

I sat on the floor with Brody and a rope. Of course, once I was there, Rochester wanted in on the action. Every time I got up, Rochester ignored the puppy, and Brody began to whimper.

"Can you please keep that dog quiet?" Lili asked from the top of the stairs. "I cannot concentrate."

"I'm trying," I said. "He's very demanding."

"Like Rochester isn't," Lili said, and retreated back into the office, closing the door behind her.

This was why I had resisted having a dog, I thought, as I squeezed a ball in front of Brody. They were so needy. Even Rochester, who was a sweetheart, had to be fed and walked and played with, his coat groomed and his teeth brushed. He needed regular reinforcement that he was a good boy, lots of belly rubs and ear scratches and sweet endearments.

With two dogs in the house, it was as if the needs had been squared, not doubled. When one wanted to sleep, the other wanted to play. When one wanted to go out the other wanted to stay in. When Rochester didn't eat his bowl food fast enough, Brody nosed his way in, creating skirmishes that could lead to war.

Outside the wind picked up, bringing sleet with it. Not a day to go outside and tire the puppies out with a walk. They gobbled treats within seconds and got bored with balls between tosses. When they did play together I had to watch them carefully to make sure no one suffered mortal wounds.

By the time Lili came downstairs for dinner, they were both finally asleep, curled together beside the sofa. But at the sound of Lili's arrival, Brody jumped up and tried to tackle her.

"This puppy is a pain in the *tuchas*," she said, gently pushing on his snout. "Down!"

"At least you've been locked up in the office. I can't get anything done with the two of them here."

"You're the one who said we could take the puppy."

"No. I said I was leaving it up to you."

"And I said you weren't going to make me into the bad guy." She stopped. "We're all getting a bit of cabin fever. It's miserable outside and not that much better in here."

"Why don't we invite Rick and Rascal over for dinner?" I asked.

"So I can cook even more?"

"I'll cook," I said, trying not to get angry. One of the many useful skills I'd learned in prison was how to defuse arguments. "Rascal can herd the other two dogs around, and the three of us can act like humans."

It looked like Lili was going to argue again, but she said,

"There's a meat loaf in the freezer you can heat up. With a salad and baked potatoes, we can stretch it to three."

I kissed her cheek. "It'll get better, I promise," I said.

"Don't make promises you can't keep," she grumbled, but she smiled.

10 – Joe Hardy

I CALLED RICK. "Gee, I'd have to give up this Lean Cuisine I've been thinking about all day," he said. "I can be there at six."

I got the meat loaf out and the dogs gathered around me as I put it in a pan and covered it with tomato sauce. "It's frozen, puppies," I said. "You'd break your teeth on it."

That didn't deter them. I prepared the baking potatoes and slid them into the oven beside the pan. The dogs settled once all the food was out of sight, and I used the lip balm on my chapped lips. Something about the size and shape of the tube reminded me of the vials of potassium that had been stolen from Dr. Horz's office, and I went online, where I looked up veterinary uses of potassium. They were similar in animals and humans, used to treat a deficiency. But the potassium that vets used was in a liquid solution, in an injector.

Why would someone steal it, though? I remembered the last time I'd gone to the drugstore to buy cold pills, and found that I had to show my driver's license to the pharmacist in order to buy a blister pack of pseudoephedrine. Junkies had figured out a way to use it to make methamphetamines, so sales were restricted, and drugstores had to keep records of who bought the pills and in what quantity.

Could the same thing be happening with potassium? Were junkies in North Philly shooting it up? I did some more searching but couldn't find anything before Rochester and Brody jumped up and began barking at the arrival of Rick and Rascal. True to his heritage, Rascal ran the other two dogs around the downstairs, trying to corral them into behaving. The puppy yelped and barked, but it looked like they were all having a good time.

I handed Rick a Dogfish Head Midas Ale from the refrigerator, and uncapped one for myself. It was sweet yet dry, made with ingredients found in ancient drinking vessels from the tomb of King

Dog Have Mercy

Midas. It was a good brew for a cold winter night, somewhere between wine and mead.

"What's new on the police beat?" I asked as we sat in the living room and the dogs raced up and down the stairs.

"Picked up Bethea again at the corner of Main and Ferry," he said. Bethea was a middle-aged woman with mental problems who liked to stand at the one intersection in town with a traffic light. As soon as the light turned yellow against her, whichever side she was on, she began a slow, painstaking transit, tying up cars until she made her way across. By the time traffic could move, the light had changed, and horns honked and people yelled.

"She's out even in this weather?" I asked.

He shrugged. "She's been living with her sister-in-law in one of those run-down duplexes at the north end of the Flats." The Flats was a low-income pocket of Stewart's Crossing squeezed into a couple of acres of land downtown. It was sandwiched between the fancy houses along the river and the eastern bank of the canal, and it flooded regularly. Rick had once told me that neighborhood accounted for at least fifty percent of the crime in town, from illicit drug deals to domestic disputes.

"Last month the two of them got into a fight, and the sister-in-law kicked her out," he continued. "She's been sleeping in that thicket of maple trees behind DeLorenzo's hoagie shop, dumpster-diving for food."

Lili joined us, holding a glass of white wine by the steam. "That's terrible," she said, as she sat beside me on the sofa. "Isn't there somewhere she can go?"

"Not if she doesn't want to," Rick said. "I got the judge to put a psych hold on her and we took her over to the hospital. Hopefully they can find something wrong with her, and keep her there over the holiday."

"Doesn't the county have social workers?" Lili asked.

Rick sighed. "I've driven her to the mental health office myself. But she denies she has a problem, and as long as she seems coherent there's nothing they can do to force her. Statistics say that at least thirty percent of the homeless have mental problems. It's a way bigger problem than just Bethea and Jerry Cheseboro and Stewart's Crossing."

Lili started to talk to Rick about the man she'd met who was living behind the florist's, and I got the food from the oven and brought it to the table. After dinner we moved to the living room and I said, "I've been wondering about the potassium that was stolen from Dr. Horz's office."

Rick groaned. "You're not playing Nancy Drew again, are you?"

I crossed my arms over my chest. "The name is Hardy. Joe Hardy."

He snorted. "Dr. Horz is pretty baffled about the theft, which makes two of us."

Rochester jumped up onto the sofa beside me and Brody nosed around my feet. Rascal ignored them both and dozed on the tile. "I was thinking about those vials of potassium that were stolen from Dr. Horz's office," I said to Rick. "Could somebody have stolen it to get high? The way junkies are using cold medicine to make meth?"

"You have the most vivid imagination of anyone I've ever met," Rick said. "I haven't heard of anything like that. And since potassium isn't a schedule one drug, a vet isn't required to lock it up. She kept these vials in a cabinet in the lab room along with other medications."

"Anything else taken?" I asked.

"Not that she can tell. A lot of the supplies, she just reorders when they get low. She only noticed this potassium was gone when she went to get a vial and couldn't find any."

"It seems like such an odd theft," I said. "Is she making a big deal out of it?"

"At first she was worried that other stuff was taken, which was why she called the police. But since the vials weren't worth that much, it's only petty theft, and she isn't going to push it. I wouldn't be surprised if more stuff goes missing in the future, as long as she has that kennel assistant on her staff."

"Felix?"

"You know him?"

"Yeah, he was filling in for Elysia when I took Rochester in. I've been helping him improve his writing and grammar so he can apply to a vet tech program." I didn't add that Felix had been at my office, and my house. My parole was over, so I could associate with whoever I wanted to, but I didn't want to distract Rick and possibly get a lecture from him.

"So you know about his background?"

Dog Have Mercy

"His time in prison? Yeah. But that doesn't mean he stole the potassium."

"Makes him the most likely suspect. If I were Dr. Horz I'd can him, but I'm not her. If you want my honest opinion, I think somebody on Dr. Horz's staff used the last of the stuff up and forgot to tell her."

"But I thought you said she was missing five vials. That's a lot to forget about."

"Not if it happens one by one," he said. "Anyway, it's over, unless more drugs go missing. I've got enough real crimes on my plate without worrying about misplaced pharmaceuticals."

The conversation shifted to Tamsen and her son, and then to our dogs, and after a while Rick left, but I couldn't stop thinking about Felix. This job with Dr. Horz was his chance for rehabilitation, to start a new life and a new career. I hoped the vet would see that, and not fall prey to suspicion. I knew in my heart that Felix deserved the same chance for change I'd received.

Tuesday morning I was still thinking about Felix, so I turned on the desktop computer in the office and emailed him to ask how he was coming with his exercises and his summaries. I said that I was looking forward to seeing him again, and eventually to helping him with his application for the vet tech program.

The question of why someone had stolen those vials of potassium from Dr. Horz kept gnawing at me. I Googled everything I could think of, and one of the links I followed was intriguing. I learned that potassium chloride was one of the three chemicals used in carrying out the death penalty.

First sodium thiopental was injected at a high dose, rendering the person unconscious quickly. Then pancuronium bromide relaxed the muscles – that alone would eventually cause asphyxiation. To be more humane, potassium chloride was injected next. That stopped the heart almost immediately, before the lungs gave out and the person suffocated. The process took no more than a few minutes.

The first two were very controlled substances, and I doubted someone would be stealing the potassium to complete that triumvirate. Another link, though, was more sinister. Apparently potassium could be used to induce heart attacks. Hyperkalemia, that term for high potassium levels, disrupted the electrical conduction activity of the heart, resulting in myocardial infarction, or heart attack. I couldn't find any clear data on how fast an attack would come on – it depended a lot on the patient's overall health, weight and so on. Could someone have stolen the potassium in order to commit murder?

From downstairs I heard Lili yelling. "No, Brody! That is not yours!"

I hurried down. "What's up?"

"He grabbed a pile of photos from the dining room table and shredded them," she said. "I know, I shouldn't have left them out. But now I have to print them all again."

"Sorry," I said. "I'll take care of them now."

"I could make some suggestions on how you could take care of Brody," she said. "But I'm reminding myself that he's going home in a few days." She stalked upstairs, and I focused on the dogs, who romped around the living room together like long-lost siblings.

It took some rough play between the dogs, and some treats, but eventually they both curled around me. I opened the laptop and checked my email. "I'm over the whole grammar thing," Felix had written. "Even if somebody wants to give you a 2nd chance, somebody else screws you over."

Not even a smiley face at the end, or a "Thanks for your help, Steve."

Had Dr. Horz fired him? Or was he pissed off that suspicion had fallen on him because he was an ex-con? I started to type another email in response, but I stopped. I'd have to see him in person. I called Dr. Horz's office to see if he was there, but I got a recording that the office was closed until Monday for the Christmas holidays, and a referral to a twenty-four-hour emergency clinic.

Well, then I'd have to figure out where Felix Logato lived, and go over there. I'd take Rochester with me, because my golden had the ability to soften up anyone, especially a dog-lover like Felix.

But where did he live? I did a quick Google search. He wasn't the Felix Logato on Facebook or LinkedIn or any of the other social networking sites. One of the search engines that charged for results gave me a dozen choices, but none of them matched what I knew about Felix.

I remembered a previous search I'd done, for an elderly hippie who lived off the grid – no phone, no electric bill, no social media. I'd figured out that he was using his middle name as a first name, and once I knew that I had discovered his property records.

But Felix was a different kind of guy. It was logical that he wouldn't have social media accounts; depending on where he had been incarcerated, and under what conditions, he could have had Internet access restrictions. And I'd read articles about Facebook shutting down prisoner accounts.

It was also unlikely that he'd have set those accounts up once he was released. I remembered the months after my own discharge; I had wanted nothing more than to curl up by myself, not have to face people from my previous life.

If he was a parolee, though, maybe the parole officer I'd dealt with myself could help me find Felix. I picked up my cell and dialed Santiago Santos.

My last conversation with Santos hadn't been completely positive. He'd told me that despite his efforts, I was still an arrogant prick, that I thought I could outsmart the police and do whatever I wanted. He hadn't said it quite that way, but that's the way I'd heard it.

He answered briskly, "Santos."

"Santiago? It's Steve Levitan." I hesitated. "I'm not in trouble or anything, but a guy I know might be."

"I'm not a cop, Steve," he said. "Call your friend Rick Stemper."

"It's not like that," I said hurriedly. I explained that I had met Felix at the vet's, that I'd been helping him improve his writing so that he could apply to a vet tech program.

"And?"

"There was a theft, at the vet's office where he worked. I don't think Felix did it, and I'm afraid he's going to let the suspicion derail his progress. I want to go see him, try to convince him to push through this."

"So why call me?"

"The office where he works is closed for the holidays. I don't know where he lives, and I'm fighting the temptation to look behind closed doors on the Internet."

He sighed. "Well, at least you're trying," he said. "What's this guy's name again?"

"Felix Logato."

I heard Santiago's fingers clicking on his keyboard. "He's not on my list. And his PO is on vacation."

"Can you give me his address?"

"I'm not your personal assistant. And I couldn't do it without his permission."

I waited. I wanted Santos to make the next move.

"I suppose I could call him and ask," he said.

"Great! I'll hold."

"I have my own clients to worry about," he grumbled.

"But you care about your clients, I know that," I said. "And I'm figuring by association you care about people in general. It would be a real kindness to help me get in touch with him."

"Hold on."

I listened to some irritating music that was supposed to relax me, but just made more anxious. I didn't need to go home for the holidays, and I didn't need Rudolf to light my way anywhere.

What if Felix refused to let Santos give me his address? What if he got angry and did something stupid? I drummed my fingers on the desk.

"He says there's nothing you can do or say," Santos said, when he got back on the line. "But he let me give you his contact information." He read me out an address and phone number.

"Thanks, Santiago," I said. "Merry Christmas."

"Hold on. Before I let you go. How are things going for you?"

"Really good," I said. "Lili moved in with me, and she and Rick have been keeping me on the straight and narrow." I hesitated, but then pushed on. "I made a mistake a few weeks ago, but I recognized it right away, and I told Lili and Rick about it. And I joined this online hacker support group, too. That's been really good for me."

"This is a good thing you're doing for this guy, Steve. But remember, you've got an addiction, and nobody ever got over one of those easily, or without a few missteps along the way. You can't justify bad actions because they're for a good cause, as I know you've done in the past. If you focus on your own rehabilitation first, you may end up one of my success stories."

"You mean I'm not already?" I asked, only half joking.

"Happy holidays," he said, and hung up.

11 – Cobalt Ridge

I HEARD LILI YELLING from upstairs. "Brody! That's my shoe!" I jumped up and began up the stairs, as Rochester and Brody barreled down past me.

I found Lili at the desk in the office, holding up one of her Icelandic wool slippers. "He had this in his mouth. He didn't chew it, but it's kind of damp."

"It'll dry," I said. "Suppose I take both dogs out for a ride?"

She looked suspicious. "A ride where?"

"Levittown. I spoke to Santiago Santos, and he gave me Felix's address. It'll get them out of the house for a while, and they can sleep together on the back seat."

"Right," Lili said. "Good luck with that."

The address Santos had given me was on Calicobush Road in Levittown, and I went back to the laptop to figure out how to get there. Levittown was not a city of its own, but forty-one different neighborhoods sprawled over four different municipalities and three school districts. It had been built in the 1950s for returning World War II vets and employees of the Fairless Works, one of the largest open-pit steel mills in the world.

There were only six original house models, from the Country Clubber to the Jubilee, and the meandering streets were confusing. My dad used to tell a joke about a Levittown man who got confused on his way home, parked in the wrong driveway, went into the wrong house, and ate dinner at the wrong table. When he had an over-18 audience, Dad added the man had slept with the wrong wife, too.

Each of the divisions had a name, from Appletree Hill to Yellowwood, and within that community all the streets began with the same letter. For some developments, such as Quincy Hollow and Upper Orchard, that was a good thing—if someone lived on Quaint or Quail, you knew where you were going.

I knew there were two "C" developments, Cobalt Ridge and Crabtree Hollow. Even though I knew that in Levittown East the streets were called *Lanes*, and in Levittown West *Roads*, I still needed the map to tell me that Calicobush was in Cobalt Ridge.

The easiest way to get there appeared to be following US 1 to the Oxford Valley Mall, then taking a left on Oxford Valley Road. It was familiar territory for me, because as a teen I hung out at the mall with my friends, many of whom lived in Levittown.

A half hour later I was ready to go. The residue of snow on the roads didn't bother me; I'd been driving in those kind of conditions since I first got my license. I led both dogs outside, and let them pee. Then I opened the back door. "Go on, everybody inside."

Rochester looked up at me. He was accustomed to riding in the back when Lili was with us. But when she wasn't, he rode shotgun. Neither dog was willing to move, so I had to pick up Brody and hoist him inside. "You next," I said to Rochester. "You've got to keep an eye on the puppy."

He looked at me reproachfully, but he went in, pushing Brody forward with his big square head and taking up most of the real estate on the back seat.

When I slipped into the driver's seat, Brody stood on his hind legs and sniffed me through the bars of the headrest. "Rochester, control the puppy," I said, as I put the car in gear. Of course Rochester did nothing, so I had to gently push the puppy back before I could head for the road my dad had always called Useless One.

Cobalt was one of those substances I only remembered vaguely from the high school chemistry class I had shared with Rick Stemper. I knew it was a shade of blue, and that it had something to do with nuclear weapons, but that was about it.

When I turned into Cobalt Ridge Drive, I didn't have the trouble the guy in my dad's joke had. In the over fifty years that had passed since Levittown was built, each home had been modified, expanded and painted. Carports had been enclosed and yards landscaped. One house had a miniature windmill in the front yard, another a fake well. Most of the houses had some kind of Christmas decorations, from whole dioramas of Santa, sleigh, reindeer and elves to a single strand of colored lights.

The address Santos had given me was a single-story house with an attached garage, a sloping gray roof, and light-blue shutters. It looked well maintained, though the three cars in the driveway were all old and beat-up, with mismatched paint and big dents. I parked on the street and let the dogs out to sniff.

The front door opened and Felix stepped forward wearing a pair of sweat pants and a worn sweatshirt with the arms cut off that showed off his biceps as well as his tats. I waved at him and turned the dogs toward him. They both rushed forward, pulling me along like the tail of a kite. "You shouldn't let them pull you like that," Felix said, as we got up to the door.

"Maybe you can give me some training tips," I said.

He stood there in the doorway for a minute as if deciding whether to let me in or not. But Rochester nuzzled his hand, and Felix relaxed. "Come on in. The place is a mess."

It wasn't that bad. Some dirty clothes were thrown over the back of a well-worn sofa. The two armchairs were ripped, the carpet stained. But it was more like bachelor digs than a pigsty.

"I live here with two other guys," Felix said. "They don't care about the way things look." Brody began to sniff around the whole room, and I was hoping he was housebroken enough that he wouldn't piddle anywhere.

"It's all right by me." I took my coat off as Felix played with Rochester and Brody.

"You heard about the theft at the vet's, I guess," Felix said as I sat in one of the old chairs.

"Yeah. But you didn't steal that potassium."

Rochester and Brody clustered around him, then climbed up beside him as he sat on the sofa. "What makes you so sure?"

"Because I know where you're coming from. I see how hard you're working to turn things around. You're not stupid. You wouldn't jeopardize everything for such a dumb theft."

"Yeah, I wish everybody felt that way."

"Dr. Horz?" I asked. "Does she blame you?"

He shrugged. "She says she doesn't, but she still fired me."

"No," I said. "Why would she fire you if she thinks you're innocent?"

"The other people don't agree with her. Minna and Sahima and all the rest of them. They don't live having an ex-con around. Dr. Horz said she'd give me a good reference, but I don't care. I don't want to do that shit anymore anyway."

Brody rolled onto his back and waved his legs in the air, and Felix stroked his belly.

"You can't let a couple of small-minded people get you down," I said. "I know there's a great program in Philly for ex-offenders. Maybe they can help you get a new job, maybe even help with the tuition for that vet tech program."

He just sat there. Rochester sat up and nuzzled him, but Felix ignored him.

"You have a parole officer, right? Mine really helped me out. You can use this time to work on your writing, and after New Year's I'll help you with your application letter. You have a GED, right?"

He nodded. "I finished it up while I was in prison."

"Then between that, and your experience with animals, you should be a shoo-in for that program, especially if Dr. Horz will write you a nice letter." I could tell from the way his shoulders relaxed that he was back on track. "Now, let me see what kind of writing you've been doing."

I stayed there nearly an hour, showing Felix a couple of mistakes he'd made and talking to him about how to correct them. As we worked, the roommate with the computer, his buddy Dan, passed by. Dan was a rangy guy in his late forties, skinny and tough-looking, with an attitude I recognized from my own time inside.

Felix told the guy who I was, and he shook my hand. "Dan Symonds You get Felix all hooked up, maybe you can help me."

"Felix knows how to find me," I said.

Dan left, and Felix said, "I'll work on this tonight. I promised Yunior I'd help him with something in Philly tomorrow, and then I'm going to my mom's for Christmas the day after that. I don't want to let this slide."

Before I left, I remembered that Felix had once been a drug dealer. "I'm curious about something," I said. "I know people can use cold medicine to make meth. Could somebody do the same thing with potassium?"

He shrugged. "Not that I know of."

I thought about asking him to check with people he knew – but then I remembered that would be putting him back in touch with the those who had gotten him in trouble, and avoiding those bad influences was very important for a parolee.

Dog Have Mercy

Even so, I couldn't help thinking about the question as I drove home with Brody and Rochester. I wanted to do some more online research, but my first responsibility was keeping the dogs out of Lili's way, so I spent the rest of Tuesday afternoon playing with the dogs and keeping them out of Lili's way. Shortly before dinner, Joey called from Cozumel.

"Your puppy's a handful," I said. "Thank God Rochester was older when I got him, or I'd never have let him stay beyond a couple of days."

"But you're going to keep him until we get home, right?" Joey asked.

"Oh yeah. I'm sure he'll settle down once he gets accustomed to our house." I marveled at my ability to lie so smoothly.

"We'll be in Belize tomorrow," Joey said. "I can call you when I get there."

"Don't stress," I said. "Relax and enjoy your vacation. Don't worry about Brody."

After I hung up, I thought that if I had a puppy like Brody, I'd need a vacation, too. I felt sorry for Mark, who, like Lili, had fallen in love with a dog-lover. I knew he'd been that route before, and things hadn't worked out – if I recalled, with a guy who owned a dachshund named after Judy Garland. I hoped things would be better for him with Joey.

After Lili and I ate, I fed the dogs and took them for a long walk around River Bend. The snow flurries hadn't stuck, and the air was warmer, though the skies were still cloudy. By the time we got home, they were both panting and I hoped that meant they were going to collapse for a while.

"Why is there a yellow streak from Brody's head down his back?" Lili asked, as I was taking off my coat.

"What do you mean?"

"Look for yourself."

Brody's pristine white coat had been ornamented by a bright yellow line from the crown of his head down his neck to his back. "Rochester!" I said. "We don't peepee on company!"

"I'll get a couple of puppy wipes," Lili said.

I shook my head. "I'm going to have to bathe him. Crap." I went upstairs to the big Roman tub in the master bathroom and began to run the water. I stripped to my shorts and then went downstairs to get the puppy.

"Stop wiggling!" I said. "Resistance is futile. You will be assimilated into the collective."

"You really think the dog knows *Star Trek?*" Lili asked.

"Hey, Joey's his dad. I wouldn't be surprised."

I climbed into the tub with the puppy and filled my plastic pitcher with warm water. I poured it over his head with one hand, while restraining him with the other. I soaped him up with Rochester's shampoo and rinsed him off. As soon as I let him go, he shook all over me. "Lili! I need help."

She arrived like an angel of mercy carrying an armful of towels, accompanied by her furry golden assistant. Together we dried the puppy, constantly having to elbow Rochester out of the way. By the time we were done, the only one of us who was completely dry was Rochester.

Dog Have Mercy

12 – Gifts

IT WAS STILL GLOOMY AND OVERCAST on Wednesday morning, the day before Christmas. Lili left to get groceries before the stores closed, and I sat in the living room and supervised the dogs, who were going at each other like wild beasts, growling and locking jaws on collars and ears. "I still have Rochester's crate in the garage, Brody," I said. "If you don't behave you're going inside it."

Rochester rushed over to play with me, Brody right behind him, and I scratched and petted them both. Then Brody got bored and raced away, and Rochester chased him into the dining room. "Nobody kill anybody!" I yelled.

That reminded me of the deadly properties of certain types of potassium. Pushing aside the idea that the potassium had been stolen by a drug gang, I wondered if one of Dr. Horz's staffers had stolen the vials with the intent to kill? I eliminated the vet herself; she had no reason to report the theft if she was planning a murder.

It was a small office, and I'd met everyone who worked there at one time or another. As the dogs continued to play, I opened my laptop and started to make a list of Dr. Horz's employees.

Because of his criminal record, Felix Logato was the first suspect on my list. I believed he was trying to turn his life around. But suppose someone from his past asked for his help? Or pressured him into stealing the potassium? Could the other staff members have been right in pressuring Dr. Horz to fire him?

As a kennel assistant, he was responsible for keeping the boarding area clean and well-stocked as well as feeding and walking animals who were staying there. In the course of his work, he might have witnessed Dr. Horz giving injections. She was the kind of doctor who explained exactly what she was doing to her patients, so he might have heard her describe potassium and its effects. Or someone from his past might have wanted the drug either for murder, or as a component of something else?

Elysia, the vet tech, collected case histories, took specimens, and so on. As a tech, she'd know the uses of potassium, and most likely the consequences of an overdose. She'd recently gone to visit her mother. Had she left before or after the theft? Because Elysia was in her fifties, I assumed her mother was at least seventy, if not older. Suppose Elysia had decided it was time for Mama to leave this earthly realm? It would be hard to prove that a heart attack wasn't natural, especially if you used a naturally-occurring mineral to cause it.

The other vet tech, Jamilla, was a heavyset black woman in her late twenties. She took X-rays and helped Dr. Horz with minor surgical procedures. I assumed she was trained in the use of medications, and would know the effects of potassium.

Neither of them seemed like great suspects. Rochester liked Elysia, and I trusted his judgment. We'd first met Jamilla when Rochester had an intestinal bug, and she gave him a shot. Since then, we'd seen her a couple of times at the vet's office and while he wasn't as friendly with her he didn't seem to dislike her.

There was also a veterinary assistant, a quiet guy named Hugh who appeared to be somewhere on the autism scale. From what I'd seen, he helped out by restraining animals for procedures, cleaned up the premises and kept all the equipment clean and in good repair. He rarely spoke to patients and liked his routines. But he was very good with dogs, and Rochester had cozied up to him several times.

The office manager, Minna, was an Israeli woman with a heavy accent, blonde hair pulled up into a knot, and lots of eye makeup. She was often the one who checked us out, and I assumed she also handled billing and other administrative matters. I wondered how much medical background she had.

Sahima, the receptionist, was a new employee. Rochester hadn't had much contact with her or Minna, so I couldn't rely on his impressions. Suppose Sahima had taken the job for the access to various medications? I'd have to so some snooping to determine if she could be a suspect. And as long as I kept my investigation legal, I wouldn't get into trouble.

When I heard Lili's car pull into the driveway, I shut down the laptop. I grabbed my parka and went out to help her carry bags and bags of groceries inside. I was always amazed at how much food we went through. When I lived on my own, I ate frozen dinners and takeout food, but Lili cooked real meals for us every day.

The dogs remained behind the courtyard gate, barking, and darted around our feet as we struggled inside. I closed the front door behind us, happy to shut out the cold for a while. After we unloaded the groceries, Lili put a brisket in the oven, and we spent the afternoon on the sofa together, reading, with the dogs on the floor beside us.

Every now and then, one of them would get up and kneel down on his front paws, in the classic play posture. The other would jump up, and they would wrestle, or tug a rope between them, and then, almost as mysteriously, they would quit playing and sprawl on the floor again.

Through the sliding glass doors onto the courtyard, I could see the snow beginning to pile up, pristine and white. Around five, my cell rang with Rick's *Hawaii Five-O* tone. I picked it up and said, "This is Steve. I can't take your call right now, but leave a message and I'll think about getting back to you."

"Big comedian," he said. "Hey, can you do me a favor?"

I was sure he wanted help with the mysterious theft from the veterinarian's office, so I agreed.

"Great! I'm going to Tamsen's tomorrow for Christmas dinner, and she's got a houseful of guests coming – her sister Hannah and her family, and lots of cousins and random Quakers without anyplace else to go. Rascal doesn't cope well with so many strangers in one place. Can I drop him off with you for a few hours?"

Oh. Dog care, not investigative advice. "Hey, what's one more dog when you've already got two?" I looked over at Lili. "You don't mind if Rascal comes over for a visit tomorrow, do you?"

"The more the merrier," she said, her lip curling up in half a smile. "Rascal can keep these two wild creatures in line."

As the snow continued to fall, we took the dogs out together earlier than usual. "Be careful of that white puppy," I said. The plows hadn't come through yet, and passing cars had pushed up drifts along Sarajevo Court. "We could lose him in the snow."

"I'm sure he'd wiggle out eventually," Lili said.

I put my gloved hand in hers. "Joey and Mark are in Belize today," I said. "Probably snorkeling and sunning."

"And we're in Pennsylvania, freezing." She smiled. "But I

wouldn't be anywhere else but with you."

"Me too, sweetheart." I leaned forward and our cold lips met, warming each other from the inside out. Back home, we fed the dogs and ate the delicious brisket in the growing glow of the Hanukkah candles. I was glad that Lili's frustration with Brody had eased. There was a lot less stress when neither of us had more to do than relax, read and play.

Lili went to bed early, and the dogs followed her. I hadn't felt the need to log in to my hacker support group for a few weeks. But talking to Felix, I realized that an important part of my rehabilitation had to be helping others. It wasn't just that I was a teacher at heart; seeing what others were going through was a reminder to me to stay out of trouble.

Brewski_Bubba had posted recently about how the holidays reminded him of the time he'd hacked into local store's database and stolen credit card numbers, and then used those to shop online for extravagant presents for his family and friends. He hadn't counted on the cops showing up at his father's house, tracking the purchaser of the big-screen TV.

Stinger23 was a regular on the site. He had a hair-trigger temper, and almost anything seemed to set him off. He had written a long rant about Christmas and how all the empty time for a single guy around the holidays was a big temptation to mess around online. I wrote back, under my online ID of CrossedWires – a reference not only to Stewart's Crossing, but to the idea that all of us had some wires crossed in our brains that caused our addictions. Only half in jest, I suggested he get a dog.

"Mine keeps me out of trouble," I wrote. "Anytime I'm tempted to play around on my computer, I play with the dog instead."

Female hackers were relatively rare. I wasn't sure if that was because girls had historically shied away from technical studies like computer programming, or because the female brain was wired differently from the male in some crucial way. We had one regular poster, though, MamaHack, and she wrote about how much pressure the holidays brought for wives and mothers like her. "Sometimes I feel like I'm putting on a face for everyone around me, while underneath I'm falling apart."

Most people used the site as a release valve, and there wasn't the kind of artificially induced bonhomie that characterized a lot of

Dog Have Mercy

twelve-step programs. So it was sweet to see how so many of the group members had chimed in with messages of support.

I added my own. "My girlfriend and my best friend staged an intervention a couple of months ago," I wrote. "That triggered my joining this group. And I did feel that the pressure was lowered once I had someone to share with. I hope you have supportive people around you who can help you in the same way."

I logged off and pushed back from the computer, then climbed the stairs to the bedroom. Rochester was on the floor by Lili's side, and Brody was curled beside her on the bed. I got undressed, shoved the little dog out of my parking space, and cuddled up beside Lili, grateful for all the gifts in my life.

The snowplows came through while we slept, and when we awoke on Christmas morning Sarajevo Court was clear, and the lawns, houses and trees had a full coat of thick white snow. It was a real shame to have the dogs stain it yellow. Brody assumed his regular pose – tail up, head forward, legs at a slight angle. "Man, you've got a lot of pee in you for such a little dog," I said.

He looked up at me, those brown tracks staining his cheeks, as if to apologize, and I praised him copiously when he finished.

Rick arrived around eleven with Rascal. He parked in front of the townhouse and walked up the driveway carrying shopping bags from the pet superstore out on US 1. The Aussie shepherd had his nose up proudly, his tail erect, as if he knew he was on his way to work herding rambunctious dogs.

Rochester and Brody erupted into welcoming barks, which caused Rascal to emit a series of sharp yips. The dogs took off into the house, and Rick followed us to the living room. "Consider these a bribe for keeping Rascal." He handed one glossy red bag with a black lab in a Santa hat on it to Lili. "These are for you and Steve."

He handed the other to me. "This is all for Rochester. Luckily, the high school pep club was wrapping gifts yesterday for donations. Otherwise you'd be getting these naked."

I laughed and he blushed. "You know what I mean."

He'd gotten me a burnished metal picture frame in the shape of a doghouse, with a white ceramic bone glued to the front. Lili's gift was a key chain that looked like a charm bracelet, with a metal golden retriever at one end, and a tiny food bowl, heart, enamel bone, and other dog-related charms.

The real bonanza was reserved for Rochester – a rawhide bone, a red vinyl octopus squeaky toy with a nubby head, a rubber tire complete with treads, and a small bag of organic training treats.

"You really went to town," I said.

"I did get carried away. Bought way too much for Rascal, too." He shrugged. "But hey, it's Christmas."

"I had a feeling you were a secret shopper," Lili said. She walked into the kitchen and returned with a wrapped package she handed to him.

"You didn't have to," he said.

I didn't know she had. I watched as he tore open the Hanukkah paper to reveal a T-shirt with a picture of a cartoon dog sitting in a canoe, with a raised oar in one paw. The words beneath it read "Dog Paddle."

"I love it!" he said. He leaned over and kissed Lili's cheek. "Thank you. Merry Christmas and Happy Hanukkah."

It wasn't until he'd left that I asked, "How did you know he'd be bringing us gifts?"

"I didn't. That was for you."

I laughed. "I love a woman who can think on her feet."

We kissed, and then Lili said, "This woman needs to get into the kitchen and start cooking. My mother's roast chicken with apricots and prunes takes a couple of hours."

I joined her in the kitchen and began preparing my mother's noodle kugel, one of the few dishes she had learned from her own mother and passed down to me. Lili and I worked companionably together, with all three dogs sprawled on the floor around us. It was awkward to have to step around them, but we managed.

We ate dinner, fed the dogs, and then walked them in the last light of the winter afternoon. "I wouldn't mind a house with a fireplace," I said, as we walked back inside. "Someday."

"Or a house in a place where you don't need a fireplace," Lili said. "Where are Joey and Mark today?"

I looked at the schedule I'd posted on the refrigerator. "Isla Roatan," I said. "What country is that?"

"Honduras," Lili said. "Off the northern coast. There's a huge reef there, second largest in the world, I think, so it's a big diving spot. Van has been there a couple of times for vacation."

Van Dryver was a reporter for the *Wall Street Journal*. He and Lili

Dog Have Mercy

had worked together on a number of assignments, and had a brief fling in there somewhere. I thought he was a pompous prick, but I was still jealous of him.

I was saved from irritating thoughts of Van by Rick's return. "Man, those Quaker girls can cook," he said, pretending to stagger inside. "Between Hannah and Tamsen there was a mountain of food."

"Which you conquered, I'm sure," I said.

"I had to be a good guest." Rascal rushed over to him and began sniffing and licking him. "There are some leftovers for you in the car," he said to the dog as he ruffled his ears.

"Nothing for us?" I asked.

"I'm sure Jewish girls cook as well as Quaker ones," Rick said.

I knew my cue. "Probably better," I said.

13 – Suspect List

SEEING RICK REMINDED ME that the question of the missing potassium was still unanswered, and I went upstairs to the computer in the office to do some more research on the mineral and its uses. Potassium was the third most abundant mineral in the body, and as an electrolyte very important to its functions.

I read about an elderly woman in Missouri whose autopsy revealed hyperkalemia – potassium overload – and how her daughter had admitted fiddling with her mother's pills in order to inherit more quickly. The case had only come to police attention because the mother had voiced some fears about her daughter to a neighbor, who had reported them to the police after the woman's death.

A doctor interviewed by the newspaper had indicated that since the woman was elderly and died of a heart attack, no one would have thought twice about an autopsy if it hadn't been for the neighbor's comments.

I sat back and wondered how many other vulnerable people had been killed in a similar way. Could you buy a big bottle of potassium tablets and slip them in with the pills you were giving to a patient who was either too trusting, or too out of it, to notice? And if so, why go to the trouble of stealing it in liquid form?

By the time I finished, I'd learned a lot about potential poisoning, and I was proud of myself for figuring out how to find the information I wanted without illegal means. That night, for the first time, Brody slept on the floor beside Rochester instead of in bed with Lili and me. I felt like I was making progress on multiple fronts.

Friday morning Lili was downstairs and I was up in the bedroom. Rochester and Brody were rampaging through the downstairs despite Lili's pleas to them to calm down. Then I heard a crash.

Dog Have Mercy

"Brody!" Lili yelled. I jumped up and ran downstairs. She was standing over a pile of broken glass. "Stay away from here, you rotten dogs!"

"What happened?"

"Brody knocked down that photograph of us at Bowman's Tower and the glass shattered," she said. "Don't just stand there. Get a broom and a dustpan while I keep the dogs away."

I hurried to the garage. "How did he get up there?" I asked. "I thought that shelf was too high."

"Well, you thought wrong."

I knew it wasn't Brody's fault, and that he was pretty well-behaved for a puppy. But he was eight months old, and he loved to put his furry white paws up on any table he could reach, sniffing for food and chewables. He jumped on Rochester when my dog wanted to sleep. His sharp toenails dug in as he climbed over us when we were between him and something he wanted. I was looking forward to his going home something fierce.

I could tell that Lili felt the same way. She herded the two dogs out of the living room and I swept up the glass, then ran the vacuum cleaner to pick up any loose fragments. By the time I was done, Lili looked frazzled. "I need a break," she said. "I'm going to take my camera and go for a drive."

"And leave me with the crazy dogs."

"You're the one who wanted to take Brody in," she said. We began to argue about who was responsible for the disasters of the week, and Rochester ran up to the staircase landing and Brody hid under the dining room table.

We both stopped at the same time. "I don't want to argue," I said. "I'm sorry the dogs are going wild. I'll try and tire them out while you're gone."

"I shouldn't have yelled," she said. "I was looking forward to a quiet holiday and a chance to chill after the end of the semester."

"I know. Things will be back to normal as soon as Brody goes home."

I felt like putting up a chart on the refrigerator, tracking the number of hours until Joey returned to take Brody off our hands. Though we were both kind to the little dog, petting him and telling him he was a good boy, he was still a handful.

Lili came back downstairs with her parka and her camera bag

Neil S. Plakcy

and I looked around for the dogs. Rochester was by my feet, but Brody was nowhere in sight. "Where's the puppy, Rochester?" I raised my voice and called "Brody!"

He came trotting out of the kitchen, his toenails clicking on the tile floor. He had the end of a banana in his mouth, holding it like a drooping cigar.

"Brody!" I said. "Dogs don't eat bananas." I reached down and took it from him, and he wagged his tail eagerly.

"Bananas are a good source of potassium. Maybe he's the one who stole those vials from Dr. Horz's office," Lili said, laughing. "You should see if Joey has had him at the vet's recently."

Could people who'd brought their dogs in for treatment have access to that storage cabinet? I knew it was in the vet's work room, as I'd passed the open door a few times on my own visits to the clinic. It seemed awfully risky, though, because what if one of the staff found you there? And you'd have to have a science background in order to recognize the right drug quickly.

By then Brody had curled up beside Rochester, resting his head on my dog's golden flanks. He looked like such an angel that I had to smile.

Lili left, and I played with both dogs for a while, tossing balls and tugging ropes. Then they slept. Watching them, I thought, if only Dr. Horz could give us something so Brody would sleep until Sunday afternoon, we'd be fine.

That reminded me that I didn't know most of the last names of the staff at Dr. Horz's clinic. The old Steve would have immediately turned to hacking – breaking into the vet's online billing system, for example. But the new Steve was trying to change those bad habits.

Instead, I began with the basics – at the website for The Animal House of Stewart's Crossing. Unfortunately, it was very basic, and didn't list the names of staff members. So I turned to Facebook. I typed the name of the practice into the search box and hit the enter key, hoping that at least one of the staff had a page there.

The first few entries were from fans of the 1970s movie with John Belushi and Kevin Bacon, but then I got a hit with Jamilla McCarthy, the surgical vet tech. I learned that she lived in Levittown, and had graduated from Pennsbury High, and then a vet tech program. She was single, had lots of friends, and had most recently been photographed at a restaurant in Bristol with a group of women her own age. The caption read "celebrating Omari Jefferson's release from the hospital."

When I hovered over the picture, I saw that Omari was a skinny girl in a wheelchair, with oxygen tubes in her nose and a colored bandana wrapped around her bald head. My first reaction was one of pity – the poor young woman, who looked like a cancer victim. Then I thought, at least she has friends who have stuck by her.

I sat back in my chair. How far might Jamilla go to help her friend? Suppose Omari was terminal, and Jamilla had stolen the potassium to help her make a gracious exit? From her training, I was sure that Jamilla knew what an overdose could do, and it did seem like an easy way to die, especially if Omari was on painkillers that might knock her out.

I skipped down to the list of Jamilla's Facebook friends. In addition to Omari and the other women in the picture, Hugh Jonas and Sahima Das were both listed. Hugh's page was nearly empty, with the generic icon in place of an actual picture. But it did list his workplace and his hometown – Stewart's Crossing. It wasn't much, but with his last name, his place of residence and his job, I could do more advanced searching.

Sahima Das was a recent graduate of Neshaminy High, Pennsbury's rival. She was a student at Bucks County Community College, which my friends and I had called BC Cubed when we were in high school and fancied ourselves clever. Sahima was a huge social media user. There were dozens of photos of her, her family and her friends, dozens of "check-ins" at movie theaters, restaurants, even the Sesame Place Amusement Park, where she'd had her picture taken with Big Bird.

Most of her family appeared very traditional – the men in those long white coats with high collars, the short, plump women in colorful saris. There were several photos of Sahima with her grandfather, Dadaji, a small, wizened man who looked like a cross between Yoda and Ben Kingsley in *Gandhi*. The most recent showed him in a hospital bed, with an IV in his arm and lots of high-tech monitoring equipment around him. He looked very ill; was it possible Sahima had learned about potassium and stolen it to use on him?

I switched over to the local obituaries but couldn't find one for Sahima's grandfather – though it was possible that he had a different last name, and that her name hadn't been mentioned in a death notice. I realized that between Jamilla and Sahima, I was coming up with more and more desperate and outlandish ideas, but they were all I had.

When Lili came home, she went upstairs to download the pictures from her camera to the computer, and I continued my research on Dr. Horz's staff. Hugh Jonas was an enigma. My limited contact with him had given me the idea he was somewhere on the autism spectrum. I knew that people with that condition often became very familiar with one or two particular subjects, like trains or dinosaurs. What if Hugh's obsession was chemistry?

Beyond his basic Facebook page, he didn't have much of a digital footprint. No property in his name, no pictures that matched him. Perhaps he still lived with his parents? I searched for a Jonas family in Stewart's Crossing and discovered that a Richard Jonas owned a residence on Hill Street. I did a quick search for Richard, and discovered that he was a Realtor in town, and his website had a photo of his family. In the picture, which had been taken several years before, Hugh appeared to be the oldest son. He had to be in his late twenties, an age when most kids would have moved on.

Would his condition make him easily influenced? What if his father wanted someone to die so he could gain a listing for his real estate business? Would he have asked Hugh to steal the potassium? And could Hugh have done it?

More wild feats of speculation. I shifted focus to researching local deaths as a result of heart attacks, but it was difficult to gather much data – often an obituary didn't list cause of death, or said something vague like "natural causes." It was impossible to tell if any death had been suspicious. I thought about emailing Rick and asking him to look through police records, but there was no evidence to justify such a search. I could always ask him later, if I found anything suspicious.

It was time to return to basics. For any crime to occur, there have to be means, motive and opportunity. I knew the means; did any of the people at Dr. Horz's office, who had the opportunity, also have a motive? I made a list:

Dog Have Mercy

SUSPECT LIST

Felix Logato	Blackmail or other force by criminal associate?
Elysia Camilleri	Eliminate elderly mother?
Jamilla McCarthy	Mercy killing of sick friend?
Sahima Das	Ditto, for beloved grandfather?
Hugh Jonas	Person or persons unknown influencing him?
Minna	Who was she? Did she have a motive?

I still needed Minna's last name. The office manager didn't appear on Facebook or LinkedIn or any of the other social media sites I searched, using different combinations of her first name, the animal hospital, her homeland of Israel, and Stewart's Crossing.

While I was puzzling over how else I could track her, Rochester nuzzled my leg. He had a red stuffed starfish hanging limply in his mouth. It was a toy he'd had for as long as he'd lived with me, and he'd always taken loving care of it. Now, though, all the stuffing was gone, along with one of the starfish's arms and both its eyes.

"What happened here?" I asked. I took the starfish from him. "Did Brody do this?"

He sat on his butt and stared at me.

"I guess he did. Well, we can fix that. I'll get you a new one."

I turned to Google and typed in "red starfish dog toy" and then selected to view images. I shifted the laptop's screen so Rochester could see, and pointed to one that looked similar. "You want that one?" I asked.

He nuzzled my hand. "I'll take that as a yes," I said. I clicked the image and was taken to the site where I could order one for him. When I finished with that, Rochester wasn't satisfied. "I'm sorry, puppy. But toys can't come out of the computer." I closed the order window and shifted the screen so he could see the Google search page. "See? All you can do is look for things."

He woofed, and nodded his head. Of course. I hadn't tried a simple Google search for Minna, because I thought I'd probably get a million hits, none of them useful. But as Rochester had pointed out, sometimes the simplest solution is the right one.

Neil S. Plakcy

Rochester slumped beside me and I stared at the results on the screen. There were over forty-seven million hits, beginning with a company that offered "innovative sexual health products." A San Francisco art gallery, a bridal shop in the United Kingdom, a Brooklyn company that sold hand-made textiles. There was nothing that looked promising.

However, one of the results I got came up in Hebrew. Though I'd taken three years of the language in preparation for my bar mitzvah, all I had retained was a grasp of the alphabet. I stared at the screen for a moment and then remembered that the letters read right to left, not left to right as in English. It still didn't make much sense to me, but I sounded out the first word, which appeared to be Minna, or some variation.

I copied the text and pasted it into Google Translate. It's a clunky service, but I wasn't trying to create a literary masterpiece, just find out if I had the right Minna.

The translation was kind of funny. "Mini brash nick" appeared to have been a nurse in the Israeli city of Ra'anana. She had decided not to take the NCLEX examination for US licensure, she wrote, because she was tired of dealing with people. She preferred animals.

Rochester got up and padded away, and a moment later I heard the sound of puppy wrestling in the kitchen. At least Rochester was keeping Brody occupied.

I did some more searching and figured out that Minna's last name was Breznick, and that she lived in Crossing Estates, the high-end suburban neighborhood outside town. Her husband was a cardiologist and she had two teenaged children.

Since she had been a nurse, she'd know about potassium. But I didn't know enough about her to guess at a possible motive. What I did know, though, was that I was going to put together enough suspects so that if Felix was innocent, he didn't pay for someone else's crime. He deserved the chance to keep moving forward with his life.

14 – Support

LILI CAME DOWNSTAIRS as I was closing my laptop. "How do you feel about New Year's Eve?" she asked.

I looked up at her. "In a general sense?"

"In a party sense."

"You want to have a party?"

She shook her head. "I just got an email from Gracious Chigwe. Do you know her?"

"Don't think so."

"She's a professor in the Sociology department. I met her during new faculty orientations when I started last year. She's originally from Botswana, but she went to graduate school in Scotland." She sat on the sofa. "She's having a party Wednesday night, a bunch of the faculty, and she invited us."

"I don't know," I said. "Rochester hates loud noises. Usually I have to stay with him on New Year's Eve and July fourth or he gets very nervous."

At the sound of his name, my big golden dog came rocketing into the living room, trailed quickly by a small white imitation. "Rick owes us a favor," Lili said. "And if he's busy, then Joey and Mark do, too."

"I guess that means you want to go."

"It would be good for both of us. We've been cooped up here for a week. Besides, it will give me a chance to get dressed up. I haven't done that in a while."

"And I certainly like to see you in all your finery." I wiggled my eyebrows. "As well as out of it, of course." The dogs settled in a heap as I retrieved my cell from the top of the china cabinet, where I'd put it to keep it out of Brody's reach.

"Hey," I said, when Rick answered. "Lili wants us to go to this

Neil S. Plakcy

New Year's Eve party, and I don't want to leave Rochester on his own because he doesn't like fireworks. Are you going to be home?"

"Yeah. I don't like to leave Rascal alone either. You want to bring Rochester over? He can stay the night. Between the two of them they should be all right."

"That would be great," I said, and gave Lili a thumbs up.

"Call me Wednesday and let me know when you want to drop Rochester off."

I wanted to go back to my research on Dr. Horz's staff, but I wasn't going to make the same mistakes with Lili that I'd made with Mary, burying myself in my work and ignoring her. "Can I see some of the pictures you took today?" I asked.

"There's nothing to see yet," she said. "You know my process. I take a lot of pictures and then I throw most of them away, and eventually I find the ones I want to work with. So all I have now is a whole lot of pictures of snow."

Instead of going upstairs to look at the computer, we snuggled together on the couch and talked. "I went past the Chocolate Ear when I was out, to get a hot chocolate and a croissant," she said. "Your matchmaking efforts this summer seem to have worked out. Gail is still seeing that guy from New Zealand. They spent Christmas with Gail's mother and her grandmother."

The Chocolate Ear was a café in the center of Stewart's Crossing, and Lili and I had become friends with the owner, Gail Dukowski. During the summer I'd convinced her to give a guy from her past, a friend of her ex-boyfriend, a chance.

"And Mark and Joey are still together," I said. "What can I say? I'm a born *shadchen*."

"Born yenta, more likely," Lili said, and I started tickling her. Rochester and Brody wanted in on the action, and we ended up in a group romp that I hope washed away all the residual tension from our argument that morning.

* * *

Saturday morning was bright and sunny, so I took both dogs for a long walk around River Bend. When we returned Lili was in the kitchen frying bacon, and the aroma drove the dogs nuts. They kept nosing her and sniffing her, and Brody tried to get his front paws up on the counter beside the stove.

Dog Have Mercy

She expertly flipped an omelet onto a plate, and handed it to me, and I picked a couple of rashers of bacon from the plate where they were draining. I fed a bit to each dog. "This is a nice treat," I said.

"Would you mind if I went out for dinner tonight?" she asked, as she began making her own omelet.

"Not at all. Who are you going with?"

"Van called while you were out with the dogs. He's going to be in the neighborhood, and he wants to get together."

"In the neighborhood? What possible reason could globe-trotting reporter Van Dryver have to be in the neighborhood of Stewart's Crossing?"

"He's researching a story," she said. "On the New Homeless – families displaced by the economic crisis. When he mentioned that, I thought he and I could share some ideas."

"Have I ever mentioned that I don't like him or trust him?" I asked.

She groaned. "Not this jealousy again. Van and I are just colleagues, Steve. I keep telling you that."

I took a deep breath. Lili had been steadfast in denying any romantic interest in Van, that their brief dalliance years before had been enough to convince her he wasn't relationship material. It was time for me to man up and trust her.

"Have a good time," I said. "You can even tell him I said hello."

"I will." She leaned over and kissed my cheek. "Thank you."

"No need to thank me. We both have lives, and pasts, and that's not going to change."

While it was still sunny, I wanted to fix a loose gutter on the townhouse, and I discovered that I'd run through my entire roll of duct tape. My dad had been a big believer in the power of duct tape to remedy almost any household problem, and I'd inherited that notion. The closest place to get a new roll was at the drugstore in the center of town, so I told Lili I'd be right back and drove over there.

Though most of the holiday snow had melted, there were still piles of it around the edges of the drugstore parking lot, and I walked carefully across the pavement, wary of ice. Once inside, I loosened my scarf and put my gloves in my pocket, and headed for the catch-all aisle, where locals who didn't head out to the superstores along the highway could buy everything from ice scrapers to drain cleaner. I found a good-sized roll of tape and headed for the register.

I stopped short at the vitamin aisle. Did they really sell potassium in drugstores? In what form? I meandered down the aisle until I realized the supplements and vitamins were all in alphabetical order, then pushed past dietary fiber, goldenseal, and neroli oil, until I reached the Ps.

There were four different brands of potassium supplements, on its own or mixed with calcium and magnesium. I picked up a bottle of potassium and looked at the label. It contained 99 mg of potassium, "from potassium citrate and potassium aspartate."

Was that the same as what had been in the vials stolen from Dr. Horz's office? I made a note of those names, paid for my duct tape, and drove home. I opened my laptop and went to the student's best friend, Wikipedia, where I learned that potassium citrate was a potassium salt of citric acid. Not helpful, since the last time I'd taken chemistry was back in high school. I did understand that it was used to control kidney stones.

Since Wikipedia had no entry for potassium aspartate, I had to look farther for a definition. It was a nutritional supplement that combined potassium with another salt compound, aspartate, which helped the body absorb the potassium more effectively.

None of that made much sense to me, so I pushed it aside and focused on what I did understand: that when you don't pay attention to dogs, they get into mischief.

Lili was upstairs in the office doing some research on homelessness so I stayed downstairs, reading and playing with the dogs. She joined me in walking them that evening. "There's stuff for salad in the fridge," she said. "And a couple of TV dinners."

"I'll be fine," I said. "I have the dogs to keep me out of trouble."

I bypassed both the options Lili had mentioned and boiled up a big pot of elbow macaroni, topping it with butter and grated parmesan cheese. My mother had gone back to work soon after I was born, and hired a live-in housekeeper to take care of me and do the housework. Roxie lived with us for about ten years, and when I was sick and had to stay home from school, she made me elbow macaroni that way, though back then the only way we bought grated cheese was from one of those green cans that didn't need refrigeration.

Now I bought artisan pasta, organic butter and shaved Parmesan that came in plastic tubs with an artist's rendering of an Italian farm on the label, but the end result was the same: comfort food. Since I had time to kill while I waited for the pasta to boil, I pulled a box cake mix, left over from my bachelor days, from the cabinet. I added eggs, oil, water and some vanilla extract, and popped it in the oven before I sat down to eat.

By the time I'd eaten and fed the dogs, the cake was done, and I set it on the counter to cool – far back to keep away from inquisitive canine noses and tongues. I played fetch with the dogs until the cake cooled, then iced it with a can of chocolate frosting. Both dogs were desperate to join me in licking the spoon and bowl, but I had to shoo them away.

By nine o'clock, I started to worry about Lili. A lot of the country roads around Stewart's Crossing ice up at night, and I kept imagining her, slightly tipsy after a dinner lubricated by alcohol, sliding out of control on a bad patch of road. I thought about calling her cell, but I didn't want to seem like I was checking up on her, and if she was on her way home, that momentary distraction could be enough to send her careening off the road.

I wasn't jealous; I knew deep down there was no way that Lili had scooted off to some no-tell motel with Van Dryver. And I knew that Lili was a strong, capable woman who could take care of herself. So what was I worried about?

Opening my heart and my life to Lili had been a big leap forward for me. Mary had served me with divorce papers as soon as I was arrested, and it hurt not to have her stand by me during my trial. After all, what I'd done had been for her as well as for myself.

I comforted myself at the time by calling her a bitch and a variety of less printable names. After a while, I admitted that our marriage was on the rocks anyway, and would have ended sooner or later. But the experience had scarred me more deeply than I knew at the time.

In prison I closed in on myself like a turtle, hiding in my shell and protecting my tenderest parts. When Rochester came into my life, he forced me to care for someone else, and he returned my attention with love.

That emotional unfurling allowed me to open up further, to Lili. I was scared of losing her or Rochester. When I paced around the living room, the dogs sensed my agitation and followed me, getting underfoot.

To calm them down, I had to sit on the floor rubbing bellies and scratching ears and telling them what good boys they were.

The dogs raised a huge ruckus when Lili's car pulled up in the driveway, and I had to stand by the front door and body block them from lunging at her as she walked in. I kissed her hello; her cheeks were cold, as if she'd been driving with the windows open.

"How was your dinner?" I asked as I helped her off with her coat.

"The food was great," she said. "We went to Le Canal in New Hope. I remembered why I liked that place so much. We should go again, soon."

I couldn't help myself. "And what about the company?"

"Van was as self-involved as ever," she said. "Every time I asked him a question, he'd say he was protecting his sources or something equally pompous. I realized that the only reason he invited me was to grill me about living down here. Were there a lot of properties for sale? Did I know anyone who was underwater on a mortgage? Anyone who'd gone through foreclosure? I felt like I was back in graduate school, being badgered by a cranky professor."

"The way our students probably feel."

"Speak for your students," she said. "Mine love me. Five stars on Rate My Professor."

"They think you're hot, too," I said. "I've looked."

"And what about you?" she asked.

"You get five stars from me, too," I said. I kissed her again, and then we went upstairs to bed and I demonstrated exactly what those stars meant.

15 – Goat in the House

SUNDAY MORNING, I LEFT LILI IN BED and fed and walked the dogs. In the snow it was very evident where dogs had passed. When the grass was green, especially when it was overgrown, the poop and the pee could be hidden. But against a blanket of white it was clear that a dog had mushy poop, another had urine a bright yellow. The visibility of the poop in winter was kind of like the way an ex-con like Felix or I could keep our backgrounds private, but periodically something happened so that everyone could see where we'd been and what we'd done.

I returned to the kitchen with the newspaper, in a thoughtful mood. I nibbled on a slice of the cake I'd baked the night before and flipped through the pages.

Disasters far and wide filled the pages of the international section – an avalanche in the mountain west, a capsized ferry boat in Asia, a rebel group in Africa shooting up a village. I was grateful to be warm in my own house, well-fed, and surrounded by the love of a good woman and a good dog.

I reached down to pet Rochester, who was sprawled at my feet. I would have petted Brody, too, but he was a few feet away, snoring on the kitchen tile, and I didn't want to disturb him.

I wasn't quite old enough to begin the paper with the obituaries, but I did get to them eventually. That morning one name stuck out: Malavath Divaram. It took me a moment to remember she was the East Indian woman I'd met on my second visit to Crossing Manor. Her obit was brief; she had died suddenly the day before, survived by son Adeep, of Sunnyvale, CA, and two grandchildren.

I tried to remember what was wrong with her, if I'd even known. She had seemed very alert when we met, and her only complaint was that her son had warehoused her a continent away, preventing her from seeing him or her grandchildren. But I assumed she had some underlying health problem – cancer, a bad heart, liver or kidney dysfunction, that kept her at Crossing Manor, and eventually had taken her life. Or could it have been a heart attack – one caused by an overdose of potassium?

Lili came down soon after, and the dogs jumped up to greet her. "Yes, you're going home today!" she said to Brody as she scratched behind his ears. "You'll be happy, and so will we."

I got up to get her a muffin and make some coffee, and she petted Rochester on her way to the table. "You're not reading the obituaries, are you?" she asked me. "That's morbid."

"Rochester and I met Mrs. Divaram when we went back to Crossing Manor, after Edith went home," I said. "He liked her."

I handed her the muffin on a yellow Fiestaware china plate, another of the things she'd brought to the house. "I remember her saying that her son lived far away," I continued. "She felt abandoned."

"Families spread out," Lili said. "Look at my brother and me. We haven't lived in the same time zone for years."

"Even so, it's sad. She's the third person we've met from Crossing Manor to die. That's sounding very suspicious to me."

"Maybe Rochester really is a death dog, the way Rick says," Lili said. "Keep taking him there, you could clear out the place."

"That's not what Rick meant and you know it," I said, but I smiled.

"Seriously, Steve. The people who are at Crossing Manor are there because they're very sick. For some of them, it's the last place they'll stay before their final rest." She began to howl something that sounded like an African chant, and both of the dogs jumped up. It was only when she got to the English part that I realized she was singing "The Circle of Life" from *The Lion King*.

Both dogs were up on their hind legs. Lili grasped Brody's forepaws, and I got Rochester's, and we danced around the kitchen together, celebrating the joy of life and the power of the almighty Mouse to penetrate every part of our lives.

After breakfast, we relocated to the living room, where Brody kept pestering Rochester to play. My dog looked up at me with baleful eyes. "Don't worry, he's going soon," I said.

"Not soon enough," Lili muttered as Brody tried to nibble on her shoe.

"Look at it this way," I said. "My dad used to tell this joke, about a man in some shtetl in Russia whose house was too small for his family—kids, in-laws and all. He went to the rabbi and the rabbi asked him, 'Do you have a goat?' The man said yes, and the rabbi told him to take the goat into the house, and come back in a week."

"You are not a goat, Brody!" Lili said. "Leave my shoes alone." She curled her feet under her on the sofa.

"So the man does what the rabbi says, and then goes back a week later. 'Rabbi, it's even worse! The goat smells and tries to eat everything.' The rabbi tells him to go back home, bring his donkey inside, and come back in a week."

"This is an awfully long joke," Lili said.

"Maybe it's a fable more than a joke," I said. "It goes on for a couple of weeks, until the man has all his farm animals in the house and he's going nuts. The rabbi tells him to take all the animals out and come back in a week. He does, and he says how wonderful his house is now without all the animals inside."

"And the moral of this story is? Don't bring livestock into your house?"

"The moral is to appreciate what you have, because things could always get worse," I said. I leaned over to kiss her.

"And by worse you mean Joey could fall overboard and we'd have to keep Brody forever?"

"Something like that," I said. I faked spitting three times, the way my elderly relatives had when mentioning anything especially good or bad. "Pooh, pooh, pooh. It shouldn't happen to a dog."

"Or to us," Lili said. "My *bubbe*, my mother's mother, used to tell stories like that."

"You've never talked much about your grandparents," I said. "I didn't realize you knew them growing up."

"Not for very long, unfortunately," she said. "My father's parents, the Weinstocks, came from a small town in Poland, along the border with Germany. They were on their honeymoon when the Nazis rounded up all the Jews for the concentration camps. They came home and found the village nearly deserted."

"That must have been awful," I said.

"My father says that the smartest thing his father ever did was spend every penny he had on the honeymoon and the wedding rings, because that saved their lives. They missed the Nazis by a day, and then they sold my father's ring to smugglers who took them through the Alps to Trieste, where they got passage on a ship to Libya. They were told that there was a Jewish community in Cyrenaica, what's called Benghazi now."

"How did they get from there to Cuba?"

"It wasn't easy, but they were lucky again. The British took control of Cyrenaica in 1941 for a brief time, then lost it. But my grandparents were able to be evacuated with the British soldiers. They couldn't get to Palestine so they tried for the United States. Couldn't get in here either, so they ended up taking a ship to Cuba. But all that moving around really took a toll on them, and my father's father died right after he graduated from engineering school. His mother died a year later, and when I was born he gave me her name."

"Wow. Those stories always make me so grateful for all that my grandparents did so my parents and I could be born here."

"I know how you feel. I was so overwhelmed when I got U.S. citizenship. It was like the end of a very long journey."

"What about your mother's parents?" I asked.

"They had it a lot easier. Bubbie's cousin had moved to Havana a few years before the Nazis invaded Poland, and when she and Zayde couldn't get visas for the United States they went to live with him and his wife. Of course, everyone they left behind was wiped out, but at least they survived and they avoided the camps."

"And then got out of Cuba after Castro took over," I said. "Your father was lucky he had those engineering skills and connections to get that first job in Mexico, and then to be able later to bring his family to the States."

"He always said you have to make your own luck," she said, as she reached out to squeeze my hand. "I think we're doing pretty well in that regard."

We sat together companionably reading, and about an hour later, Brody recognized the sound of Joey's truck in front of the townhouse. He went nuts, jumping up on all fours and twisting himself into wild contortions. Rochester thought he wanted to play, and was puzzled when Brody ignored him to start scratching at the front door.

I opened it, and Brody launched himself at Joey, forty pounds of white puppy airborne like one of Santa's reindeer taking flight. "Yes,

Dog Have Mercy

I missed you too," Joey said, picking up the wriggling dog and kissing him on the snout.

Mark trailed behind, carrying a duty-free bag. His normally pasty complexion was ruddier, though he hadn't tanned as well as Joey, whose skin glowed. "We hope you like rum," Mark said, handing the bag to me. He leaned forward and whispered, "Though you'd have to bring me a whole distillery to convince me to keep that puppy for a week."

"Brody was a perfect houseguest," I said. "No major accidents, nothing important destroyed."

"How was your cruise?" Lili asked as Joey got down on the floor and romped with Brody, both of them so delighted to be together again. "You both look so tanned. I'm jealous."

"We had a great time," Mark said. "Joey convinced me to go snorkeling, and I didn't drown. We dozed in lounge chairs and drank rum drinks. We stuffed ourselves at the buffet and the specialty restaurants. And as a bonus, neither of us had to be carted off the ship on a gurney and sped off to a hospital like one of the other passengers."

"Someone got sick?" I asked. "Not one of those cruise ship viruses, I hope."

"We were told he was an elderly man with a history of heart problems. Nothing for us to worry about."

"But Mark still worried," Joey called from his place on the floor.

Lili, Mark and I sat down at the kitchen table. I was reminded of the potassium I'd researched earlier, and how an overdose could lead to heart failure. Would a cruise ship be a good place to carry out a murder like that? The victim would be away from his personal physician, in a foreign country. It would probably be easy to cover up a crime that way, though the suspect list had to be smaller because of the confined environment.

"Where was this?" Lili asked.

"Roatan," Mark said. "An island off Honduras. God knows what kind of hospital facilities they have there. It was beautiful, but very Third World."

"Mark considers anywhere without a Starbucks as Third World," Joey called.

"No comments from the peanut gallery," Mark said back to him. I was glad to see that they were still joking with each other after a week spent together.

"I had an intestinal virus in Honduras once," Lili said. "Couldn't stop vomiting long enough to get on a plane, so the reporter I was working with took my camera and film and flew back to New York, and I stayed in the hospital there. I was lucky; it was very clean, and the nurses knew what they were doing, and in the end I wasn't that sick. But I'd hate to be somewhere like that and need advanced care."

Joey and Mark left soon after with Brody and his assorted paraphernalia, and Lili, Rochester and I were all glad to see them pile back into Joey's truck and drive away. "I'm going upstairs to read," Lili said. "Maybe I can actually get into something without having to worry about that puppy all the time."

Lili's manner told me she expected me and Rochester to stay downstairs. I sat down on the sofa, and Rochester clambered up beside me. What if the tension that had been building between Lili and me the previous week wasn't about the puppy at all, but about some deeper rift in our relationship? What if we both had become so accustomed to living on our own that we couldn't live together without rancor developing?

What if her dinner with Van the night before hadn't been about homelessness so much as Lili considering changing her home?

I took a deep breath. I was letting my imagination run away, as I often did when Rochester and I were investigating something that intrigued us, whether it was a death or a theft or something more mundane, like where squirrels went at night. Did they have nests, or just sleep on tree branches? How did they stay on the branches if they fell asleep?

I focused on my dog, stroking his silky fur and telling him how happy I was that he had come into my life. We stayed in the living room until it was time for his eleven o'clock walk, and by the time I got upstairs Lili had already gone to sleep. I undressed quietly and slid in bed beside her, and Rochester curled up on the floor. I knew that I would have him with me, by my side or in my heart, forever.

16 – Hats

MONDAY MORNING LILI'S SUNNY DISPOSITION had returned. "I have to decide what to wear to the party on Wednesday night," she said. "I called Tamsen for advice because she's always so beautifully dressed. She's coming over this afternoon to look through the closet with me."

Again, I felt that implied message that I wasn't welcome, which worried me. But I smiled and said, "I think you'll look amazing no matter what you choose."

"Good answer," she said, standing up from the table. A few minutes later she called to me, and I climbed the stairs to the bedroom, Rochester right on my heels.

Lili stood in front of the closet with her hands on her hips. "I want to clean up the closet so that Tamsen doesn't think we live like pigs. When I moved in, I threw a lot of stuff up on those high shelves because I didn't have time to sort it. I want to organize it now."

"I'll get the stepladder from the garage," I said. Rochester was right on my heels, as if he was afraid that if I got out of his sight I'd let that puppy back in.

When I returned with the stepladder, I saw that Lili had already begun tossing the items she could reach onto the bed. Rochester settled in the bedroom doorway and watched everything we did intently. "Don't worry, boy, there's no puppy hiding up there," I said.

I began handing down a collection of crazy hats, starting with a sombrero, a Viking helmet, a French beret and a pointy-topped straw hat that looked like it was from the Philippines. "These hats are great," I said. "Why don't I put up some hooks on the wall in the office, and you can hang them there."

"You think it won't look too dorky?"

"Who cares? It's our house."

I liked the sound of that – "our house." Lili's, mine, and Rochester's. We worked together for a while, getting everything down and then organizing it. We began mugging for selfies with various hats, trying the smaller ones on Rochester and getting him to pose.

Then I found a package of decorative hooks in the kitchen and hung the hats on the office wall, while Lili began to come up with potential outfits for New Year's Eve.

It struck me that I'd worn a lot of hats in my life – from son to student to teacher, from husband to hacker to convict. My engineer father had worked at the same job, most of the time for the same company. I hadn't been able to stick with anything that long. Even if I hadn't had my career path jolted by my stint as a guest of the California penal system, I probably wouldn't have stuck with my tech writing job forever. Mary would have pressed me to get a better job, a higher-paying one. I might have had to go back to school to refresh my tech abilities.

What kind of hat could Felix find, I wondered? He had gone from kid to drug lookout and dealer, from homeless to convict to kennel tech. He was great with dogs, but that wasn't going to be enough to create a whole career. He needed more education and a few more good opportunities. I was happy to be part of that.

It had been nearly a week since I'd been to his house with the dogs, and I hadn't heard from him since then. I figured he was busy with the holidays, and frankly I'd been busy myself so I hadn't followed up with him.

I sat down at the desk and sent Felix an email reminder. I hoped that being back home over Christmas hadn't hurt his resolve, but I tried to be non-judgmental in the message, offering to see him as soon as he could make it so we could keep moving forward.

I hit "send" and pushed back my chair. I had known a lot of restless people in my career, and I admitted that I was one of them. Many of the guys I'd worked with in Silicon Valley had tried the start-up route. A few had begun their own businesses, and more had joined nascent ventures. Most of them had either crashed and burned, or settled into a perennial scramble for funds or a chase for the newest, best tech.

How long would I stay at Friar Lake? Would I get bored with

organizing programs and running the center? Would some external force derail my career again? Suppose Lili was offered a terrific job somewhere and asked me to move with her?

My reveries were disrupted when Tamsen arrived shortly after two, and Rochester rushed downstairs. I followed and opened the door to her, holding on to Rochester's collar so he couldn't tackle her.

"You would not believe how much trouble an eight-year-old can get into when your back is turned," she said, as she shrugged off her wool-lined trenchcoat.

"I would believe it," I said. "We had an eight-month-old puppy visiting for a week, and he was a handful."

I took her coat and she unwound her long, multi-colored scarf. "I know I should cherish every moment with him, because someday, if I'm lucky, he'll grow up and go to college. But some days I can't wait for that day to arrive."

"I think all parents feel that way," I said. "I can imagine mine were glad to send me off to Eastern."

Lili joined us, and then she and Tamsen went upstairs to look for party outfits. I was getting into a book when my phone rang. "Hey, Rick," I said. "You'll never guess who's here right now?"

"I hope it's Felix Logato," he said.

"Sorry to disappoint you," I said. "Tamsen's here helping Lili find an outfit for that New Year's Eve party. Remember, you're dog-sitting Rochester. Why are you looking for Felix?"

"I need to talk to him, and it looks like he skipped town after he got fired. You went over to Logato's house last week, right? While you were there, did he say anything about leaving?"

I thought back to my conversation with Felix. "He was going to Philly Wednesday to help a friend," I said. "Then to his mother's for Christmas. Why do you need to talk to him? I thought Dr. Horz wasn't going to make a big deal out of that theft."

"The chief takes his dog to Animal House and he's friendly with Dr. Horz. He got on my case this morning about following up on that potassium theft, so I started tracking down the staff from the vet's office. Felix was number one on my list. I went over to his house, and his roommates said he got fired, and left Wednesday morning and hasn't been back since. Looks like he might have done a runner."

"I'm sure he'll turn up. Rochester really likes him and I trust my dog's instincts."

"The dog doesn't know everything, Steve," Rick said. "If Felix gets in touch with you, will you let me know?"

"Of course. I emailed him earlier today to set up a meeting and go over his writing."

When Rick hung up, I turned to Rochester. I liked Felix, and I hoped he wasn't in trouble. Had I been wrong about him? We had a couple of shared connections – we had both served time, we both loved dogs. But I had been ignoring the vast differences in our backgrounds, and how the way he'd grown up had formed him, just as my own upbringing had done for me.

"What do you think, boy? You think Felix ran off?"

He didn't have an opinion, just wanted to play. As I tugged one end of his rope, I thought about my last conversation with Felix. What was name of the friend he'd mentioned? Maybe he might know where Felix had gone.

Since Lili and Tamsen were busy upstairs, I sat at the dining room table and turned my laptop on. Rochester sprawled beside me in one of his standard positions, his front paws outstretched and his body at a forty-five degree angle, like the top of a Z.

Z, I thought. Zero. Zeno. Junior Zeno. No, Yunior Zeno. That was the name Felix had mentioned. I went online to see if I could find an address or phone number for him.

Yunior Zeno, whoever he was, kept a pretty low online profile. I quickly found that article from the Inquirer about the grow house bust where his name had been mentioned, but there was no follow-up about the incident.

The only useful thing I could find was a brief mention in an online blog of Yunior as an up and coming businessman in North Philly. His company was called Z Man Group. But there was no indication of what Z Man Group did, or where it was located.

I flexed my fingers. I loved a good computer-based challenge. Just then, Lili appeared at the top of the staircase and began to descend. "How do I look?" she asked.

She was wearing a slinky black dress that opened up to a swirl just above her knees. It was sleeveless, with a scooped neck, and she'd pulled her hair up into a knot and added a string of pearls. "Ravishing," I said. "Why don't you send Tamsen home so I can

Dog Have Mercy

ravish you?"

She laughed and went back upstairs. I took a deep breath and remembered the promise I'd made to Lili and to Rick not to hack. I had to use my brain instead of my hacking tools.

I tried a bunch of different searches until I found a corporate registration for Z Man Group, Yunior Zeno, president and chief executive officer. The address of record was a post office box in Philadelphia. Another dead end, though I felt like I was closing in.

I tried a bunch of different public databases, and finally hit pay dirt with the City of Philadelphia's Office of Property Assessment. Yunior Zeno didn't own any property in his own name, but Z Man Group did. A lot.

There was no website for the company, which I found suspicious. If Z Man rented apartments, for example, how would prospective tenants find them, or investigate them? I knew from my own experience, and that of the students I'd taught at Eastern, that most people looked on line for information first, whether from a computer or a smart phone.

I made a list of all the addresses, then opened a new window for Google Maps, where I plotted them out. They were all in North Philadelphia, around the area where Felix had said he'd grown up. Yunior owned houses on Ruffner, Sydenham, Birch, and Rowan Streets. From a street view, the neighborhood didn't look too bad; there were lots of trees, a park and a stadium nearby. But I was sure the view was deceiving.

I wasn't sure what else I could do, so I started putting those addresses into Google, and I was stunned when I got a hit from the Philadelphia *Inquirer* from Christmas day. A drug-related shootout had occurred at 404 W. Birch Street on Wednesday afternoon, Christmas Eve; there were four unidentified victims.

It seemed like too much of a coincidence to be anything but true. I called Rick. "Listen, there was a shooting in Philly on Christmas Eve," I said. I gave him the details. "Can you call the Philly cops and see if Felix Logato was one of the victims?"

"Where'd you get this from?" he asked.

"Too complicated to explain over the phone," I said. "Can you just check?"

"Fine. But I want to hear it."

"If it's him, I'll tell you all the details. Don't worry, I found everything legally. Oh, and check to see of one of the other victims was named Yunior Zeno."

"It sounds like you know a lot more than you're letting on. I'll talk to the Philly cops and then get back to you if there's a positive ID."

After Rick hung up, I paced around the downstairs, too edgy to focus on anything. Rochester sensed my mood and kept following me. I felt like I had failed Felix in some way. Could I have done anything more? I took the dogs out for a long walk in the cold, but my mind was still on Felix. Was he one of those unidentified victims? Would that explain why he'd left home and hadn't come back?

What if Yunior was a drug dealer, and he'd found a way to use the veterinarian's potassium to create that street drug, Cat or Charlie or whatever it was. Say he'd recruited Felix to steal those vials. It wasn't a long-term method of supply; Dr. Horz had already noticed them missing and alerted the police, and since Felix had been fired he wouldn't have any further access. But what if this was just an experiment? Could this be another example of Philly drug gangs infiltrating the suburbs?

I was still edgy when Tamsen and Lili came downstairs. "We've been invited to Tamsen's for dinner on New Year's Day," Lili said.

"Sounds like fun."

"And you have to bring Rochester," Tamsen said. "Rick's bringing Rascal. Nathaniel keeps bugging my sister for a dog, and I want him and Justin to both see how much trouble having a dog is."

"So are you telling me you want my dog to misbehave?" I said, in mock surprise.

"He doesn't have to misbehave, he just has to be himself," Lili said. "Eighty pounds of big happy dog. Maybe he can knock the boys over a couple of times."

"I don't know that we'd go that far," Tamsen said. "I've already done the holiday-emergency-room drill with Justin and I don't want to repeat it."

We all hugged and kissed, and Tamsen left. When she was out the door, Lili turned to me. "What's the matter? You look like something's wrong. You don't want to go to Tamsen's for dinner?"

"It's not that. Felix Logato has disappeared, and I'm afraid he's dead."

"Really? How do you know?"

She sat with me at the table, and Rochester came over to nuzzle my hand as I explained what I'd done. "Do you think I could have done anything more to help him?"

Lili shook her head. "If he was shot in some drug deal, then his problems were a lot worse than not being able to write well," she said.

"But I knew what he was going through. I could have tried more. Been his friend. Gotten him to open up more about his problems."

Lili reached over and took my hand. "I know you could relate to him, and I'm sure you feel bad that he might have gotten himself killed. But it wasn't up to you to save him."

"Then who?" I asked.

17 – A Nose for Clues

"I KNOW WHAT YOU NEED," Lili said. "Follow me."

We went upstairs together. "That black dress I showed you is pretty form-fitting," she said. "I'm not sure what to wear underneath it. Think you could help me decide?"

"I'd be delighted to assist." I sat back against the pillows on the bed, ready for a show. Before she started, Lili sat beside me and we kissed.

Then suddenly Rochester jumped up and skittered down the stairs, barking madly.

"Crap," I said. "That's probably Rick. Can we table this process for a little while?"

"The Hardy Boys are on another case," she said. "Far be it from me to stand in their way." She kissed me again. "That's so you remember what you're missing out on."

Like I needed the reminder.

I went downstairs and let Rick in. "It was Logato," Rick said. "They matched his prints."

Maybe it was the news, or the cold air that had rushed in the house when I let Rick in, but I was chilled. I went into the kitchen and started boiling water. "Hot chocolate?" I asked Rick. "Or tea or coffee?"

"I could do with something warm. Hot chocolate."

While the water boiled, I asked, "Was Yunior Zeno with him?"

"The guy I spoke to said Zeno wasn't one of the dead, but he wasn't the investigating detective. That guy, Holland, is supposed to call me back."

I started preparing the hot chocolate. I stirred in powder, and then a dollop of Godiva chocolate liqueur. "Not for me. I'm still on duty," Rick said when I showed him the bottle.

I topped the mugs with whipped cream, chocolate syrup and chocolate flakes. "You're killing me here," Rick grumbled. "This is at least an extra hour at the gym."

We both sipped from our mugs, which had different pictures of golden retrievers on them. Finally I sighed, and I began to tell Rick what I knew. "I didn't think anything of it at the time," I said. "He told me he had one friend who'd stood by him while he was in prison. This guy, Yunior Zeno. When you told me that Felix was missing, I went looking for information on Zeno, hoping he might be able to tell you where Felix was. That's when I found the information on that shooting."

"Did Felix look like he was using any kind of drugs?" Rick asked.

"I'm no expert," I said. "But his eyes weren't red, he wasn't jittery or anything. He spoke clearly, he played with Rochester. Did you talk to his roommates?"

"Yeah, they both said that he was clean, that he was trying to turn his life around. They were surprised that he'd booked."

His phone rang then. "This must be the detective from Philly." He introduced himself, then listened for a moment. "Yeah, that's the name I was given, Yunior Zeno."

He shifted the phone so I could hear. "He's a slippery one," Holland said. "Never been able to pin anything on him. He wasn't one of the victims but it's possible he was there. What makes you ask about him?"

"My source told me that Zeno owns the property where the shooting happened," Rick said. "Through a company called Z Man Group."

"You've got a pretty knowledgeable source. He or she know anything else?"

"Just that Felix Logato was a friend of Zeno's and was supposed to see him Christmas Eve."

I grabbed a piece of paper and scribbled "potassium?" on it.

"This may be completely irrelevant," Rick said. "But is there any trade in stolen potassium by you?"

"Potassium? Like in bananas?"

"Yeah. Some vials of liquid potassium were stolen from the veterinary office where Logato worked. That's how he came to my attention in the first place."

I wrote "methcathinone" on the paper as Holland said, "Haven't heard of anything like that. What do you do with them? Inject them?"

"If you want to give somebody a heart attack, you do," Rick sad. "Apparently there may also be a way to use potassium in manufacturing a street drug called methcathinone. You know anything about that?"

"Just heard rumors. Supposedly it's a Russian drug that gangs are trying to figure out how to manufacture here. You think there's a connection?"

"I was wondering if maybe Logato stole the potassium vials for his friend, if he was handing them off on Wednesday."

"From what we can tell, this shootout was about cocaine, not potassium," Holland said. "But stranger things have happened in the Badlands."

Rick thanked him and promised to pass on any other information he found, and Holland said that he'd look into the ownership of the building and see if he could bring Zeno in for questioning.

Rick left, and my bad mood remained. I kept wondering if there was something more I could have done for Felix Logato. Rochester stayed close to me, nuzzling me and licking my hand, and I felt blessed for the opportunities I'd had, that Felix hadn't.

"Steve?" Lili called from upstairs. "Are you just going to ignore me?"

That was certainly not my plan. I hurried up the stairs, Rochester on my heels, and found Lili lounging on the bed wearing some very sexy lingerie. We spent the rest of the afternoon together, though first I helped her remove the bra and panties.

Tuesday morning I still felt haunted by Felix Logato's death, and I decided that rather than sit around and obsess, I'd take Rochester back to Crossing Manor, see if we could cheer up some of the patients who didn't have a lot of family to visit.

"You go," Lili said. "I want to make rum balls for Tamsen's party and they need to steep in the rum for a few days."

Rochester was happy to jump into the car with me. I think he missed going to up to Friar Lake, all those construction workers saying hi to him and petting him.

The snow around the Crossing Manor parking lot had been piled into dirty clumps, though the lot itself had been salted and was pretty clean. I was careful walking Rochester up to the door; I didn't want to end up like Edith, in the Manor as a patient.

The lobby was deserted when we walked in. The receptionist's desk was empty, and there were no patients sitting in the big chairs. "Hello?" I called.

No answer. I was debating what to do when Marilyn Joiner appeared, in her white coat, wearing the same intricate gold chain around her neck. "Sorry, we're short-handed today," she said. "A couple of staffers are out sick, and we're trying to cope."

"If this is a bad time, we can come back," I said.

"No, it would be a real help if you could sit with the patients in the lounge," she said. "We need to clean the rooms and I don't have enough staff to keep them company there."

Rochester and I walked back to the lounge, where we found Mr. MacRae and Mrs. Vinci engaged in an argument. "I tell you, there was nothing wrong with that lady," Mrs. Vinci insisted. She waved an arthritic finger.

"We all got stuff wrong with us," Mr. MacRae said. "Me, I got a bad heart. You can't see that from the outside." He saw us in the doorway. "Here come my favorite doggie. How are you, boy?"

"You feeling all right, Mrs. Vinci?" I asked as I let the dog go toward Mr. MacRae's outstretched hand. She was wearing a yellow sweater dotted with fake pearls over a polyester blouse in a pink and yellow floral print, with dark blue sweat pants and white terrycloth slippers. At least her clothes were cheerful.

"Malavath died," she said. "My roommate."

"Yeah, I saw that in the paper. I'm sorry."

"Something fishy is going on here," she said. "She wasn't hardly sick at all, just that her family needed a place to park her. Her son married a white lady, you know, and didn't want some old woman in a sari around her house."

I sat in the chair beside her, as Mr. MacRae petted Rochester. "What happened to her?" I asked.

"They say it was a heart attack," Mrs. Vinci said. "But she didn't have no problems with her heart. She was here for the rheumatism."

I remembered my great-aunt used that term for arthritis. She always used to ask for her "rheumatiz medicine."

"Well, like Mr. MacRae said, we all have stuff wrong with us, and you can't see it all from the outside. I used to have high blood pressure, before I got Rochester and went for walks all the time."

Actually, I'd had the high pressure back in Silicon Valley, between the stress of my job and of living with Mary. I'd lost a lot of weight in prison and the pressure had evened out, but I was sure that walking the dog helped keep it down.

"Seems like a lot of people having heart attacks here," Mrs. Vinci said. "But when you ask Mrs. Joiner about it she brushes you off."

Rochester moved on from Mr. MacRae to Mr. Watnik, the gin rummy player, and I talked to a couple of the other patients. Mr. Fictura was in a corner of the room, grumbling because he'd had to leave his room. "How are you today?" I asked him. "Looking forward to the New Year?"

"What have I got to look forward to?" he asked. "My son didn't even come see me for Christmas. Went to some resort in the islands instead. You know what, screw him. I'm changing my will. I'm going to leave everything I got to the dogs and cats. My son, he'll get a dollar ninety-nine, he should buy a rope and hang himself."

Rochester jumped up and placed his paws on the arm of Mr. Fictura's chair and leaned forward to lick the old man.

"Rochester!" I said, and I yanked on his leash.

"You're a bossy one," Mr. Fictura said to him. "I can relate."

Rochester wagged his tail and sat on the floor beside Mr. Fictura. The old man stroked his head for a while. "We should get going," I said. "Come on, Rochester."

My dog wasn't willing to leave, though. He kept looking up at Mr. Fictura as if he was trying to tell the old man something. Eventually Mr. Fictura slipped back in the chair and his hand hung down alongside it. He began to snore lightly.

Mrs. Joiner and an orderly came in to start taking the patients down to the cafeteria for lunch. Mr. Fictura grumbled that he'd just finally gotten to sleep, and Rochester pulled to go back over to him but I tugged his leash and we walked out of the lounge.

There was still no receptionist at the front desk when we passed, but Rochester tugged me over to the front desk, then put his paws up on the counter and sniffed at the computer keyboard.

"What's up, boy?" I asked. "Somebody leave a treat over there?"

He cocked his head and I recognized that look. "What? Is there something on the computer you want me to look at?"

I glanced around the room. Nobody was around. Rochester

Dog Have Mercy

moved away from the keyboard and I stood beside it. The screen saver was engaged, and when I hit the space bar the screen came to life. Whoever had been sitting there had begun entering information on Mrs. Divaram into a state form for deaths at nursing homes and extended care facilities.

A box at the bottom of the form was used to list similar deaths within the same month. Mrs. Tuttle's name was there, along with another I didn't recognize. Like Mrs. Divaram, the cause of death in each case was heart failure.

I heard a door open and quickly stepped away from the computer. "Rochester, don't rummage in the garbage can!" I said, tugging at his leash. I looked up to see Marilyn Joiner approaching, holding a cell phone in one hand and a clipboard in the other.

"Sorry, he's usually much better behaved," I said. "Come on, boy, let's go."

He looked at me reproachfully. When we got outside I said, "Sorry, puppy, had to think on my feet. I know you're a good boy."

As we drove home, I thought about the deaths I'd seen on the form. Did that indicate some kind of pattern? It wasn't unusual for an elderly person, already ill enough to be in a nursing home, to die of heart failure. I had no idea if three deaths in a month was a few, or a lot.

I turned to Rochester. "What do you think, boy? Was there something on that form that you wanted me to see?"

He shook his big golden head from side to side, and the tags on his collar jangled.

"What? Some other computer thing?"

His tongue rolled out, and he yawned. Had he been trying to tell me to look for something online, and seeing Mrs. Divaram's form was coincidental? I found it hard to believe that he'd intuited something from a computer with the screen saver running.

But he did have a nose for clues. If it wasn't the form, could it have been the computer itself? Was he trying to tell me to hack into the nursing home's system for some reason? Or some other computer?

Not for the first time, I wished the dog could just tell me what he wanted.

18 – Black Bridge

ALL THE WAY HOME my brain buzzed, trying to make a connection to computers. As I was pulling into River Bend, I remembered that Felix had used his roommate's computer to email me and to access the grammar materials. Was it possible there would be some piece of information on that computer that could help find out who killed him?

I made a U-turn and drove back out the gate toward US 1. I remembered meeting one of Felix's roommates the day I visited, and I hoped he might be there, and willing to let me take a look at Felix's email account.

Traffic was heavy, and I was stuck for a while behind a panel truck advertising a company as "The Picasso of Plumbers." I wondered if that meant your pipes would come out all weird and twisted. At the entrance to Cobalt Ridge, a teenaged girl slouched on a bus bench, her rats nest of dreadlocks pulled up into a bun on the top of her head and secured with a rubber band. Her neck was wreathed in tattoos.

"And people say cursive writing is dead," I said to Rochester.

An old Toyota was parked in the driveway of the house on Calicobush Road, with a bumper sticker for a Christian Exercise group called Witness Fitness. I walked up to the front door, where Dan Symonds answered my knock. "If you're looking for Felix, he's gone," he said. "The cops came by and said that he's dead."

"I know," I said. "I was hoping to take a look at his emails, if you don't mind. He was using your computer, right?"

"Yeah, he had a Gmail account and I let him use my laptop for that, and for writing that stuff you asked him for."

"You think I could take a look at it?"

"What for?"

Dog Have Mercy

"I don't know," I said. "I keep feeling that there was something more I should have done for Felix. And now that he's dead I feel like the only way I make up for that is to help the cops figure out what happened to him."

"You work for the cops?"

I shook my head. "I have a friend who's a cop in Stewart's Crossing," I said. "Sometimes I find out information and give it to him."

Dan Symonds still looked suspicious. "Please?" I asked. "I need to do this."

"All right. If you can make it quick. I've got to get to work soon." He reached down and scratched behind Rochester's ear. "You're welcome, too, bud."

Dan's laptop was on the dining room table. "Felix didn't know much about computers," Dan said. "He wasn't real sharp on computer security. His password was felixthecat, which I kept telling him was dumb and too easy for somebody to crack."

I sat at the laptop and logged into Felix's Gmail account. The first thirty messages or so were spam that had come in since the last time Felix checked his email. The first email that was personal was a response from Scott Higley, a staffer at Paws Up, the agency that had worked with Felix when he was in prison, teaching him to train dogs.

I started at the bottom of the message, where the email correspondence began about a week before Christmas. Higley had emailed Felix to check on him and see how he was doing. "I know the holidays are tough," Higley wrote. "Maybe we should get together sometime and talk."

Moving up, I read Felix's response. He told Higley that he'd lost his job and asked if he knew of any openings. From the date of the message, I realized Felix had sent it soon after he and I had talked, and I was glad he'd taken some action to look for new work.

The most recent was a response from Higley that he had a couple of ideas, and that it would be a good idea for them to meet somewhere soon. So Felix had had some good news, I thought. I was pleased about that. I didn't like the idea that he had died in despair.

I checked the "sent mail" folder and found that Felix had replied to Scott Higley. He was going to be in North Philly on Wednesday, if Scott wanted to meet with him then.

There was nothing further either to or from Higley. Rochester came over to sniff at the laptop, and he nudged my elbow with his nose. That caused the cursor to move, and to hover over the email address.

While the display name was "Scott Higley" the actual sending address was negroponte@hotmail.com. I doubted that someone writing from an organization would use a different email account with a different name, which meant that someone had spoofed Felix into believing he was this Scott Higley.

"Do you know if Felix knew anyone named Negroponte?" I asked Dan.

He shook his head. "He didn't bring friends over, and we didn't talk about his life," he said. "Listen, can you wrap it up? I need to get moving."

"Sure. Just give me two seconds." I scanned quickly through the rest of Felix's email but there was nothing else that looked interesting. I Googled for Paws Up and discovered that they had an office on Roosevelt Boulevard in Northeast Philly. I wrote down the address and phone number, thanked Dan, and took Rochester outside.

While he sniffed and peed, I called the phone number for Paws Up. A woman answered. "Paws Up. This is December."

"Can I speak to Scott Higley?" I asked.

"He stepped out for a few minutes, but he should be back in about a half hour. Can I have him call you?"

"No thanks. I'll call back." I hung up. It wasn't that far from Levittown to Northeast Philly – I thought I could make it to the office in about half an hour. And I figured Scott Higley would be more willing to talk to me in person than over the phone. I was curious to know if that message had really come from him, or if he knew who might have been impersonating him online.

I made a U-turn on Calicobush, careful to avoid running over a little girl in a pink bicycle helmet with a glittery silver tiara glued on top of it. As I head south on US 1, I was hit by a pang of nostalgia, for all the years my parents had taken that road into the city, before I-95 existed. Most of the landmarks I remembered were long gone, but where the road changed names, from Lincoln Highway to Roosevelt Boulevard, I saw the familiar sight of a pair of cemeteries, then a big hospital.

I passed the signs for the Northeast Philadelphia airport and then started checking street numbers. Just beyond the Rolling Thunder Skating Center, I found the office of Paws Up, in a single-story house. I pulled into the parking lot and let Rochester out.

He lifted his snout and sniffed the air. "You smell other doggies around?" I asked.

He didn't answer, but he did tug me over to a leafless tree and peed copiously at its base. Then we walked up a short ramp to the front door. A young woman at a plain metal desk looked up. "Can I help you?"

The office was small, with one door that led to a bathroom and another to an office behind her. "I was hoping I could talk to Scott Higley. My name is Steve Levitan and I'm a friend of someone who was in the program."

A middle-aged man in a wheelchair rolled to the doorway. "I'm Scott. How can I help you?"

He rolled back into his office and Rochester and I followed. A female German Shepherd was on the floor beside Scott's desk, and she stood up. Her ears were raised and she was focused on Rochester. She had a black snout and a triangle of black fur above her eyes. The rest of her alternated between brown and black.

"Sophie, down," Scott said. "She gets kind of protective of me."

"Rochester's very friendly," I said. "Can he say hello?"

"Sure." Rochester moved slowly toward the female, keeping his body low, as if in submission. Sophie sniffed him, and he sniffed back, and very quickly he was sprawled on the floor beside her.

"You have a good dog," Scott said. "You train him yourself?"

I shook my head. "I adopted him at about a year old. He was already way smarter than any ever dog I've ever met."

Scott nodded. "What brings you here?"

"I was a friend of Felix Logato's," I said. "I understand he was in your program?"

"Felix is a good guy," Scott said. "He got a rough start in life but I have a lot of faith in him."

"When was the last time you saw him?"

He looked at me curiously, but said, "About six months ago. He finished his time and told me he had a job lined up at a veterinarian's office. What's this about?"

"I guess you don't know, then." I told him about Felix's death.

"That's awful. We try our best to help the guys while they're inside, and give them skills they can use in the world. But sometimes it doesn't work out."

"I think Felix was set up." I explained about the message trail I had read. "You didn't email him last week?"

Scott shook his head. "And if I had, I'd have used our server."

"Do you know anyone named Negroponte? That was the name on the account."

"Negroponte? Italian name, sounds like South Philly to me. Felix didn't get down that way, as far as I know. Italians and Puerto Ricans clashed a lot in prison."

Rochester pawed the German Shepherd's back, and she rolled onto her side. He kept his golden paw on a black patch on her side. The contrast in the colors was sharp.

"Black," I said out loud. "Negro is Italian for black, right?"

Scott nodded. "And ponte means bridge." His eyebrows raised. "Black bridge," he said. "Negroponte, black bridge."

"You know someone with that name?"

He nodded. "Jimmy Blackbridge. He was in prison with Felix. Both of them were in Paws Up, but Jimmy kept breaking the rules and we had to kick him out."

"You think he might have blamed Felix for that?"

"Hard to say. Felix was a good worker, one of our stars. It might have been him who reported Jimmy. Or they could have had some other beef unrelated to the program."

"I think it has to be related," I said. "Because it was your address that was spoofed."

"And you think that Felix went to this house to meet me, and instead Jimmy killed him?"

"Felix was already planning to go to that house. Maybe once Jimmy Blackbridge knew that, he did something that led to Felix's death. But I'm not a cop, and the first thing I'm going to do is pass this information on to a friend of mine who is. I know he's been in touch with the Philly cops investigating Felix's death. I imagine they'll want to talk to you."

"We'll be open tomorrow morning, but then closing early for New Year's Eve."

"Trust me," I said. "When the police have information, they move quickly."

19 – Final Justice

AS SOON AS I GOT BACK IN MY CAR, I called Rick and told him what I'd learned. "How do you know that this Jimmy Blackbridge is the one who emailed Felix?"

"I don't know that for sure. But the email address was from an account called Negroponte, which translates into black bridge. Since he and Felix knew each other, and this guy Scott Higley says the two of them argued, it seems worth investigating, right?"

"Why didn't Felix get suspicious about the email?"

"Felix didn't know much about computers," I said. "Even if he had accidentally hovered over the email address and seen the real sender, I doubt he'd have recognized it was a problem."

"I'll call Detective Holland and pass this on. Where are you now?"

"Just left Paws Up, heading home."

"You're not going to track down this Blackbridge guy, right? Because you know that's police business."

"I know. I'm not stupid enough to go ask some stranger if he killed Felix." I reached over and scratched Rochester under his neck. "At least not with Rochester with me."

"Thank God for that," Rick said dryly. "And while I appreciate your help here, I don't want you to get yourself in trouble again. No snooping online in places you shouldn't be, all right? Even if you think it's the right thing to do."

"I know. I feel bad about Felix but at the same time I know he was trying to turn his life around. It seems like I'd be diminishing that somehow if I did something that got myself in trouble."

"That's a good thought," Rick said.

On the drive home, I felt at loose ends. I kept thinking about Felix Logato, and wondering if there was something I could have done that might have changed the trajectory that had led to his death.

It was clear that I couldn't do any more investigating; the police would have to talk to Yunior Zeno and Jimmy Blackbridge, and see what they could discover. I was proud of myself for that understanding, and for the realization that I had to honor Felix's memory by doing my best to stick to the straight and narrow. Rick believed that I kept interfering in his cases because I couldn't help myself, and here I was, willingly backing away.

By the time I got home, my emotions were still confused. "Where were you all day?" Lili asked. "You didn't spend the day at Crossing Manor, did you?"

"No, we were all over the map." I told her about our visit to the nursing home and Mrs. Vinci's suspicions, then about the trip to Cobalt Ridge to look at Felix's email account.

"Hold on," she said, when I got to the part about the spoofed email address. "You think someone lured him to that house in North Philly in order to kill him?"

"He was already going there to meet his friend Yunior," I said. "But he did tell whoever sent the email where he was going to be, and when, thinking that it was the guy from Paws Up."

I told her about Paws Up, and driving down there to meet Scott Higley. "He says he didn't send that message. But he gave me the name of somebody he thought might have."

Lili had her hands on her hips. "Don't tell me you went to see that person, too."

I shook my head. "I called Rick and gave him the information. I'm not chasing ex-cons all over Philadelphia."

"Well, that's progress," she said. She leaned over and kissed me. "I've got some more photo manipulation to do. I'll be upstairs."

I went into the kitchen to get a bottle of water. There were three mason jars of chocolate balls on the top shelf, and I opened a jar and pulled one rum ball out. The rum smell was strong, the texture crumbly, with sprinkles of white sugar against the dark chocolate. I popped it in my mouth and the flavors exploded. The rum brought out the richness of the chocolate.

"Those rum balls are for the party!" Lili called from upstairs. "And they need to steep before they're ready to eat."

"I only had one and it tasted fine to me," I hollered back. I grabbed a bottle of cold water and poured some for Rochester, then

Dog Have Mercy

opened my laptop on the kitchen table. My fingers were itching to do something about Felix's death and I knew that if I didn't change gears I'd get myself in trouble. So I logged on to my support group to see what everyone else was up to.

In addition to the message boards, there was a chat room that wasn't often populated, but that afternoon MamaHack was there, chatting with another hacker whose ID was Fizzy_Water. I logged in and typed, *hey.*

We chatted about the weather and the holidays for a few lines, and then I typed, *do either of you hack just because you're curious?*

You mean nosy? Fizzy responded.

I guess.

Mama wrote, *my shrink sez she thinks I hack for power & control. Hubster makes the cash, kids dictate the schedule w/ school, sports, dance, etc. When my fingers itch it's so I can be in charge.*

She and Fizzy got into a debate about kids and whether they should be reined in to do what their parents told them, and I sat back and thought. Back in Silicon Valley, I had been a technical writer for a big catalog sales company. One of my jobs was to create manuals for all company procedures, including any new software we instituted. The company had discovered a hole in its merchandise tracking operations, and bought a packaged program to fill that need.

The shipping department staffers needed instructions on how the system operated, so I was given a log-in ID and password, and I learned how to operate it. Then I started writing my instructions, but I needed some additional documentation that apparently existed on the company's website, but was behind a firewall. I had emailed and called the company for access, but the company had recently been bought out and most of the staff let go, and no one I spoke to was able to help me.

I was expressing my frustration to one of my co-workers, a heavy-duty programmer named Bruce, and he said, "I can help you out."

This was back before the days of jump drives and elaborate security precautions at companies and in the online world. Bruce slipped a floppy disk into the drive of my PC and walked me through what was on it.

It was a door to a whole new world. The program sniffed out an open port on a computer at the software company's office and let me log in as an administrator. I downloaded the files I needed and logged off.

My pulse was racing. I'd broken into a protected site and stolen information. Well, it wasn't theft, exactly, because it was material that my company had purchased and couldn't get hold of. All afternoon I kept expecting some law enforcement guy to walk into our cube farm and come up to my desk with a pair of handcuffs.

That didn't happen. Bruce took his disk back, but the files had been copied to my hard drive. I copied them to another floppy of my own and took them home, and that night, while Mary was watching TV, I installed them on my computer and began playing around.

I became obsessed. I surfed the Internet looking for additional tools, learning how to use them, becoming conversant with terms like IP address, honey pot, and sniffer. I broke into a genealogy site and researched my family. I got into one of those reunion sites and looked up information on classmates and old friends.

I mentioned something in passing to Bruce about what I'd been doing, and he said, in a low voice, "You can't go around talking about that stuff, dude. That is seriously illegal."

"But you gave me those tools."

"Yeah, and I don't want your big mouth to land me in jail. So keep it quiet."

I felt chastened, and didn't say anything more until Bruce came to me a few weeks later. "I've got a friend," he said. "Needs some information. I can't handle it because I'm going out of town. You want to pick up a few extra bucks?"

Of course I did. No matter how much money Mary and I made, it was never enough to support the big mortgage, the car payments, the credit card bills. Over the next year or two Bruce slipped me a job now and then, and I began to build up my own clients. I never stole anything dramatic – a company wanted to see what a competitor was doing, a divorce attorney wanted to know about hidden assets.

It wasn't about the money; it was about the thrill of the chase, of gathering this information, of knowing something I wasn't supposed to. I had always been a curious kid, the kind who was constantly asking questions and snooping around. Discovering the world of computers opened new doors for me, new places to look for information. I was always Googling people that I met, looking at maps and photo albums. Then Mary miscarried for the second time,

Dog Have Mercy

and my world fell apart.

Back then, like MamaHack, I had felt powerless, almost emasculated. Mary was the driving force in our marriage. We had followed her career to California, and she made all the major decisions, including choosing when to start making a baby. I was a low-level functionary at work, well-paid but under-utilized. I was bored a lot of the time but didn't have the authority to create new projects for myself that would be more challenging.

Prison, for me, was the ultimate loss of control. The schedule governed when I ate, when I slept, when I worked. I did manage to exert a bit of power, because as I had told Felix, I could help other prisoners with their appeals, and they protected and rewarded me.

When I came back to Stewart's Crossing I was rudderless. I simply didn't remember how to manage my own time, my own life. It had taken Rochester, and my jobs at Eastern, to bring me back to life. It was important to me that I recognize all I had regained in the last couple of years, and how easily I could lose it if I made a mistake.

Rochester nuzzled me and I realized that I'd been ignoring him all the time I'd been online. I signed off the computer and played tug-a-rope with him for a while, then took him for a long walk.

Rick called after dinner. "That Blackbridge guy has quite a record," he said. "Holland looked him up and verified that he'd been at Graterford at the same time Felix was. He used that information you gave me to log into Felix's email account, and he saw the spoofing. That gives him enough to pull Blackbridge in for questioning, even though Holland still thinks that Felix died during a drug deal."

"Thanks, Rick," I said. "I appreciate your following up with Holland, and with me. I'd like to see some justice for Felix."

"The only real justice is the final one," Rick said. "If God believes in Felix, then he'll be okay."

I remembered that Rick had been brought up as a Roman Catholic, and was a bit surprised that he still believed, after years as a cop. But all I said was, "I hope so."

Neil S. Plakcy

20 – Very Agatha Christie

THE NEXT MORNING, after I had fed and walked Rochester, I couldn't resist the impulse to go online and look for information on Jimmy Blackbridge. I wasn't going to confront him. I just wanted to see what he looked like, know what kind of guy he was.

I did a couple of general searches, and one of the sites that I pulled up listed other people who might be connected to the person I was searching for. A couple of the names there were Negroponte. That reassured me that I was on the right track.

Jimmy didn't have a Facebook account, but he was tagged in a photo of a group of twenty-somethings celebrating a birthday. He was slim and wiry, with dark hair combed back from his forehead. He had a square jaw and a chipped front tooth.

He was wearing what I'd grown up calling a wife-beater, a form-fitting white T-shirt without sleeves. His right arm showed off impressive biceps, and a tattoo of a lion's head, mouth open in mid-roar, with the words "Take the Lion's Share" in script beneath it.

He had his left arm around a big-busted, big-hipped girl named Merlys, and when I zoomed in on the photo I saw his fingers had been tattooed with the word G A M E in a Gothic script. I recognized that; a guy I'd known in prison had that on one hand, and the word O V E R on the other.

I repressed a shiver. Was he the guy who had killed Felix Logato? Was the tattoo on that fist the last thing Felix ever saw?

I shut down the computer. I had to get that image out of my head. So I did what I often do when something bothers me; I played with my dog. I tossed a tennis ball and he retrieved it, though after two runs he refused to give it back to me. We played tug-a-rope and then I scratched his belly.

By then, I had started to believe, against my heart, that Felix had

Dog Have Mercy

stolen the potassium from Dr. Horz, and that he'd been planning to hand it over to Yunior in North Philly the day he died. I didn't know the specifics, but I assumed that Yunior wanted to kill somebody and have it look natural, and that he'd forced Felix to steal the vials.

By late afternoon I was still depressed and didn't feel like going out to a party that night, but I'd promised Lili and I knew she was looking forward to it. I fed Rochester and drove him over to Rick's, then returned home. Lili was already in her slinky black dress by then, though she was barefoot and hadn't put up her hair yet. "What time is it?" she asked.

"Only eight. We've got plenty of time."

"For you, maybe. It takes a lot of work to make me beautiful."

I took her hand. "My darling, you look beautiful to me all the time."

"That's sweet," she said. "But I still need to get ready."

It was close to ten by the time we left the house, carrying a platter of Lili's homemade brownies as a hostess gift. The night was cold and clear, and there wasn't much traffic as we drove to Crossing Estates, where Gracious Chigwe lived. As we approached the gate, though, we were stuck behind an RV with "Jesus is Lord of All" written in huge letters across the back.

"Hard not to miss that message," I said.

We parked down the block from the house and walked up. It was a big split level, all lit up, and from the driveway we could hear the sound of classical music. I put on a smile and we walked inside.

Gracious met us at the door, a pleasant woman with what Alexander McCall Smith would have called a "traditional build." She took our coats and directed us to the refreshments in the living room. I got cups of punch for Lili and myself, and then she walked over to one of her colleagues to talk art.

Across the room, I saw Jackie Conrad from the biology department. It was probably the first time I'd seen her in anything other than her white lab coat. For the party, she'd worn a maroon velvet dress with short sleeves. When I got close I noticed that her dangling earrings were shimmery silver lizards.

"You didn't wear your brain cells as earrings?" I asked her.

"I figured I wouldn't need them, since this is only a faculty gathering," she said. "Most of our faculty are operating short a few brain cells anyway."

"I'll drink to that," I said, lifting my punch cup and clinking it against hers. We chatted for a few minutes about some of the others at the party, and then I remembered I had a question for her. "What do you know about potassium?"

"That depends. You want to know its chemical function? Remember, I'm a biologist, not a chemist."

"Is there a difference between potassium in liquid form versus in a pill?"

"Yes. When a doctor prescribes you a pill, it's so that your potassium levels will rise gradually, compensating for a deficiency in diet, for example. If you add potassium to an IV for delivery, the level goes up very fast. You have to watch carefully or the patient could suffer cardiac arrest."

"If you had a vial of liquid potassium, how could you get it into someone's IV?"

She looked at me closely. "Every time you come to my office you ask the most intriguing questions. Are you investigating something else now?"

I explained to her about the potassium theft from Dr. Horz's office, and how I'd been looking into it.

"You think someone stole the potassium in order to commit a murder?" she asked. "How very Agatha Christie."

"It's a solid reason why someone would steal it," I said. "So could you get it into someone's IV easily?"

"Very easily." She looked around the room and spotted a pad and a pen beside the telephone. "Let me show you." She drew two parallel lines. "This is your IV tube." Then she drew a small circle along one side. "This is a port. Every IV has one. You insert the vial into the port and release the potassium into the fluids."

"So anybody could do it?" I asked. "You don't need to be a nurse?"

"You only need to be able to get close enough to the person," Jackie said.

I saw Lili across the room motioning to me, so I left Jackie and walked over to her. She was talking to Gracious. "Thank you for inviting us," I said. "It's a lovely party."

"I'm so glad you could come," she said. "So many of our colleagues have taken off for the holidays. And I really want to get to know people better. What is it that you teach?"

Dog Have Mercy

I explained that I adjuncted in the English department, but that my primary job was at Friar Lake. "Have any ideas for continuing education programs in your discipline?" I asked.

"Gracious and I have been talking about homelessness," Lili said. "Maybe you could put together a program on that."

"I'm not sure it would be a big seller," I said. "I think it's one of those problems people want to avoid." I held up my hand before Lili could say anything. "It's great that you're approaching it in the classroom, because you can educate people. But I think we'd need a sexier topic in order to draw in older learners."

"I'd love to do something about Africa," Gracious said. "Most Americans know almost nothing about the continent, and how diverse it is. Perhaps they long to go on a safari, but that's about it."

"We'll have to talk," I said. Across the room I saw Minna Breznick, and I was surprised, but then I remembered that she and her cardiologist husband lived in the same neighborhood. "If you'll excuse me, I see someone I need to talk to."

I walked over to her. "Steve Levitan," I said. "I bring my golden in to Dr. Horz's office."

"Oh, yes, I recognize you," she said, in that sharp, guttural Israeli accent. Her blonde hair had been puffed up like a balloon, and she wore six gold chains around her neck.

"I was there the other day and Dr. Horz had discovered some supplies stolen," I said casually. "She ever figure out what happened?"

Minna looked around, then leaned in conspiratorially. "A police detective came to my house on Monday to ask me questions. But I think it's all resolved now."

"Really?"

"You probably don't know this, but Dr. Horz hired a kennel assistant who had been in prison for drug dealing. The rest of the staff didn't know at first, and once we found out we had to talk to her and eventually she let him go." She shook her head. "Dr. Horz is a sweet woman, but sometimes I think she's too trusting. And now see what happened."

I wanted to defend Felix. I really believed he had been trying to turn his life around. But it was a party, and I wasn't going to accuse Minna of being small-minded when she might very well be right. However, I was still curious to know if she understood the uses of potassium and had any motive herself for the theft.

"What exactly was stolen?" I asked. "Not anything dangerous, I hope."

"Very dangerous, in the wrong hands," she said. "But then, any medical supplies can be used to hurt as well as to heal."

She had a gleam in her eye that was unsettling, but I pressed on. "What do you mean?"

"All of the body must be in balance," she said. "Not too much or too little of any vitamin or mineral. This potassium that was stolen, you inject it into someone and poof! Heart attack. I'm sure we all know people we would like to see go that way, huh?"

Then she laughed. "But of course, we are not criminals."

I wanted to say, "Speak for yourself," but I bit my tongue. It was a party, after all. Instead, I said, "I hope the new year brings good things for all of us."

Lili was still talking to someone, so I wandered over to the food and grabbed a couple of her brownies. I thought back to what Jackie Conrad had said, about the ability to stick a vial of potassium into an IV. Who might have Yunior wanted to kill? A rival drug dealer who was hospitalized, for example? I pulled out my wallet and scribbled a reminder to tell Rick what I had learned.

When I looked up I saw Lili smiling at me, and I walked back to her. At midnight, we kissed to ring in the new year. I was so happy with the way my life had changed during the past year, and I made sure to tell Lili what a big part of that positive change had to do with her. Life was too fleeting not to say those things.

21 – Active Imagination

IT WAS LOVELY TO SLEEP IN on New Year's Day, without a big golden head breathing on me and demanding food, walk and attention. Lili and I lounged in bed together, then I made breakfast and brought it up to her on a tray.

"What a treat," she said, sitting up.

"Happy New Year," I said. We ate together and then while she sat back with my new iPad and played around, I drove over to Rick's to pick up Rochester.

"I was right," I said to Rick. "According to one of the science professors at Eastern, you can use potassium to kill someone, especially if they have an IV."

"I never said you weren't right about that," Rick said. "But it looks to me like Felix Logato stole those vials from Dr. Horz's office. Maybe he sold them to his buddy, maybe he did something else with them. But he's dead now, so the case is closed."

I didn't like it, but I couldn't blame Rick for wanting a simple solution to a simple crime.

"Don't forget dinner at Tamsen's tonight," Rick said. "Justin's looking forward to playing with Rascal and Rochester."

I had forgotten, but Rick was so eager that I didn't want to admit I had. "We'll be there. Lili made rum balls, which have been steeping in our refrigerator. I've only been taking one at a time from each jar so she won't notice."

"Women always notice that kind of thing," he said. "It's in their genes."

When I got home, Lili was in the kitchen with the jar of rum balls open, and I worried she was going to bust me. But when she turned to me, she had two in her hand, and passed one to me. "You think these are ready?" she asked.

I popped it in my mouth, and if anything, the flavor had improved since the first one I'd tasted. "I think they're awesome."

"My mother used to make these for parties," she said. "I'd almost forgotten them. I had to look up a recipe online and then tweak it to make them taste like hers."

"You are a woman of awesome talents," I said. We kissed, and I tasted the rum and chocolate on her lips. Rochester tried to nose his way in, but I kneed him away. "No chocolate for you, puppy. We've already been that route before."

A woman who had killed two Eastern College students had believed Rochester had dug up evidence against her. Before we knew she was the culprit, she had sent us a box of dog biscuits that were supposed to be flavored with carob, which is okay for dogs, but instead was heavily dosed with chocolate. I'd accidentally left the box within his reach, back before I knew how easy it was for him to get up to a kitchen counter. He'd eaten the whole box, and I had to rush him to Dr. Horz's and have him dosed with activated charcoal. The woman was serving a life sentence in prison for her crimes, and I hoped she rotted there.

Later that morning, Dr. Horz called. "I know that you took an interest in helping Felix," she said. "I spoke with his mother, and his funeral is tomorrow morning in North Philadelphia. I'd like to go and pay my respects, but I can't say I'm thrilled about going to that neighborhood on my own. I was hoping you would go with me."

"I'd like that," I said. "I feel terrible about what happened to Felix and I'd like to express my condolences to his family."

Her office was still closed, but she said she had to go in for an hour or so the next morning to catch up on paperwork. We arranged that I would pick her up there at ten and we'd drive into North Philly together.

After I hung up, Lili asked, "You're not taking Rochester to the funeral, are you? Because even if he behaves, some people there might take it the wrong way."

"No, I'll leave him here. You don't want to go, do you?"

She shook her head. "I was talking to Gracious at the party, and she told me about a great nail salon in New Hope. We're going there tomorrow for mani-pedis. I need some girl time to recharge."

I guessed my meetings with Rick counted as "guy time," so I was fine with Lili's plans. "That means you're going to be on your own

Dog Have Mercy

tomorrow afternoon, boy," I said to Rochester, who was pushing up against my leg. "You all right with that?"

In response, he sprawled on his back on the floor and waved his legs in the air. "Looks like you've got to give him a head start on belly rubs to tide him over," Lili said.

I sat on the living room floor and rubbed Rochester's tummy, and Lili lounged on the couch until we had to get ready for dinner at Tamsen's.

It wasn't far to where Tamsen and her son Justin lived, in a fifties-era split level a few blocks from where I'd grown up. "Tamsen's business must be doing well," I said, as we got out of the car. Lili had the jars of rum balls in a canvas bag and I had Rochester on his leash.

"What makes you say that?"

"Houses like this one go for half a mill these days," I said. "There must be a lot of money in tchotchkes." I knew from Rick that Tamsen helped corporate clients find and produce promotional products like towels, mugs, and mouse pads imprinted with company logos, but he'd never mentioned how successful she was.

Justin opened the door to welcome us in. He was eight, a towheaded boy with energy to burn. Behind him stood his quieter cousin Nathaniel, brown hair and glasses. He was two years younger than Justin, and too slight to play on the Pop Warner football team that Justin played on and Rick coached. Both of them were excited to see Rochester. I let Rochester off his leash, and he romped with the boys.

We found Tamsen and Hannah in the kitchen, which looked like it had been recently remodeled, with sleek appliances and new-looking cabinets. The sisters were a year apart, and a few years younger than Rick and I were. Tamsen was as tall as Lili, with lustrous blonde hair and a coltish grace. I thought her energy and cheer were a good match for Rick. She could keep up with him, mentally and physically, and keep his spirits up as well.

That evening, she looked particularly lovely, in a long-sleeved bright blue silk blouse and black slacks. Her hair looked fresh from a salon, and she wore gold earrings with tiny stars hanging from them.

Hannah Palmer, like her son Nathaniel, was quieter. She was the Clerk of the Friends' Meeting in town, and had a deeply spiritual side, as well as a commitment to the Quaker ideals she and her sister had been raised with. She was an inch or two shorter than her sister, and her hair was the same color, but pulled back into a knot. Hannah was dressed more casually, in a chocolate brown turtleneck sweater over skinny jeans and those low boots that always remind me of elves.

After we kissed hello, Lili put the bag of jars on the table and began handing them to Tamsen. "These look delicious!" Tamsen said.

Tamsen's cell phone rang with the theme from *The Lone Ranger*. "Crap, I have to get that," she said. "Can you take over, Han?" Her sister nodded as Tamsen grabbed the phone and walked out of the kitchen.

"I hope nothing's wrong," I said to Hannah.

"No, that's just one of her clients," Hannah said. "My sister is too professional sometimes. She takes calls all the time. She's a super saleswoman and she has an amazing eye for detail. And if she were here, she'd ask if you want something to drink. There's beer and wine in the fridge."

I got myself a beer, noticing that either Rick had brought some microbrews to Tamsen's, or that she was stocking her refrigerator for him. Interesting. I poured a glass of white wine for Lili. She took a plate of crudités that Hannah handed her and we walked out to the living room.

Hannah's husband Eric was on the sofa. He was a nerdy-looking guy with dark hipster-style glasses, though at the moment he was laughing at Rick. My friend was on the floor with Justin, Nathaniel and the two dogs, all climbing on top of him. A strange lump swelled at the bottom of my throat. I'd never be a dad.

"Steve! You've got to help me," Rick called, as Eric laughed. "I'm being attacked!"

I got down to the floor with him, and Rochester jumped up and put his front paws on my shoulders. Rick and I romped on the floor with the kids and the dogs for a few minutes, until Rascal had a sudden urge to lick his genitals. Rochester wanted to investigate what his friend was doing, and they began rolling around and growling at each other, a blur of gold, black, brown and white.

"They're not going to hurt each other, are they?" Nathaniel asked.

"Nah, that's the way they play," Rick said.

"Don't even think about growling and biting each other,"

Dog Have Mercy

Hannah said from the kitchen door. "Who wants to help me put out the little hot dogs?"

Both boys hollered, "Me!" and jumped up.

As they ran to the kitchen, I turned to Rick. "You have a good day off?"

He shook his head. "Right after you left, I got called in. Another death at Crossing Manor. A man named Victor Fictura."

"Mr. Fistula," I said. "The pain in the ass. What happened?"

"Looks like he had a heart attack sometime in the night. The people at the Manor notified his son, who's a pain in the ass, too. He insisted that his father's heart was fine and demanded they call the police."

Rascal was chewing on Rochester's ear, and my big dog had rolled over on his back and was waving his legs in the air. Rick stretched his legs out and leaned back against the sofa. "Mr. Fictura junior said his father told him to call the cops if anything happened to him. He said they were out to get him at that place, that people were dying there right and left."

"Which is true," I said. "Four people that I met with Rochester have died since we started going there."

"It's a nursing home. A place where you go when you're about to die."

"When we were there last, I happened to see a form being prepared for the state that listed suspicious deaths. One name I didn't recognize." I began holding up fingers as I ticked them off. "Mrs. Tuttle, an elderly woman with dementia. Mr. Pappas, who had Crohn's Disease and no close family. Mrs. Divaram, whose son lives in California and had parked here there to get her out of his wife's hair. And now Mr. Fictura."

"How did you happen to see that form?"

"We were walking out and the receptionist's desk was empty. Rochester nosed around her computer and the screen saver popped off. I got a quick look before the administrator came back."

"You're beginning to sound like the eight-year-olds I coach," Rick said. "An excuse for everything. Although most of your excuses involve the death dog."

"Don't keep calling him that," I said. "And it's not just me and Rochester. Mr. Fictura told his son something was going on. And Mrs. Divaram had nothing wrong with her. Her roommate, Mrs.

Vinci, was suspicious. She said something wasn't right."

Rick sighed and pulled a pad out of his back pocket. Immediately Rochester and Rascal mobbed him, and he had to push them away. "Spell those names," he said.

I did. "Talk to Mr. MacRae, too. He and Mr. Watnik are two of the more coherent folks there."

"What did you think of the place?" Rick asked.

"It looks and smells clean, and the staff seem kind and caring. They have lots of events for the patients, and there are always aides around." I paused to think for a minute. "You think maybe one of the staff has it in for patients?"

"Doesn't make business sense, because every time a patient dies they lose the revenue from Medicare or insurance or whatever. And I doubt families are ordering hits on their relatives to avoid the co-pays."

"Are you going to investigate?" I asked.

"I'm going to wait for the autopsy results before I go crazy," he said. "But if I have to, I can run background checks on the staff and get the Department of Health involved."

He reached around to put his pad away, and his bicep flexed. That triggered something but it took me a few seconds to make the connection.

"Was Mr. Fictura on an IV?" I asked.

"Why?"

I explained what Jackie Conrad had told me about how easy it was to get that liquid into a patient's IV. "The potassium stolen from the vet's office could have been injected into Mr. Fictura."

"You think someone at the vet's office knew Mr. Fictura?"

"I don't know," I said. "But I've been looking at each person on the staff, and every one of them has someone in his or her life who could be helped into the afterlife, to put it politely, although I admit that some of the reasons I've come up with are stretching pretty far. The killer could be practicing on people at the nursing home."

Tamsen called everyone to the table, and we stood up. "You have a very active imagination, Steve," Rick said. "Sadly, sometimes what you imagine comes true."

Dog Have Mercy

22 – Faithful

WE HAD A GREAT DINNER, the adults talking and the boys trying to slip food to the dogs. Lili volunteered to help Tamsen and Hannah clean up, and Rick, Eric and I accompanied the boys and the dogs to the den. Very quickly, both boys were on their backs on the carpet, with dogs jumping over them.

When the dogs took a break to lick themselves, Nathaniel said, "See, Dad, I get along with dogs. They like me."

I knew that Nathaniel was desperate to get a dog, but so far his parents were resisting, and I figured this was my cue to jump in. "You like to sleep late, Nathaniel?" I asked.

He nodded. "Yeah. But we have school really early. The bus comes at seven-thirty."

"You know, dogs need a walk in the morning," I said. "You'd have to get up at least a half hour earlier to manage that."

The dogs tired of their game and sprawled together beside the sofa. "And you have to clean up after your dog, too," Rick said. "Sometimes when I go to pick up Rascal's poop it's all runny and smelly."

"Yuck," Justin said. He sat up and elbowed his cousin. "You could be poop boy!"

"You're a poopy head," Nathaniel said.

"A dog is a big commitment," I said to both boys. "Not like a game you can get tired of and put away."

The kids kept playing with the dogs as the three of us guys sat around in the den talking about the Flyers and their chances for the Stanley Cup that year. My dad had gotten tickets through work for at least one hockey game a season when I was growing up, and though neither of us were big sports fans, he and I had gone to the games, cheering for the home team. When the women joined us, we talked about skating on Mirror Lake in the winter, and eventually we all began yawning.

Lili and I left soon after that. We were both tired and I was a little drunk, and in the kitchen when I went to get water for Rochester I knocked a glass off the countertop, and it shattered on the floor.

Rochester immediately wanted to investigate and I had to body-block him. "You take him in the living room and I'll clean up," Lili said. She pulled a pair of blue plastic gloves from the drawer and began picking up the big pieces of glass.

I watched her work, and the sight of those gloves reminded me of the ones the aides had worn at Crossing Manor when they had to clean up after the patients. And that reminded me of my conversation with Rick. Had those deaths at Crossing Manor been a natural progression? Coincidence? Or the work of a killer on the loose?

When Lili finished picking up the glass, she went upstairs and I sat at the dining room table with my laptop, with Rochester curled protectively around my chair. I opened up a browser and typed in "nursing home deaths" to see how Crossing Manor stacked up against similar facilities.

I was stunned at how many hits came up – over twenty-one million. More than thirty percent of nursing homes had some incidents of elder abuse, and thousands of deaths that might be the result of negligence – bedsores, starvation, dehydration and so on. Nearly one-quarter of deaths in the US occurred in nursing homes. I hadn't seen any open wounds, dirty linens or other visible signs of abuse on the people that I'd spoken with at Crossing Manor. The symptoms of emotional abuse were harder to pin down, but again, the patients I'd spoken with had been in good spirits – at least those who could communicate.

There was a big difference, though, between elder abuse and outright murder. I found an awful lot of information, though, on nurses who took matters into their own hands and committed what they called "mercy killings." Four women in Austria were alleged to have killed over two hundred patients; a VA nurse who used epinephrine to induce heart attacks; and a male nurse in New Jersey and Pennsylvania who had killed forty patients with lethal injections of Digoxin, a heart medication.

Some of those killer nurses appeared to need the validation of

Dog Have Mercy

trying to save someone, even if he or she had induced the problem. Others liked the power that drugs like Lidocaine or muscle relaxants gave them. In many cases the victims were elderly, which made their deaths go unnoticed, though I found one pediatric nurse who had killed forty-six children in her care.

The research began to upset me, so I gave up and pushed back my chair. Was someone killing off the patients at Crossing Manor? Poor Mrs. Tuttle had dementia. How could someone have a grudge against her? Could it be someone wanted to put her out of her misery? How could anyone know if she was miserable, if she couldn't communicate?

Then there was Mrs. Divaram. She wasn't happy because she felt that her son's second wife had forced him to push her aside. But according to Mrs. Vinci, her roommate wasn't sick. Had she alienated someone at the home with her complaints?

Mr. Pappas had Crohn's Disease, which had kept him in and out of hospitals his entire life. But according to Edith, he had been feeling better, and planning for discharge.

Mr. Fictura was certainly a complainer, and from the way Allison had called him Mr. Fistula, a pain in the ass. I had the feeling he wasn't loved by the staff. Was there anything in common between the four of them, besides staying at Crossing Manor? One was demented, one abandoned, one congenitally ill, one angry.

Rochester got up from his place on the floor and nosed against my knee. I reached out to pet him. "What do you think, boy? You're a good judge of humans. Could somebody be killing patients at Crossing Manor?"

He rolled over on his back in his dying cockroach posture, waving all four of his legs in the air. That was a signal that he wanted a belly rub, but could he be saying something more? He looked up at me and woofed once. "All right, bossy dog, I'm coming," I said. I settled on the floor and began scratching his soft white tummy.

I already knew that the general population was aging, but even so, the predictions that by 2050 there would be nearly three times as many people eighty-five and older were surprising. What was going to happen to all those elderly people? To me and Lili? Would medical science keep us healthy until death? Or would we be warehoused in facilities, abandoned by loved ones, cared for by minimum-wage attendants?

Rochester must have sensed my mood – or maybe I wasn't scratching well enough. He scrambled up, nodded toward the stairs and woofed once, then galloped up to the landing. "You really think you're in charge around here, don't you?" I asked.

I stood up and followed him to the bedroom, where Lili was sitting up in bed, reading. He sprawled on the carpet, his head on his paws, watching me.

Lili looked up from her book, and I asked, "What do you think will happen to us when we get old? Neither of us have children to look after us."

"That's a grim question." She put aside her book and I sat beside her. "Look at Edith. She doesn't have children either, but she has friends in the community and a long-term care policy. If we plan properly, we'll be all right."

"How can we be sure, though?" I asked. "Look at my father. He thought he'd be okay because he had me to look after him. But when he was sick, I was in prison and I couldn't even make sure he was all right."

She took my hand. "Do you think you could have done anything more to help your father if you'd been here?"

"I don't know. I mean, I could have visited him and, I don't know, poured water for him, made sure he was getting the right medications." I looked down, to where Rochester was sprawled beside me on the floor. "What if my going to prison made him worse? Like he gave up or something?"

"Steve. Did he ever say anything like that?"

I shook my head. "I know he was disappointed in me, because he didn't like Mary and didn't think I should have married her. He wasn't happy when we moved to California, and he said often that he wanted grandchildren. I couldn't even do that for him."

She let go of my hand and pulled me close to her, and I snuggled up, resting my head on her shoulder. "My father had a heart attack when I was living in Rome with Adriano," she said. That was her first husband, an Italian photographer she had met while studying in Italy. "By the time I got a flight to Miami, he was already gone. We had argued about my dropping out of college and marrying Adriano, and we never had a chance to make up."

"That must have been very tough," I said.

"It was. I was a real Daddy's girl. He called me *princesa*, you

Dog Have Mercy

know."

I sat up. "I didn't know that. You don't seem much like the princess type."

"I wasn't spoiled. But I was named for my father's mother and he always said that I looked just like her. We had a special bond."

"What about Federico?" I asked. "Was he more attached to your mother?"

"No, Fedi was a real boy, and he and my father were both mad for soccer and used to go to games together, when my father wasn't working." She crossed her arms over her chest. "My mother wasn't the warmest woman in the world. Her parents had been poor in Poland and they were poor in Havana. That experience formed her. Especially as we moved around from country to country she was obsessed with how we were going to live. She was always complaining to Fedi and me about how much we ate, how we always needed new clothes. Her favorite saying was '*On gelt is keyn velt.*' Without money, there's no world."

"That's sad," I said. "But your father was an engineer, like mine. Didn't he make a good living?"

"When he could work," she said. "In Cuba we had a nice house, and then in Mexico we lived like kings. But when we moved to Kansas City, my father worked as a janitor until his English was good enough to get an engineering job. My mother took in sewing. She had a real talent for clothing design, but she never had the chance to get herself established, because we moved so much."

"What happened to her after your father died?"

"She stayed in Miami. There was a whole Juban community there, Cuban Jews, and she could speak Spanish and get *cafecitos* at a stand a block from her apartment. When Fedi graduated from architecture school he got a job in Miami, and so he was nearby, eventually with his wife and his kids."

She rolled her legs off the side of the bed and stood up. "I admit that I tried not to have much to do with her. As she got older, the anger that she always had inside began to curdle. She had these crazy ideas, that Fedi's wife wanted to kill her, that Fidel was spying on her because her parents had left a fortune behind in Havana."

"Dementia?" I asked.

"Yes. There was nothing we could do, the doctors said. One day the Miami Beach police called Fedi. She was walking down Lincoln

Road in a torn housecoat and flip flops, and she got agitated when an officer tried to talk to her. She didn't remember her name or address, but she always carried Fedi's phone number with her in case she wanted to call him. Which she did, sometimes a couple of times a day."

"I can see why you wanted to stay out of the picture. It must have been a tough situation."

"I was a terrible daughter," she said. "She used to say to me, '*A hunt iz a mol getrei'er fun a kind.*' A dog is more faithful than a child."

She looked down to Rochester. "Is that true, boy?" He stood up and nuzzled his head against her hand. "After that, Fedi had her put into a nursing home with a special locked floor for dementia patients. When I visited I had to use a code for the elevator."

"But you did go visit her," I said.

"Oh, yes. But out of guilt, not out of love. Fedi bore the brunt of things. Soon after she went into the home I broke up with Philip and jumped into photojournalism, and I started traveling around the world. I was in the Sudan when Fedi called me to say she had died. It takes a really long time to get from Khartoum to Miami, you know. I told Fedi to go ahead and bury her, and I'd be there for the shiva."

"How did Fedi feel about that?"

"Fedi has always been the responsible one. I was the one who couldn't stay married, who flew around the world at the drop of a hat."

"Remind me not to marry you, then," I said. "I wouldn't want to lose you."

"I'm not that person anymore," she said. She sat back on the bed beside me. "I'm more comfortable in my own skin now. And what we have feels different from my marriages. More right, somehow."

She looked at me. "How do you feel?"

I turned on my side. "I feel the same way," I said. I leaned over and kissed her, and we moved on from there.

23 – Soft Spot

By Friday morning, River Bend had come back to life after the holiday quiet. Our neighborhood was like an obstacle course that morning between the recycling bins out for collection, garbage trucks, delivery trucks, contractors' vehicles, and of course, other people walking dogs that either barked or snapped or strained at their leashes.

A car that passed had a paw-shaped bumper sticker in purple that read "Rescued is my favorite breed," and I wasn't sure how I felt about that. Rochester had been a rescue dog, so of course I was in favor of such efforts. But the bumper sticker seemed to be a slap at those of us with purebred dogs, even though purebreds could be rescued as easily as mixed-breeds.

Or maybe I was taking things too seriously. The holidays were about to end, I'd be back at work on Monday, and I needed to enjoy the last time I had. That is, after Felix Logato's funeral was over.

Soon after Rochester and I returned from our walk, Lili left for her mani-pedi appointment with Gracious Chigwe. An hour later I told Rochester to behave and drove to Animal House. The door was locked, and I rang the bell.

The doctor answered the ring wearing a long-sleeved black dress, with a winter coat over her arm. It struck me that I was seeing a lot of people without their traditional garb—first Jackie Conrad, now Dr. Horz.

"Thank you for agreeing to take me," she said as she stepped into her coat. She was so short that she might have been mistaken for a child if not for her white hair.

"Not a problem. I'm glad you called me."

She didn't speak again until we were almost at the highway. "My staff isn't very happy with me at the moment," she said. "Between the police activity after the potassium disappearance, and now Felix's death."

"Did they know that he was an ex-con?" I asked, as we got onto I-95.

She shook her head. "He asked me to keep it quiet, and I did. It didn't come out until the theft. And then several people were so upset that I had to let him go. I feel terrible about that."

"You don't think he stole the potassium, do you?"

"No. But the whole thing is baffling. There's no reason to steal something like that. I'm starting to believe the vials were misplaced, or accidentally disposed of."

"You know what those vials looked like," I said. "Could one of them have been attached to an IV?" I fumbled through the explanation Jackie had given me.

"What a horrible thought," Dr. Horz said, when I was finished. "I can't imagine any of my staff doing something like that."

I thought back to the research I'd done on the people who worked at the vet's office. "How long has Sahima been working for you?"

"Just a few months. She's not the sharpest receptionist I've ever had, but she's learning."

"Her grandfather is very sick, isn't he? Do you think she knows enough about medicine to understand what potassium could do?"

"Sahima? But she's just a girl. And she has no medical background at all."

"What about Jamilla?"

"Have you been investigating each of my staff members?" Dr. Horz asked. She turned toward me with an accusing look on her face.

"I have," I said. "I felt strongly that Felix was innocent so I wanted to see if anyone else might have a motive for the theft."

"Jamilla has been with me for four years," Dr. Horz said. She faced forward again and crossed her arms. "She's an excellent tech and a very caring human being. She'd never kill someone."

"Never say never," I said. "Has she ever spoken about her friend Omari Jefferson?"

"That's such a sad story," Dr. Horz said. She looked out the window as the barren roadside sped by. Farms and suburban developments abutted the highway, and the trees were bare, the grass and fields brown. "Omari is her best friend, like a sister to her. She has a very aggressive form of brain cancer, and the outlook isn't good."

"So the very caring Jamilla might want to spare her best friend so much suffering," I said. "A potassium injection could cause a heart attack and a very quick death."

Dr. Horz didn't say anything, but I noticed that she pulled her coat closer around her.

The farms and suburbs gave way to industrial developments and weedy lots as we got closer to Philadelphia. I exited I-95 where a stretch of highway would take me up to US 1. Apartments along the street still had their holiday decorations up, though they looked sad and bedraggled.

"I'm sorry to be such a pain in the ass and keep badgering you," I said to Dr. Horz, "but I think it's important to consider who had access to your medicine cabinet, and who might have had a motive for the theft. Minna was a nurse in Israel, wasn't she? And her husband's a doctor. So she'd know about potassium."

"She would."

"And Hugh? I know he's not quite all there, but could someone have influenced him?"

"I've been thinking about retirement," Dr. Horz said. "Maybe I should do that. Move to Florida, take in some rescue dogs. Stop dealing with people altogether."

"Don't do that," I said. "Rochester would miss you too much."

"What do you think I should do?"

"I don't think there's anything you can do," I said. "But if someone on your staff loses someone to a heart attack…"

"I can't even consider that."

We didn't speak again until we approached the funeral home and I pulled into the parking lot. There weren't many cars there, and I worried that perhaps we'd gotten the time or date wrong.

It was bitter cold, and I pulled my scarf closer around my neck as Dr. Horz and I walked through the parking lot to the front door. Once inside, though, we saw a bulletin board with a listing for *el servicio funeral* for Felix Logato. Dr. Horz and I both signed our names in the book of memory at the front of the chapel, then walked in.

The room was small, with a single stained-glass window at the far end. In front of the window, on an elevated dais, rested a simple black casket, with a podium to the left side.

About a dozen people stood or sat in the wood pews. As a devout reader of mystery novels, I knew that sometimes killers attended the funerals of their victims – especially if the killer was someone close. Could it be that whoever killed Felix was there in the room with us?

Dr. Horz took the lead, walking up to a short, heavyset woman a few years older than I was. Several young people stood beside her.

We waited in line until it was our turn to speak. Dr. Horz introduced herself, and Senora Logato burst into frenzied Spanish.

One of the young women interpreted. "I'm Yesenia, Felix's sister. My mother says thank you for giving Felix a chance." She wore bright red high heels with her short black dress, and had painted her long fingernails to match. I admired her spirit and thought Felix probably had liked those shoes on her.

Yesenia shook hands with Dr. Horz and then turned to me. "My name is Steve Levitan," I said. "I met Felix when I brought my dog into the office, and I was helping him improve his writing skills so he could apply to a vet tech program."

"He spoke about you," Yesenia said. "He was so grateful for your help." She pulled a tissue from the sleeve of her dress and reached up to dab at her eye. "Not that it mattered in the end."

"I believe Felix was a good person. I know he was trying to turn his life around."

Senora Logato spoke again. I managed to catch the named Yunior in there. Yesenia turned to her mother and spoke to her in a low, soothing voice.

"Is he here?" I asked Yesenia. "Yunior Zeno?"

Felix's mother's eyes blazed and she said what I assumed were derogatory things about Felix's friend.

"He's not here," Yesenia said. "My mother believes that Felix's death is Yunior's fault. Felix was trying to be good, but Yunior wouldn't let him."

"I spoke to Felix a few days before he died," I said. "He told me he was going to see Yunior on Christmas Eve."

"I knew it!" Yesenia said. "I knew Yunior had to be connected with Felix's murder. He never would have gone to a place like that on his own." She turned to her mother and translated in rapid-fire Spanish.

There were others in line behind us, so Dr. Horz and I moved on. We sat several rows back and I looked at the crowd—only a few were Felix's age, more young women than men, and I wondered if the young men of his community were dead or in prison.

One of the women looked familiar. She had black hair piled up on her head in an elaborate beehive, like the late Amy Winehouse, with heavy black eye shadow and black lipstick. She wore a very low-cut white blouse which showed off her ample breasts, and black hip-huggers that left a line of flesh visible around her hips. Black stilettos and a gaudy black-and-silver belt completed her outfit.

I tried to place her. She was too tough-looking to have been an Eastern College student. Her makeup and accessories said South Philly much more than Stewart's Crossing. Who was she, and how did I know her?

The funeral service was in Spanish, so I didn't understand much beyond the obvious grief of Felix's family, and I kept glancing over at the young woman. It took a few minutes to make the connection, from the young woman's South Philly look to Jimmy Blackbridge to the woman in the Facebook photo with him.

Discreetly, I pulled out my phone and accessed Facebook, then searched for that picture again. Yes, that was her. Merlys.

I looked back to Jimmy's picture. Was he there at the funeral, too? That would take brass balls, I thought. But no one in the sparsely populated chapel matched his look.

What was Merlys doing there? Had Jimmy sent her to spy? See who showed up to mourn the man he'd killed?

I took a deep breath. Once again, I was letting my imagination run away with me. Felix's family appeared to believe that Yunior was responsible for Felix's death. The police thought a rival drug gang had carried out the murders. I couldn't assume anything. But I could talk to Merlys. Maybe she'd provide a clue I could pass on to Rick.

When the service ended, Dr. Horz and I stood. "I'd like to say something to Felix's mother," she said.

"I'll meet you in the lobby," I said, and I followed Merlys out. She didn't appear to have come with anyone else, and just before the exit door she stopped to put on a black leatherette trenchcoat.

"Can I help you with that?" I asked.

She turned to look at me. I hadn't had a woman size me up that way, so overtly sexual, in years, and I could see I fell short. "Sure," she said, and it sounded like shoo-ah.

"Were you a friend of Felix's?" I asked as she slipped her arms in the sleeves.

"I knew him," she said. "You?"

"He worked at the vet's office where I take my dog," I said. "The vet asked me to drive her here."

"Good Samaritan," she said. She pushed the door open, and I followed her.

I couldn't let her walk away without trying to learn something. "Do you know Jimmy Blackbridge?" I asked.

She stopped just outside the door. Mourners moved around us as she stared at me. "How do you know Jimmy?"

I shrugged. "Felix talked about him."

She fished in the pocket of her trenchcoat and pulled out a pack of unfiltered Camels. She expertly knocked one into her hand. "Like what?"

"He said they had a beef when they were both inside," I said. My breath was coming out in misty clouds. I knew I was on delicate ground but I pushed forward. "Said if he ever saw Jimmy again he'd make sure he was fucked up good."

Merlys laughed harshly. "Shows you what a dipshit he was," she said, as she lit the cigarette. "Felix broke Jimmy's arm so Jimmy had to drop out of that damn dog program, and Jimmy was pissed as shit. For a tough guy, he has a real soft spot for dogs." She took a drag on her cancer stick. "Anybody gets fucked up, it was gonna be Felix. And see what happened."

She leaned forward, and her cigarette breath floated in front of me. "Take it from me, Mr. Good Samaritan. You don't want to get on Jimmy's bad side." She turned sharply on one stiletto heel and stalked away.

Dr. Horz joined me as I watched Merlys leave. "Friend of yours?" she asked.

"Nope. Just sharing memories of Felix."

We chose not to follow the family to the cemetery. Neither of us spoke much on the drive back to Stewart's Crossing. It was two thirty by the time I dropped Dr. Horz at her office. After I backed out of the parking lot, I called Rick to give him a report on the funeral.

As I drove down Main Street past the police station, I told him about finding the photo of Jimmy Blackbridge, then recognizing Merlys among the mourners.

Dog Have Mercy

"Tell me you didn't talk to her," Rick said. "This woman you think might be a killer's girlfriend."

"It's not like I gave her my name or anything," I said. "I wanted to find out if Jimmy Blackbridge was carrying a grudge against Felix the way the guy from Paws Up said. And Merlys said he was."

Rick exhaled deeply. "Why don't you apply to the police academy, Steve? If you're so damned determined to be a detective."

"I couldn't pass the physical. I was thinking of going private. Rochester and Steve, Dog Detectives."

"Don't joke about this, Steve. This is serious."

"She was a South Philly girl with big hair and stiletto heels," I said.

"And she probably had a .32 in her pocket, or a switchblade. Wake up and live in the real world, Levitan."

"You forget," I said. "I spent a year behind bars. I know how to deal with criminals. I am one."

"I keep forgetting that," Rick said. And then he hung up.

24 – Social Justice

"It was nice of you to go to Felix's funeral," Lili said that evening, after I had admired the French manicure on her fingernails. "That impulse is one of the things I love about you. The way you care so much about people, and about social justice."

"I wouldn't say that I'm more interested in social justice than the next guy," I said.

"Yeah, and that's why you spend so much time investigating crimes," she said. "Tell me another."

"To me, caring about other people is wrapped up in being Jewish," I said. "Like Rabbi Hillel said, when he was challenged to define the essence of Judaism while standing on one foot. Love thy neighbor as thyself. My attitudes were formed by all those years in Sunday School, Hebrew school and synagogue. Wasn't it the same for you?"

"We didn't belong to a synagogue in Cuba or in Mexico," Lili said. "So all I learned about being Jewish was from my grandparents. It wasn't until moved to Kansas City and it was time for Fedi to start studying for his bar mitzvah that my parents joined a temple. I remember my mother was mortified that we were a charity case because we were so poor. And there were all these things that we didn't understand, so Fedi and I kept to ourselves."

"Like what?"

"Well, I remember we studied this unit on Jewish last names," she said. "And how many of them were derived from common German words. Weinstock is easy—it means grapevine. The teacher listed a bunch of others, with their English equivalents, and ended with Schwartz, with no definition. So I raised my hand and asked, 'What is a Schwartz?'"

I laughed.

Dog Have Mercy

"That's what the class did, too. My teacher asked me if I knew what a *shvartze* was, and I said no. She explained that it was a term Jewish people used for black people, and I said something like 'not *negrito*?' which was what my parents said. She went into this whole diatribe about using bad names for people – things I'd never heard, words for Italians and Poles and blacks. How Jews were called all kinds of names like kike, and that we shouldn't perpetuate those stereotypes. When we got home that day and told our parents what had happened, they were horrified. My mother said that anything she said in the house shouldn't be repeated, that people would think badly of us."

"It's a Jewish thing," I said. "My parents always taught me that I belonged to a minority that had been persecuted throughout the ages, from ancient Egypt to the Spanish Inquisition to the Holocaust. And everything that happened in the world had this kind of "is this good for the Jews" concept attached to it. Whenever somebody Jewish was arrested, or ran for office, or anything, they'd ask that."

"My parents said the same thing, only in Spanish," Lili said. She stood up. "I'm going to catch up on emails. Call me when you're ready for dinner."

Lili went upstairs and Rochester jumped up on the sofa beside me and settled his head against my lap. As I stroked his smooth golden coat I thought about what Lili had said. I'd always believed that my investigations came from my basic nosiness, the same inquisitive nature that had led me to prison. But what if there were some nobler motives buried inside me? Some concept of social justice that I had learned at the synagogue?

Was that what I'd been doing all along? Or was that a rationalization? My musings were interrupted by the persistent drumbeat of the *Hawaii Five-O* theme.

"Hey, Rick."

"I'm sorry I was rude to you before," he said. "The truth is, you think outside the box, and sometimes I get irritated when you figure things out before I do."

"No worries," I said. "We're both on the same side, right?"

"Truth, justice and the American way," he said. "Listen, I got the autopsy results back on Mr. Fictura. Heart attack, caused by an overdose of potassium."

"Holy crap," I said.

"My feelings exactly. You mind if I come over and brainstorm with you?"

"Not at all. Bring Rascal and come for dinner."

I hung up and hollered upstairs. "Rick's on his way. What do we have to eat?"

Lili appeared at the top of the stairs. "It would be nice if you asked me first before you invite company over. We don't have anything prepared and the house is a mess."

"Rick isn't company. How about if I order a pizza and have him pick it up, and then I do some cleaning?"

"Make sure you vacuum," she said, and I heard her go into the office and close the door.

"How do I get myself into these situations, Rochester?" I asked. The dog stared at me balefully. I called to order the pizza, and then texted Rick to pick it up. Then I vacuumed the downstairs, put away the pile of towels from the dining room table, plumped up the sofa pillows and even dusted the bookshelves. I heard the shower upstairs, and when Rick arrived with the pizza and the garlic rolls, Lili came downstairs looking beautiful.

Rascal and Rochester besieged Rick as he carried the food to the dining room table. "You'll get yours, monsters," he said. "Chill out. Hi, Lili. Thanks for letting me come over."

"*Mi casa es su casa*," she said. "In other words, you're always welcome here."

We sat down to eat. "I know you're bursting to know what's going on at Crossing Manor, Steve," Rick said, between bites.

"Hey, you're the one who wanted to brainstorm," I said. "But yeah, you're right."

"You asked if Fictura had been on IVs before he died. I checked with the nurse on duty New Year's Eve. She said he was throwing up earlier and she put him on IV fluids to keep him from getting dehydrated."

"How about Mrs. Tuttle and Mrs. Divaram?" I asked.

"One step ahead of you, Brother Joe," he said, making another Hardy Boys reference. "I checked with the nurse about them, too. Same pattern. Both of them had been vomiting earlier in the day, and were put on IV fluids."

"So that's how the killer got the potassium into them. Adding it to their IV drips."

Dog Have Mercy

"But why?" Lili asked. "Why those particular patients? Did they have something in common?"

She and I both looked at Rick. "I'm working on that, but I haven't found anything yet. It doesn't look like they knew each other before they ended up at Crossing Manor. Mrs. Tuttle lived in Stewart's Crossing all her life and so did Mr. Pappas, but she was a lot older than he was, and lived in a different neighborhood. Mrs. Divaram was from Philadelphia, and her son picked out the facility for her. Mr. Fictura was from Levittown."

"Mrs. Tuttle was Edith's roommate," I said. "And Mrs. Divaram shared a room with Mrs. Vinci. Were the four of them in any therapy groups together or anything?"

Rick shook his head. "Mrs. Tuttle had dementia so she stayed in bed. Mr. Fictura needed dialysis so his activity was limited. Mr. Pappas was limited by his Crohn's, and Mrs. Divaram was depressed about her son, so she didn't participate in anything."

"Have you looked into the staff?" I asked. "Anybody stick out?"

"I'm working on it, but you'd be surprised at how many people work there, from the administrator and the director of nursing down to the cleaning staff. There has to be an RN on duty all the time, so there are three shifts as well as floaters who come in per diem. Then there are the certified nursing assistants – there are nearly twenty of them, as well as physical, occupational and speech therapists."

"Do you need any help looking at them?" I asked.

"Thanks for the offer but I'll manage," Rick said. "Mr. Fictura's death seems to wipe out Felix Logato as a suspect. Too bad he didn't live to see that."

"I wonder if his being suspected of the theft drove him to go back to his old friends in Philly," I said.

"What do you mean?"

"He might have gotten frustrated that people judged him because of his record."

"Do you feel that way?" Lili asked, and I saw Rick was interested in the answer, too.

I didn't have to think long. "Felix and I came from different circumstances," I said. "People saw him, the way he looked, his tattoos, the way he talked, and they formed an impression of him. Add that to his record, and I'm sure people thought the worst of him—that he was a murderer or something. But I was a lot luckier than Felix. Usually when people find out I have a record they automatically assume it's for white collar crime, and they don't seem to be all that frightened of me."

Lili took my hand and squeezed, and Rick nodded. "Yeah, I can see that. I know a lot of cons get a rough deal when they get out of prison, which just pushes them back to their old friends and old habits."

We talked about the staff members Lili and I had met at Crossing Manor, and the three of us threw out a bunch of ideas, but nothing seemed to work. None of the nurses or CNAs had any disciplinary actions against them. Everyone who worked there had been investigated and bonded, even the receptionist.

After Rick left, I opened my laptop and went back to the reports I had found on nursing home deaths. Was there any commonality to them, perhaps something we might have overlooked?

I found one case that looked interesting. An elderly woman with no life-threatening issues had experienced convulsions, followed by a loss of consciousness and then death. The police had ordered an autopsy, and the ME found a recent puncture wound in her arm. Further investigation revealed that a large bubble of air had lodged in one of the arteries to the brain, cutting off blood flow.

The woman had no close relatives, and no one appeared to benefit from her death. The police investigation was stymied until the wife of a man with Alzheimer's requested an exhumation of her husband's body. He had died of a stroke at the same facility, and the autopsy revealed a similar puncture wound.

The police then began going back over all the recent deaths and found four more patients who had died in the same way, by having an air bubble injected into a vein. The cases had nothing in common except the same nursing home. Just like ours in Stewart's Crossing. Dogged police work had traced the cases back to the first incident, and charged a local man with the murder of his mother-in-law. He then admitted that he'd discovered he enjoyed killing people and had focused on those at the home no one would miss.

I copied the URL for the article and pasted it into an email to Rick, then sat back to consider. Could the same thing be happening at Crossing Manor? How many more people would have to die before the killer was caught?

Could there be a victim zero, and all the other deaths follow

Dog Have Mercy

from that one? The first person I had met who died was Mrs. Tuttle. I realized that I didn't even know her first name, and so searched the local obituaries by last name.

Myrna Tuttle, I discovered, had been eighty-nine when she died. She was survived by two sons, Elliott and Everett, and a daughter, Eileen.

When I was a kid, I knew several families who gave all their kids names that all began with the same letter. I used to daydream about having brothers and sisters—Sam, Sarah, Sally and so on.

I looked back at the obituary. After Eileen's name, Richard Jonas was in parenthesis. Why did that name ring a bell? I kept reading, and saw that one of Myrna Tuttle's grandchildren was named Hugh.

Of course, Hugh Jonas, the veterinary assistant at Animal House. Could Mrs. Tuttle be patient zero? Perhaps Hugh had stolen the potassium to put his grandmother out of her misery, and then discovered he loved the thrill of taking a life?

I sat back in my chair. Hugh didn't seem swift enough to know about potassium, and once his grandmother passed away he would have had no reason to go back to Crossing Manor. But had he? Rick could certainly ask Marilyn Joiner. I sent him another email.

Was there any other link between the dead people and the veterinary hospital? I read through the obituaries of the other patients who I knew had died and couldn't find anything that linked them to any of the staff at Animal House. Had one of them had a pet that they'd taken there?

It didn't make sense, though. The people we'd met at Crossing Manor had all liked spending time with Rochester, but they couldn't have had a pet of their own at the facility.

I kept coming back to Animal House, and the fact that only staff member fingerprints had been found on the cabinet where the potassium was stored. I thought again of Minna, and her nursing background. Why hadn't she renewed her credentials in the US? Was it just that she married a rich doctor? But she was still working, wasn't she?

I went back to searching. I typed in her name with as many different certifications and licenses as I could think of, and I finally hit pay dirt with "certified nursing assistant."

A CNA, I discovered, was the liaison between the patient and the registered nurse or the licensed practical nurse, often in care settings like nursing homes. With her nursing background, Minna could have moved easily into such a position, perhaps while processing her paperwork for additional education or accreditation.

But all I could find was her name, and the fact that she had been licensed by the state of Pennsylvania as a CNA.

Minna was an unusual first name, though. Suppose I eliminated her last name and searched for Minna and CNA? I got a few results, most of them for "Minnie" rather than Minna. But one blog post caught my eye. A woman wrote about her mother's time in a rehab center, and how several of the staff, including an Israeli woman named Minnie, had been very helpful and caring.

I read backwards in the blog, and found that the woman's mother had been a patient at Crossing Manor.

So Minna Breznick had worked there at some point before joining the staff at the Animal House of Stewart's Crossing. That was a very clear connection. She hadn't been working there at the time of Mrs. Tuttle's death, but suppose she still had friends who worked there, or she returned to see certain patients? With her nursing background she had to know about potassium and its effects.

One last email to Rick, and I was finished. Rochester wanted a bedtime walk, and I needed to push this investigation away before it consumed me.

25 – D-10 Forms

SATURDAY MORNING, THE *COURIER-TIMES* ran a story in the local section about Mr. Fictura's "suspicious" death at Crossing Manor. No one from the police or the corporation would comment, so there wasn't much substance to the article.

"I think I might take Rochester back to Crossing Manor this morning," I said to Lili. "Give you some time on your own."

"And give you a chance to snoop around about that poor man's death," she said. "I know you, Steve Levitan." She smiled. "But better to snoop in person than in online places you shouldn't be. Go to town. I'm going to catch up on my reading."

I leaned over and kissed her. Rochester and I left a few minutes later. The sun shone weakly and it had warmed up a bit, and most of the snow had melted. Many people had taken down their holiday decorations and the barren trees looked grim. I thought about which tropical location Lili and I would choose for our winter vacation, and my head was full of rumrunners and tanning lotion by the time Rochester and I arrived at Crossing Manor.

As I signed in, I saw Allison in the lobby playing gin rummy with Mr. Watnik again. He had a heavy black cardigan over his shirt and I worried that he was too cold out there. Allison wore a dark green sweater with a white reindeer on it, and her earrings were little red and green Christmas balls.

"Where did you learn to play like this, Miss Brezza?" Mr. Watnik asked, as Allison laid out three runs to gin out. "You're a little card shark."

Something about the name he called her was familiar to me. Did I know someone else by that name? Someone in my neighborhood, an old classmate?

Then I remembered. Brezza was the name on the torn

permission slip from Pennsbury High that Rochester had found at the veterinarian's office. "You have a Yorkie, don't you, Allison?" I asked. "Do you take him to Animal House?"

"Oh, yeah, I took my puppy there a couple of weeks ago because he was acting funny."

So that piece of paper must have fallen from her pocket at the check-out desk. That put her at the vet's around the time of the theft of the potassium, didn't it? I'd have to ask Dr. Horz if Allison was the teenager she had mentioned.

"How's everything going here?" I asked.

"Mr. Fistula died," she said.

"You shouldn't call him that," Mr. Watnik said, his breathing labored. "Yeah, he was an asshole, but he's dead now."

"The police have been here," Allison said to me in a low voice. "They think maybe he was murdered!"

"Really?"

She nodded. "I think it's kind of dumb. I mean, the people here are almost dead anyway, right?" She looked at Mr. Watnik. "No offense."

"None taken," he said. "I got one foot out the door and the other on a banana peel."

"People here didn't like Mr. Fictura," I prompted.

"He was always making a fuss," Allison said. "Ringing his call button non-stop until someone answered. He complained about the food at every meal."

"Don't forget the son," Mr. Watnik said.

"Yeah, he used to brag about how rich and successful his son was," Allison said. "Some of these people here, they don't have kids, or they don't talk to their kids, and you could see that upset them."

"I got two kids, and neither of them has a pot to piss in," Mr. Watnik said. "I used to hate hearing him talk about his son's Beemer and his trips to Europe. I hope the son is as miserable as the father."

He placed a run of cards on the table. "Gin."

"Mr. Watnik!" Allison said. "I only had two pair."

She picked up the cards and shuffled them, and Rochester and I walked down the hall to the lounge. Halfway there, we met Marilyn Joiner. Today's turtleneck was dark brown against the white of her lab coat and the gold of that glittering necklace.

"How sweet of you to keep coming back," she said. She leaned

Dog Have Mercy

down to chuck Rochester under his chin. "We've been getting some bad publicity, and we've had reporters from several newspapers and TV stations here. I'm afraid that may cause some of our residents to be transferred, and some visitors to stop coming."

"What do you think?" I asked.

"I can't say," she said. "We're under strict orders from corporate not to talk about Mr. Fictura's death at all. I've had to reprimand several of the staff this morning. And that's while trying to keep up with all the paperwork that corporate wants."

She brandished a clipboard and I could see the heading on the top sheet of paper was "Form D-10: Report of Client Death." It was a different form from the one I'd seen on the computer, the one for the state of Pennsylvania, and I wondered which would be more honest. Would Marilyn Joiner be more candid with her employer? Or would she hide things to keep her job?

"I work at Eastern College," I said. "I'm very familiar with paperwork. At least most of ours has gone digital. I still remember the days of putting carbon paper between sheets to make multiple copies."

"Actually, I need to fill these out online," she said. "But I'm a two-fingered typist so it's easier to fill them out by hand and then give them to my assistant to type in."

She continued on, and Rochester and I walked toward the lounge. He stopped in front of Mr. Fictura's room and wanted to go inside. "Sorry, puppy, he's gone," I said, and I scratched his neck. He looked up at me and I thought there was sadness in his eyes.

"But there are lots of other people who want to see you," I said. "Come on, let's go to the lounge and see who's there." We walked inside, and Rochester stopped at the first patient, an elderly woman in a heavy green sweater with a reindeer on it.

Through the big window that looked out to the backyard, I saw brown grass and small clumps of dirty snow, a patio with a few wrought-iron tables and chairs. A couple of stunted pines did an ineffective job of blocking the chain-link fence that separated the home's property from the back of an auto repair shop. I knew that the grass would rejuvenate in the springtime, unlike the patients at the Manor, many of whom had probably seen their last spring.

Mrs. Vinci and Mr. MacRae were sitting by the TV set, though neither of them appeared to be watching the program, one of those pseudo-reality shows about a bunch of strangers plunked down somewhere, trying to win a pot of money by being as obnoxious to each other as they could be.

"Hey, boy," Mr. MacRae said, and Rochester hurried over to his outstretched hand. He had a tattered brown cardigan over a plaid shirt and he looked chilled. His cheeks were sunken and what little hair he had was white.

While Mr. MacRae petted Rochester and talked to him, I turned to Mrs. Vinci. "How are you today?"

"Not a good day," she said. "With Malavath gone, they moved me into a new room with an old lady who sleeps all day." She wore a housecoat spangled with large orange flowers and terrycloth slippers.

Mrs. Vinci had to be at least eighty, and I wondered how old an "old lady" would be to her. I figured it was more a matter of attitude than age. "Well, that's almost like having a private room," I said.

She waved an arthritic finger at me and I moved in closer. "I talked to my son yesterday," she said in a low voice. "I told him he gotta get me out of here or I'm gonna end up like Malavath."

"Are you that worried?" I asked. "This seems like such a good facility."

"Everything gives me the creeps now," she said. "I can't hardly sleep at night. I keep looking around wondering who's gonna go next."

Rochester moved over to Mrs. Vinci, and he licked her hand. "You're a sweet boy," she said to him.

I moved over to Mr. MacRae. "How are you feeling?" I asked.

"That chariot's swinging close," he said. "Jesus is coming for me soon, I can feel it. My kidneys done cut out and now my heart's going."

I didn't know what to say.

"But don't worry 'bout me," he said. "I'll see my Essie Mae again in heaven and we gone sit at Jesus's feet." He smiled his gap-toothed grin.

"I wish you all the best," I said.

Rochester and I continued our circuit. There were fewer patients than ever before; I hoped that some of the ones who were gone had recovered enough to return home. I felt sorry for the ones who were left, who seemed more disheartened than in the past.

We talked Mr. Bodnar, the man who'd been a paraplegic for

Dog Have Mercy

years. "I want to go somewhere else," he said. "But it's hard to move from one facility to another when you're on Medicaid. And I don't have anybody outside to make the phone calls for me."

"But you said they've taken good care of you here," I said. "Why would you want to leave?"

"Because I want to live. "I haven't come this far to give up."

My heart was heavy by the time we left. Even Rochester, who was normally such a happy dog, seemed saddened by the people we spoke to. On top of that, the holidays had been grimmer than I expected, with the deaths of people we knew and the stress of Brody's visit. "How would you like a new toy, puppy?" I asked him. "A little retail therapy might make both of us feel better."

I drove out to the big pet superstore on US 1 and Rochester and I shopped the aisles for treats and toys. The Christmas-themed ones were half price, and I bought him a squeaky Santa, a blue rubber bone with stars of David on it, and a candy cane made of alternating layers of red and white rope. I threw in a couple of bags of his favorite organic treats, too.

By the time we got home, Lili was ready for a nap, and I joined her in bed, with Rochester sprawled on the floor beside me. I had trouble falling asleep, though. I kept thinking of the patients at Crossing Manor, and how trustingly they had lived there before this spate of incidents, hoping that human kindness, Medicare and the fees paid by their families would keep them safe.

I remembered Marilyn Joiner's comment about paperwork she had to fill out for "corporate." I wondered if there might be a database somewhere that I could check to see how many deaths there had been at Crossing Manor, and how many of them had been a result of heart attack. I finally gave up on the idea of a nap and went downstairs to my laptop. Rochester followed on my heels, then promptly fell asleep at my feet.

While I waited for the computer to warm up, I thought of my father. Soon after I began my sentence in California, he had a stroke. It was a mild one, and he recovered fairly quickly, but in hindsight it was the beginning of his decline. Once again I felt that that old guilt about not being able to be there for him.

I had seen, from the patients I'd spoken with, that many of them were in the same situation as my dad had been back then. Either no family at all, or family unwilling or unable to spend much time looking after them. When I was a kid, I had several friends whose families had taken in elderly relatives. My own grandfather had stayed with us for a month or two at a time, often when recovering from some illness.

In the twenty-first century, though, that kind of family caretaking was rare among those I knew. Many people my age were struggling to balance their own lives and careers with raising kids and looking after aged parents. The sandwich generation, we were called. One of the women at Crossing Manor had told me she'd outlived her husband, her siblings, and her two children, and all she had left were grandchildren—who had their own kids to raise. Enter the corporations to do what we couldn't do for our families anymore.

Maybe I was more interested in social justice than I had believed.

I found the website for Associated Manors, the owner of Crossing Manor. They owned nursing home/rehab facilities in twelve states, almost all of them with the word "Manor" in their name. Their website was full of corporate blather and faux caring, with lots of information on how to choose a nursing home, how to pay for care, and so on.

There was something so smarmy about it that I hated everything, even the colors they'd used. I knew that people considering the care of a loved one needed information, and would want the reassurance that the person would be in good hands. But I couldn't get over the feeling that someone with a psychology background had designed the site to maximize that reassurance, and that put my teeth on edge.

I had done some basic web development work in California, and then, when I returned to Stewart's Crossing, I had tried to set up a freelance business doing web design and technical writing – mostly to avoid having to fill out job applications where I had to list my felony conviction.

So I understood the basics of interface design, of the way you could lead a visitor through your site, directing his or her attention, using colors and fonts to reinforce the impression you wanted to create. Associated Manors had taken that to the Nth degree.

There were no statistics on safety at the website, just a lot of bragging. I knew that those forms Marilyn Joiner had filled out had to be stored somewhere, and the only way to see them, and discern any patterns at Crossing Manor, would be to hack into the site.

When I had hacked in the past, I practiced something called

moral disengagement—using neutralizing definitions to justify behavior that I knew was wrong. I came up with excuses like protecting Mary's and my credit rating in order to avoid feeling bad about what I'd done.

I felt the same way that afternoon. It was righteous for me to hack into the Associated Manors database. And if I was careful enough, no one had to know what I'd done. That meant that I couldn't do any serious hacking from my own home, anything that could be connected with my personal IP address.

The library was one of the best places to launch a hack because of all the computers and the mostly clueless users there, but it was already closed for the weekend. Many of the other places in town where I could get free Wi-Fi were closed by then, too. And Lili would be awake soon, and wonder where I was.

Rochester nuzzled my lap. I petted his head but kept thinking. Finally he jumped up and placed his front paws on my knees and tried to lick my face.

That's when I realized what I was doing. I couldn't break the promises I had made to Rick and Lili. The smart thing to do was to tell Rick what I had learned, so that he could prepare a subpoena for the death records at Crossing Manor. It was a longer, less-rewarding process—but it was the way I had to act if I wanted to be the person my friends expected me to be.

My head was jumbled with so many conflicting emotions. I felt guilty that I had not done more to help Felix Logato stay on the straight and narrow. I worried about the nice elderly people I had met at Crossing Manor. If someone was targeting them, didn't I have a moral imperative to help?

But society had determined that my actions in hacking into databases were illegal, and I had already been punished once for acting with impunity. How could I balance those two positions? Was I some kind of Lone Ranger of hacking, the only one who could figure out what was going on at Crossing Manor? Certainly not.

But there had to be something I could do that was legal. What was it? I was staring into space when Rochester left my side and padded to the kitchen. He returned a moment later with a piece of paper in his mouth.

He dropped it on the floor and I picked it up. It was a form Lili had to use to authorize a new adjunct professor to teach a particular course, and I realized she had found someone new to teach the pottery course in place of the previous instructor, who had disappeared without inputting grades.

"What are you trying to tell me, boy?" I asked. "Does this adjunct have something to do with the case? Something about grading? Pottery?"

He shook his big golden head and settled on the floor beside me. I read through the form, trying to make a connection to people at Crossing Manor, and got nowhere. Did potters use potassium? I Googled it. I discovered that potassium chromate was occasionally used as an acid-green colorant in raku pottery. But potassium chromate was very different from potassium citrate or potassium aspartate, and I doubted some rogue potter was killing people at Crossing Manor.

"I don't get it, boy," I said. "What is it about this form?"

He looked up at me with his big brown eyes, and I noticed again, as I often did, how his pupils covered most of the eye, with little white around them. "Of course!" I said. "It's a form. A form like the ones from Crossing Manor. Maybe if I search for the form I can find some online."

Rochester rolled over on his side and went back to sleep, and I searched online for copies of the D-10 form Marilyn Joiner had been filling out. I found one on a woman's website, which detailed the death of her late mother at Valley Manor, one of the corporation's facilities in Nevada. She had been able to get hold of her mother's complete medical records and uploaded them.

It was more than a single form; there were pages of information required, including the complete medical history of the patient, copies of recent charts, and interviews with staff personnel.

The woman had circled several places on the PDF, with notes like "lies" and "who are they kidding?" scrawled in places.

I didn't know the specifics of her mother's case, but it was clear that there were some real discrepancies on the form. I saved it as an example for Rick, and then wrote up an email for him. I suggested that he subpoena the D-10s from the past year at Crossing Manor to look for patterns. "I could probably get this stuff for you, but you know, that would be wrong," I wrote. Then I hit send and shut the computer down, before I could make myself into a liar.

26 – Open House

WHEN I WOKE THE NEXT MORNING I was alone – no Lili beside me, no dog on the floor. I looked at the clock and realized I'd slept past Rochester's normal walking time. When I went downstairs Lili was on the sofa with the Sunday paper, Rochester snoozing by her side.

"He's already been fed and walked," Lili said.

"You're an angel." I leaned down to kiss her.

"Muffins on top of the fridge for breakfast." She handed me the front section of the paper and went back to reading.

As I ate my muffin, I read about unrest in Russia's outlying regions, terrorist threats in the mountains of Afghanistan, monsoons in Bangladesh and a viral epidemic in West Africa. At least Stewart's Crossing was a safe corner of the world.

When I checked my email, I found a message from Rick. He'd already put together the subpoena I suggested, for the death records from Crossing Manor, but was waiting until Monday to put it before a judge. He said that he'd add the D-10 forms to the request and thanked me for the information.

Around noon, I took Rochester out for a walk. It was cold but the sun was out, and I began to sweat beneath my heavy coat. Annie Abogato, a Realtor friend of Gail's who I often saw at the Chocolate Ear café, was running an open house down the street. She was a thirty-something mom who occasionally dog-sat Rochester for me, a cheerful blonde with shoulder-length hair and a taste for pink clothing. Her scarf and gloves were both pink, as were her rubber snow boots.

She was showing a young couple the yard as we walked by, and she waved to me. "Steve, do you have a minute?"

I walked up to them.

"These are the Canninos," she said. They were both in their late twenties; he was a hefty guy with a wrestler's build, and she was a very pretty woman who could have been a model for plus-sized clothes. "This is my friend Steve. He can tell you what a great community this is for dogs."

"What kind of dog do you have?" I asked.

"A Great Pyrenees," Mrs. Cannino said. "It's hard to find a community that doesn't have rules against a hundred-pound dog."

"River Bend is the neighborhood for you. Lots of big dogs, and a couple of empty lots where dogs can run. Everybody's friendly and the security staff does a great job."

Rochester put his paws up on Mr. Cannino's thighs and though I tried to tug my dog down, the guy didn't mind. We talked for a couple of minutes and then Rochester and I continued on our walk, darting around several cars parked on the street.

One disadvantage to the neighborhood that I hadn't mentioned was that River Bend was shoehorned into an area around a nature preserve, so the developer had to maximize the utility of the land—which meant narrow streets. If several homes had guests parked in front, Sarajevo Court could become a real obstacle course.

I pulled off my scarf and put it in the pocket of my parka, and pulled the zipper down an inch to cool my throat. The sun was sharp, the sky a cloudless blue.

Rochester and I had circled the block and were on our way back home when an old black Chrysler with a smashed-in fender cruised past us, then stopped right in front of our driveway. A bad place to park; not only was he blocking me from getting out if I needed to, but there was a big SUV parked just ahead on the other side of the street.

The driver's door popped open and a wiry guy in a black leather jacket got out. As we approached, he pulled a cigarette out of his pocket and lit it.

Rochester began to bark. I had become such a softened suburban homeowner that my first reaction was that I hoped whoever the guy was, he wasn't going to put out that cigarette in my driveway. It wasn't until we got close to him that I realized it was Jimmy Blackbridge.

Rochester sensed my adrenaline rise, and tugged forward on his leash, still barking. I told him to sit and then said, "What do you

Dog Have Mercy

want, Jimmy?"

"You know who I am."

Rochester rested on his haunches beside me, on full alert. "Of course I do." I heard a tapping noise and looked up. Lili was in the bedroom window with a cell phone in her hand. She was watching the tableau in front of the house.

"Then you know you gotta butt out of my business," Jimmy said. He kept his right hand in his jacket pocket, using his left to take his cigarette out of his mouth.

One of the many things I learned in prison was that you can't show weakness to anyone. As soon as you do, you're as good as dead.

"What I *know* is that you have to pull your piece of shit car away from my driveway and get the fuck out of my neighborhood."

He looked surprised. Behind him, I saw Merlys in the front seat of the car. "Who the fuck do you think you are, telling me what the fuck I should do?"

Good. I had him on the defensive. "You ever hear of the Stand Your Ground laws?" I asked. "You're on my property, and you're threatening me. I could kill you right here and no court in the country would convict me."

Halfway down the block behind Jimmy, I saw Annie Abogato and the Canninos were watching us, too.

"You don't even have a gun," Jimmy scoffed.

"Don't need one." Though my nerves were on edge, I forced myself to smile. "I'm not some pussy who needs a gun to do my business. I did my time in California and I learned a few things inside."

Merlys leaned out the driver's window. Her hair was still in that ridiculously tall beehive and she had to twist her head to get it outside. "Get in the car, Jimmy," she called.

"Shut the fuck up, bitch," he said to her. Then he turned back to me. "So, you got balls. Mine are bigger than yours, guaranteed. And I ain't here to mess you up. Just to tell you to stay out of my business. Forget you ever knew that loser Logato."

"Why? Because you killed him?"

Jimmy glared at me. "You stupid or something? What the fuck did I just tell you? This got nothing to do with you."

Behind Jimmy, I saw Annie talking on her cell phone. Mr. Cannino said something to his wife and moved quickly toward us.

Jimmy began to remove his hand from his pocket. My adrenaline spiked because the bulge against his jacket pocket had the shape of a gun. What kind of a dumb ass was I, anyway, taunting an ex-con who might have killed someone?

I pulled on Rochester's leash and tried to step back, but he strained forward and slipped his collar. He was the picture of grace as he launched himself at Jimmy, snarling in a way I'd rarely heard from him.

"Rochester! No!"

He ignored me and tackled Jimmy just as Jimmy pulled the gun from his pocket. But Jimmy stumbled backward from the pressure of eighty pounds of golden retriever, and the gun flew out of his hand, skittering across the asphalt pavement.

Jimmy landed on his back in the street, with Rochester on top of him. I lunged forward and grabbed the gun, a 9-millimeter similar to the one my father had left me. Rick and I had spent some time at the local shooting range, and I was comfortable around firearms. Jimmy's gun fit nicely in my hand.

I planted my feet and used a two-handed grip to aim the gun at Jimmy. But with Rochester on top of him there was no way I was going to shoot.

Merlys jumped out of the car and hurried to Jimmy. She wore the same fake leather trenchcoat I'd seen at the funeral, and a pair of stiletto boots in with tiger-striped fur around the tops.

Jimmy was struggling to push Rochester off, but it was a futile effort. Once my dog had a goal in mind nothing could push him away.

"What's going on?"

I looked up to see Mr. Cannino approaching. "Little disturbance," I said. "You'd be best to stay back."

While my attention was distracted, Merlys pulled a switchblade out of her trenchcoat pocket and popped the blade. "Put the gun down or I stab this into your damn dog's neck," she said.

"Are you stupid?" I asked her. "I could shoot you dead long before you could do anything with that knife."

My hands trembled but I focused on holding the gun steady. In the distance I heard the high keening of a police siren. Merlys was beside Jimmy with one hand on Rochester's collar and the other holding the knife. He barked and growled at her, but he was also

Dog Have Mercy

trying to keep Jimmy immobilized, and Merlys was stronger than she looked.

"Hurt my dog and I swear to God I will kill you," I said through gritted teeth.

"You're crazy!" Merlys said. "Jimmy just wanted to talk to you. I told him you were asking about Felix at the funeral, and he had me go back inside and get your name. We looked up your address, just to talk to you."

"How'd you know which name was mine? I never introduced myself to you."

"You came with that vet. And your name was the only one that wasn't Spanish besides hers."

I heard an engine behind me and the screech of brakes, but I didn't want to take my eyes off Merlys. "You put the knife down, and I'll put the gun down," I said.

She was considering that when I heard Rick's voice behind me. "Police! Everybody stand down!"

I didn't turn around because I didn't trust either Merlys or Jimmy. "If you get the knife from Merlys, Rick, then I'll put the gun down and kick it over to you," I called over my shoulder.

Out of the corner of my eye, I saw Rick approach slowly, his gun in his right hand, his badge in his left.

"You hear him, Merlys?" I asked. "You throw the knife down, I give up the gun. Everybody walks away safely."

Rochester barked to underscore my point.

"You all are crazy," she said again. She tossed the knife aside and raised her hands above her head. I could see this wasn't her first time at the rodeo.

I lay Jimmy's gun on the ground and kicked it over to Rick. He pocketed his badge, picked up the gun and popped the cartridge. He put the gun in one pocket, the cartridge in the other. Then he walked over to where Rochester sat on top of Jimmy.

"Rochester. Let him up, boy," Rick said.

Rochester hopped off Jimmy and loped back over to me. "Good boy," I said, and I scratched him behind the ears. "But you can't go doing stuff like that. You could get hurt."

"You're one to talk," Rick said.

"You gotta arrest him," Jimmy said, as he stood up. "I was just here talking and his dog attacked me."

"We'll sort it all out down at the station," Rick said. As a police car came screaming down the street, Mr. Cannino returned to his wife and Annie. So much for showing what a great place River Bend was. I doubted she'd make that sale.

"How did you know to come here?" I asked Rick, as he pulled a pair of plastic cuffs from his belt.

He nodded toward the house. "Lili was watching and she called me because she knows the kind of trouble you get into. Fortunately, I wasn't far away."

Lili came out and took hold of Rochester's leash. Jimmy and Merlys kept arguing and complaining as they were frisked and cuffed. They both insisted that they hadn't planned to hurt anybody, just to talk, and it was my actions, and my dog's, that had escalated the situation.

"How come you ain't cuffing him?" Jimmy asked. "He's the one who was holding a gun on me."

"Because he's the homeowner and you're on his property," Rick said. He called for a tow truck to take away Jimmy's car, then had the uniforms take Jimmy away. "Steve, you have to follow me down to the station. Without the dog. I'll need a full statement from you."

Rick took Merlys with him in his truck and I followed. When I got to the station I had to wait over an hour while Rick took statements from Jimmy and Merlys. When it was my turn he led me into the interview room.

"You really are a dumb ass," he said, as I sat down. "You know what kind of a record that guy has?"

"I figured he was a low-life like Felix used to be."

"He has a sheet as long as your arm. And two outstanding warrants for assault. I called down to Philly to have somebody come pick him up."

"Did he say anything about Felix?"

Rick held up his hand. "First things first. I need you to start from the beginning and tell me the whole story." He pulled a hand-held digital recorder from his pocket and put it on the table between us. He pressed a button, stated his name, the date and time, and the reason for the recording.

I began with the spoofed email message and then discovering Jimmy's identity from the guy at Paws Up. As a green light on the recorder blinked, I described finding Jimmy's picture online, with

Merlys beside him. How I had recognized Merlys at the funeral and approached her.

"Did you make any comments of a threatening nature to Miss D'Agostino at that time?" Rick asked.

It took a second to realize that was Merlys's last name, and then another moment to reconstruct our conversation outside the funeral home. "Nope. If anything, she's the one who said that Jimmy had threatened to fuck Felix up."

"That's not the way she describes your encounter," he said. "Did you tell her that you believed Jimmy Blackbridge had killed Felix?"

I shook my head.

"You have to speak for the record," Rick said.

"No. All I said was that I knew Felix and Jimmy had a beef."

"She says you did, that she and Jimmy came out to your house today to tell you that Jimmy had nothing to do with Felix's death."

"She's lying, then."

He asked me a couple more questions and then shut off the recorder. "I spoke to Detective Holland in Philly. He said they have a witness who saw a Caucasian male fleeing the shootout where Felix died. He had her look at Yunior Zeno but she swears it wasn't him. From her description, it might be Jimmy. Holland's going to put him in a lineup."

"So Felix's family was wrong," I said. "It wasn't Yunior who killed Felix."

"Yunior Zeno is a bad guy, Steve. Even if he didn't kill Felix, he's the one who got him to that house. There's a lot of fault to go around. And some of it falls on you."

"On me?"

"You put yourself and Rochester in danger, not to mention your neighbors and anybody visiting. Can you imagine what kind of chaos we'd have had if Jimmy had started shooting? Or Merlys had taken that knife to your dog?"

I looked down at the scarred, stained table. "I thought I was getting better," I said. "I resisted my impulses to hack. I've really been trying." I looked up at him. "What's wrong with me, Rick? Why do I keep getting into trouble?"

He shook his head. "I'm a cop, not a therapist," he said. "But maybe you want to talk to one."

27 – Boys' Night

By the time I left the station night had fallen. The street lights on Main Street were off, and most of the holiday decorations were down, removing the comforting glow of colored lights. I kept thinking about what Rick had said. Did my emotional problems stretch farther than just computer hacking? Why did I keep putting myself and those I loved in danger?

I reached beside me to pet Rochester and realized he was back at home. I wanted to rest my head against his golden fur, listen to his heartbeat. Just be with him, and Lili.

It was hard to stay focused on the drive. My hands shook, my mouth was dry, and I had the beginning of a headache. When I finally pulled into my driveway, I shut the car off and rested my head on the steering wheel.

Rochester began barking and I forced myself get out of the car. The cold air hit me with the strength of a hammer blow, and I had to steady myself against the door frame. Lili opened the front door and Rochester rushed to the gate, up on his hind legs. Before I opened it I leaned forward and kissed his nose, and he licked my face.

"What happened?" Lili asked as I opened the gate.

I reached down to pet Rochester. "That was Jimmy Blackbridge and his girlfriend Merlys," I said. "He might be the one who killed Felix."

She took my arm and led me into the house. "Sit down and I'll make you a cup of tea," she said. She helped me take my coat and scarf off. I stroked Rochester's back as I heard the clatter of cup and saucer, the faucet and the ding of the microwave. Lili returned with a mug of tea and a small plate of chocolate-chip cookies.

"Eat," she said. My hand shook as I picked up a cookie, but the sugar rush helped. I sipped the coconut-flavored tea as Lili and I sat catty-cornered to each other on the sofa. Between sips, I told her the story I'd told Rick, and what he'd said.

"Do you think I'm crazy?" I asked. "That I have some kind of death wish?"

She shook her head. "I think you have a problem with impulse control. And like I said the other day, you care a lot about people, and social justice, and that combines to get you into trouble."

"I have been trying," I said. "I've been resisting my impulses to snoop around online where I shouldn't be. I check in with my hacker group. But then I go do something stupid."

She scooted next to me. "I love you, Steve. I don't want to lose you to some gun-wielding criminal. But you're definitely a work in progress. As long as you keep trying, I believe you'll make better choices."

Rochester nuzzled against my leg. "Rochester thinks so, too," Lili said. "Sometimes I think that dog is your guardian angel."

"I'm lucky," I said. "I have a bunch of guardian angels. You. Rochester. Rick. A lot of people watching out for me."

* * *

Monday morning, Friar Lake was back to life. The parking lot was full of cars and trucks, and the sounds of sawing and banging accompanied me and Rochester as we walked to the office.

My email box was full of generic college messages about the start of the semester the next day, upcoming events and deadlines. But there were also updates from suppliers, advertising confirmations, and a host of other things that needed attention.

Joey came in from the site around eleven. "I don't know what you did with Brody while you had him, but he's been angel this past week," he said. "Rochester must have taught him a couple of lessons."

"That's good to hear," I said, though I hoped Brody wouldn't start competing with Rochester when it came to crime-solving.

Joey settled in the chair across from me. "You have a good holiday?" he asked. Rochester walked over to sniff his hand, and Joey stroked his back as we talked.

"Went by too quickly, as usual," I said. I wasn't ready to tell anyone all the events that had happened, and I wasn't sure I ever would be.

We talked about his cruise, and the way he and Mark were settling into a domestic routine. "We're both trying to take things slow," he said. "Been burned before and all that."

I knew that Joey had been married to a woman when he was younger, and that Mark had had several relationships that had ended in disaster. "You want to find the person who will stand by you no matter what happens," I said. "I got lucky with Lili. I hope you and Mark will turn out to be as lucky as we've been."

"The most important thing is that he and Brody get along," Joey said. "You can tell a lot about someone by the way he treats dogs."

"Yeah, I saw that with Lili, too," I said. "Once she and Rochester bonded, I knew she was a keeper."

We shifted to a conversation about the site work and how things were starting up again, and then Joey left and I went back to work. I knew from experience that the campus would be humming all day with last-minute student registrations and course changes, and I wasn't surprised when Lili called to say she'd be working late.

"I'm going to grab a quick dinner at the Cafette later with Gracious," she said. "Will you and Rochester be all right on your own?"

I was tempted to remind her that I'd managed just fine in the past, but my better nature stepped in and told her to eat healthy and not work too hard. Late in the day, after most of the contractors had left, I took Rochester out for a walk around the site and saw an exterminator's truck parked near the building that had once housed the abbey's kitchen.

Joey was in conversation with a bald guy in a sheepskin coat over a khaki uniform, with a metal tank hung from one shoulder. "What's up?" I asked Joey.

"We found a big nest of ants," he said. "Must have grown up while we were closed. I called the exterminator and Tillis here came out to help us."

"All natural materials," Tillis said. "After some species of bees and ants die, their bodies emit a chemical called potassium oleate. Other insects respond to the smell by removing the dead body. If you spray it on living ants, then other insects start pushing them out as if they were dead, and eventually they're all gone."

"Potassium?" I asked.

"Not the kind that humans take," Tillis said. "And it's perfectly safe for dogs, too."

"Good to know," I said. As Rochester and I walked back to the office, I came back to the question of the stolen potassium. I still hadn't figured out how the theft from the vet's office connected to the deaths at Crossing Manor. Was it just a coincidence? Or was there something I was missing?

Rick called as I was driving home. "Yo," I said. "What's happening in your world?"

"Hell of a day," he said.

"Rochester and I are on our own for dinner," I said. "Why don't you bring Rascal over? I'll pick up salads for us at the grocery on my way home."

"Sounds good," he said. "I'm too beat to deal with anything more than that."

I left Rochester in the car while I ran into the market, and when I returned home to a darkened house, my dog by my side, I remembered that was how it had been before Lili. Once again, I was grateful she had agreed to share her life with mine.

I flipped on the lights, turned up the heat, and made a big bowl of salad, tossing in plum tomatoes, croutons, sliced mushrooms, and chunks of cooked chicken. By the time Rick arrived the house was warm and welcoming. I handed him a Highland Cold Mountain Winter Ale, a beer I'd read about online, and took one for myself,

Over dinner, we talked about Tamsen and Lili, about the dogs and the holidays and pretty much anything but death and mayhem. It wasn't until after we'd fed the dogs and we were out walking them that Rick brought up the topic.

"I went back to the vet's office again today," he said, as both dogs pulled ahead of us. "What's wrong with Hugh Jonas, you think?"

"When we were kids they called it slow," I said. "If you want to know what a doctor would say today, you'd have to ask one. My guess is that he's somewhere on the autism spectrum. Likes his routines, doesn't talk much."

"I tried to ask him a few questions about his grandmother, the first of those patients to die at Crossing Manor, but he wouldn't look at me, and he didn't seem affected by her death."

"That's autistic behavior," I said. "When Mary and I first moved to California, I tutored part-time at a college writing center. One of the students I was assigned to work with was a high-functioning autistic. He was the same way, and I did some research to see if I could reach him."

Rochester stopped to squat and I dug in my pocket for a bag. "And did you?" Rick asked.

"Not really. He was smart enough, one on one, but he had trouble concentrating on anything, so he never did his homework."

"You think Hugh could have been manipulated into stealing the potassium?" Rick asked as I bent down to scoop the poop.

"I doubt it, but you'd have to get a psych evaluation if you want a real opinion."

We continued to walk, and then Rascal assumed the position. "Your turn," I said, handing Rick a bag. "Who else did you talk to today?"

"Call me Hugh Jonas, but I don't multi-task well," he said. "Hold that thought."

He picked up the poop, told Rascal he was a good boy, and then all four of us turned around to head back to the townhouse.

"Back to the question," I said. "You talk to Minna?"

"Before I did I went back over my notes and I realized that when I spoke to her before I had no idea that the nursing home was connected, so there was no reason for her to volunteer the information that she had worked there."

We dumped our bags in a receptacle at the end of Sarajevo Court. "But I asked her about it this morning. She told me she didn't leave there on good terms and hasn't been back since."

"What does that mean? She got fired?"

"I asked. She finally said that she got into a fight with Mrs. Joiner, the administrator. She wanted to go to a medical conference in Vegas with her husband, and Joiner wouldn't give her the time off. So she quit in a huff."

"Which means she might have a grudge against Joiner, or the facility. Killing patients there would put Joiner in a bad light with her bosses."

"You read too many books, you know that?" Rick asked, as we walked up my driveway. "In the real world, people don't kill other people for such convoluted reasons."

"Thank you for that wisdom, Sherlock," I said.

Dog Have Mercy

"Don't get snarky," Rick said. "I checked the visitor logs at the Manor for the times when the three people were killed. Minna Breznick didn't sign in. And since she left on such bad terms I doubt she could have snuck in and out frequently enough to kill four people without someone noticing."

"What about the other staff?" I asked.

"None of them had any connections to the nursing home. No family members there, no friends or family on the staff."

I opened the front door and we let the dogs off their leashes. They rushed toward the water bowl and began lapping noisily. Rick shrugged off his coat and laid it on the sofa. I hung mine up in the downstairs closet.

As I closed the closet door, Rochester came up to nuzzle my leg. In his mouth he had one of the blue plastic gloves Lili had used on Saturday night to pick up the glass shards. "You shouldn't have that, puppy," I said, snatching it from him. "There could be glass on this."

I looked at the glove and something clicked. "Could someone have used gloves to get into the cabinet where the potassium was stored?" I asked Rick.

"Sure," Rick said. "Doctor's offices always have those latex gloves. I think there was even a box of them right on the counter near the cabinet."

"So it didn't have to be an Animal House employee who took the vials," I said. "It could have been a patient."

"Well, not a patient in the veterinary sense," Rick said. "Maybe a human there with a patient? But hold on, that cabinet was in the back room. The only people who go back there are the staff."

I closed my eyes and tried to visualize the layout of Dr. Horz's office. From the lobby, you entered a short hallway with the big animal scale along one wall. To the right there were two examining rooms, and a closed door that I knew led to the kennel in the back. To the left was another examining room, and then the door to the staff room, where the medications were kept.

Just beyond that was the door to the restroom.

"What if somebody asked to use the bathroom?" I asked Rick. I explained what I remembered about the layout of the office. "The door to the staff room was usually open, right? Somebody going to the bathroom would go right past there, and could look inside. I remember Dr. Horz telling me a while ago that patients could use that restroom."

"Thank you very much for widening my suspect pool," Rick said dryly. "Next thing you'll be suggesting I check the toilet for DNA evidence."

"I hope they clean that pretty regularly," I said. "Were you able to see if any of the people who died had pets, and took them to Animal House for care?"

"No matches for the people themselves. I suppose I have to go back and check their records for members of the victims' extended families."

"And remember, you might not even need to be there with a patient," I said. "For example, Hugh Jonas's mother could have come to pick him up from work, seen the vials and figured out how to end her mother's suffering."

"That still doesn't explain the other deaths," Rick said. "I think we have to look at someone who has a motive against Joiner, like Minna Breznick, or against the facility. Or maybe an angel of mercy, somebody committing euthanasia."

"Or is just batshit crazy," I said.

"Well, there's always that."

28 – Palliative Care

"I SHOULD BE GETTING HOME," Rick said. "Long day ahead of me tomorrow." He looked around. "Where's my dog?"

I heard the sound of water lapping again. "Rochester! Rascal! Don't drink so much or you'll have to pee again."

"Maybe they're both dehydrated," Rick said. "Cold weather does that sometimes. Not enough moisture in the air."

"Let's hope neither of them needs IV fluids," I said.

Rick and I looked at each other and the same thought went through our minds. "IVs," Rick said. "That's how the killer got the potassium into the patients, right?"

I nodded. "The patients all were dehydrated before they were killed, so that they had to have IVs. The killer could be a nurse at the Manor who is able to put in an IV."

"The killer doesn't have to be the one who put in the IV," Rick said. "Let's go back to Fictura. His records showed that he suffered from vomiting and diarrhea the day before he died, and the nurse put in an IV."

"The killer could have given him something to make him throw up, knowing that he'd get an IV," I said. "How many of those vials of liquid potassium were stolen from Dr. Horz's office? Five, right?"

"Yup."

I began ticking the victims on my fingers. "One, Mrs. Tuttle. Two, Mrs. Divaram. Three, Mr. Pappas. Four, Mr. Fictura. That means that the killer still has one vial left." I looked around the room and spotted my cell phone on the dining room table. "I'm calling Crossing Manor. I want to know if anybody there has been put on a IV recently."

"Give me the phone," he said. "I'm the cop, remember?"

While he introduced himself over the phone and asked his

questions, I petted both dogs. "Are you good boys?" I asked. "Nod your heads if you are."

Neither dog nodded. "Hmm. Does that mean you're not good boys?"

Rascal's fur was wirier than Rochester's, with a greater pattern of color, black, white, brown all swirled together. My dog's coat was more monochromatic, all golden, though in shades from light to dark.

"Look at what big brown eyes you both have." I knew that because dogs were often active in dim light, their pupils were large, with less depth of field. "And you both have moist black noses." I touched each one in turn.

The dogs and I carried on a one-sided conversation until Rick was finished. "The nurse on duty says that one of the patients has been sick all day. A Mr. MacRae."

"We know him," I said. "He was a janitor at Crossing Elementary when we were kids." I stood up. "We should go over there. Make sure he's all right."

"I can handle it," Rick said.

"The Hardy Boys are a team," I said. "We'll leave the dogs here and head over there together."

"I could argue with you but that would just waste time. Let's move."

We grabbed our coats and told the dogs to behave while we were gone.

The parking lot at Crossing Manor was empty except for a couple of cars in the staff spaces. The wind was cold and I pulled my scarf tighter as we hurried to the front door. It was locked, and Rick had to press a button to alert the nurse to buzz us in.

We walked inside, and the warmth hit me. I quickly undid my scarf and unzipped my parka. Rick stopped to talk to the nurse on duty, an older African-American woman in dark blue scrubs, but I headed directly for Mr. MacRae's room.

The halls were quiet and I assumed most of the patients were asleep. The lights were dim, casting eerie shadows as I hurried along. Mr. MacRae's door was closed, but I pushed it open very quietly. His roommate, an elderly man with dementia, dozed in the bed by the door. The overhead light was off and the only illumination was a soft uplight above his head.

Dog Have Mercy

The curtain had been pulled between the two beds, but I could see light streaming out. As I stepped forward I heard the sound of retching.

I was surprised to see Allison standing by Mr. MacRae's bedside, wearing a heavy wool sweater and jeans. She held a pink plastic emesis basin in front of his mouth.

"Isn't this a school night?" I asked Allison. "I'm surprised to see you here."

She shook her head. "School doesn't start until Thursday," she said. "I knew Mr. MacRae was sick. There's only one nurse on duty at night and she gets busy, so I came over to look after him."

He finished and she put the basin aside. "I'm not sure if I want to go into a nursing program or be pre-med," she said she wiped Mr. MacRae's mouth with a wet towel

She looked fondly at the old man, who had closed his eyes and rested his head back against the pillow. "I just know that I want to help people. I've been talking to Mrs. Joiner a lot about palliative care." She patted Mr. MacRae's hair. "Do you know what that is?"

"Helping people with pain?" I asked.

"More than that. So many sick people are suffering, you know? Poor Mrs. Tuttle with her dementia. She didn't even know her own family anymore, and she was always moaning with pain."

I began to understand. "So you helped her," I said.

"That's it exactly," she said. "I used to sit with her and hold her hand, and it was so sad. In my AP chemistry class we studied potassium and I realized that if I could get hold of some, I could help her."

"You were the teenager who went to Dr. Horz's office at the end of the day," I said, remembering the conversation I'd had with the vet.

"I read somewhere that vets had liquid potassium in their offices. So I found a picture online of what the vials looked like, and when I took my dog in I said I had to go to the bathroom, and I went into her supply room."

She shifted position and behind her I saw Mr. MacRae's IV drip. There was a small vial attached to it. Holy crap. She was killing Mr. MacRae right in front of me. Where was Rick? The nurse?

I had to keep Allison talking as I moved closer to Mr. MacRae's bed. If I could pull the IV out of his hand, perhaps I could short-circuit the effect of the potassium. "But what about Mrs. Divaram?" I asked. "She wasn't sick."

"She was heartsick," Allison said. "Her son abandoned her. She had nothing left to live for."

I had a hard time not focusing on the silver stud on her tongue each time she opened her mouth, but I kept edging closer. "Mr. Pappas?"

"He had that terrible disease," she said. "He was never going to get any better."

"And Mr. Fictura?"

"I just didn't like him," she said. "He was so mean and nasty and he upset the other patients. As long as I had the potassium I gave some to him."

I was almost by Mr. MacRae's side. Allison was on the other side of the bed, by the pole that held the IV drip, but if I could reach his hand I could pull the IV out. It would hurt, I was sure, but it was the only way I could see to save his life.

I reached across the bed for the IV tube, but Allison grabbed my hand. "You can't do that," she said. "The people here, no one loves them, no one cares about them. They're sick and in pain. Mr. MacRae's kidneys are failing and the dialysis isn't working anymore."

"It's not up to you to help them," I said. "Let go of my hand and let me pull the IV out of Mr. MacRae's hand."

"No! You don't know what it's like, watching people die," she said. "My nana had Alzheimer's, but there was nothing else wrong with her, so she just hung on like forever. She didn't remember who we were and she cried all the time."

Mr. MacRae started coughing behind Allison, and that distracted her enough that I was able to pry her fingers off my hand and pull out the IV. Blood began to ooze out of Mr. MacRae's hand. "Rick!" I called. "Where are you? I need the nurse in here!"

I heard the door swing open. "What's going on?" Rick said, as he pulled aside the curtain.

"Allison put the potassium in Mr. MacRae's IV drip," I said, as the nurse followed Rick inside.

The nurse hurried over to Mr. MacRae's side. "What have you been doing, child?" she asked Allison.

"I just wanted to help him," Allison said, and she began to cry.

The nurse began working with the IV. "Can you call an

ambulance for me?" she asked Rick. "Tell them they'll need an IV with calcium gluconate. That will move the potassium out of his blood and into his cells."

"I'll call," I said.

Rick pulled another pair of plastic wrist restraints from his belt and walked over to Allison. He gently put the cuffs around her wrists and began to read her rights to her as I called 911 and the nurse worked on Mr. MacRae.

The old man looked up at the nurse and smiled weakly. "You just hold on, my darling," she said to him. "We'll have you right as rain in no time."

Rick led Allison out of the room and I followed, my heart racing. "I'll keep an eye on Allison until a unit arrives to take her to the station," he said. "And then once she's gone I'll need to do a lot of interviews. Can you stay in the lobby and open the door for the paramedics? And then I'm going to need you to come by the station and give a statement. Can you wait?"

"Sure."

By the time we walked out to the lobby, a black and white patrol car was pulling up at the front door. A blast of arctic air swept in as Rick turned over Allison to their custody and returned to Mr. MacRae's room.

I waited at the front door until the paramedics arrived and let them in. While they worked on Mr. MacRae, I called Lili.

"Where are you?" she asked. "I got home a couple of minutes ago to find two dogs and no Steve."

"At Crossing Manor," I said. I explained what had happened.

"What am I going to do with you, Steve? You didn't put yourself in danger again, did you?"

"No, I swear. I stumbled on Allison and she wasn't going to hurt me. She just wanted to help Mr. MacRae."

"I'll see what Rick says," Lili said. "I'm glad you were able to help Mr. MacRae. Call me if you need anything."

"I will, sweetheart. I love you."

"I love you, too, Steve."

While I waited for Rick to finish his interviews, Marilyn Joiner arrived. "What's going on?" she asked me. "Marie called and said Allison tried to kill Mr. MacRae."

I resisted the urge to gossip. "You'll have to talk to Detective

Stemper," I said.

"Then it's true." The color drained from Marilyn's face. "I thought Allison was such a sweet girl," she said. "She was so kind to the patients, and so dutiful. She was here all the time over the holidays. She and I talked a lot about what kind of career she should have."

"I think she took the concept of palliative medicine a bit too far," I said.

"I should have realized something." She was still wearing her wool coat, but she shivered. "I let her have access to all those patients. I was responsible for keeping them safe and I let them down." She shook her head. "Not to mention that was negligent and I'll probably lose my job, and Manor Associates could be hit with wrongful death lawsuits."

I didn't know whether Marilyn Joiner had been negligent or not, but I felt obliged to reassure her somehow. "I know things look bad," I said. "But trust me, I've been through a lot of bad stuff, and I know that if you just do your best things can get better."

The door behind us popped open and a pair of paramedics rolled Mr. MacRae past us on a gurney. "You hang in there," I said to him. "Rochester wants to come back and see you as soon as you get better."

"You got a fine dog," he said weakly, and then one paramedic opened the door and the cold air rushed in again.

Rick came out to the lobby and saw Marilyn Joiner. "It looks like I'm going to be here for a while," he said. "Allison Brezza's parents have already called a lawyer for her, so I'll be busy sorting her out after that. You can come in to the station tomorrow to give your statement."

"Sure. I'll call Lili and have her come pick me up."

While I waited for Lili, I paced around the lobby. Was there anything I could have done to stop the train of events—to save any of the patients at Crossing Manor, or Felix Logato?

I looked up at the wall at the photo of the woman with the scrunched face, the one who the poster said was having a stroke. Some things just happened, I thought. I had done what I could to bring comfort to the patients who had petted Rochester. I had tried to help Felix as best I could. That had to be enough.

Outside, I saw Lili pull up in front of the building, and then

Dog Have Mercy

Rochester hopped out of the front seat and followed her up to the door, which I opened for them.

Rochester romped over to me. He put his front paws up on my knees and licked my face. I leaned down to rest my head in his fur. "Rascal's in the car," Lili said. "But I thought you'd want to see Rochester."

"You were right," I said, looking up again. "I wanted to see both of you." I took a deep breath. "I had it wrong. I thought whoever stole the potassium had to work at the vet's office. It wasn't until a couple of days ago that I even considered it could be someone who brought a dog or cat in."

"You aren't the cop," Lili said, taking my hand. "It wasn't your responsibility."

"I know. But if I'd figured it out sooner, maybe fewer people would have died." I sat up. "And then there's Felix. I wish I could have helped him more."

"I'd say you have your hands full," Lili said. "You have me, and Rochester. You have your job at Friar Lake." She squeezed my hand. "You're a good man, Steve. But you can't take on the problems of the world by yourself."

Rochester pressed his body against my thigh. "Not by myself," I said. "I have Rochester to help. And you for backup." I leaned over and kissed her, and Rochester did his best to snuggle between us.

Neil S. Plakcy

I hope you enjoyed spending time with Steve and Rochester! Have you read the previous books in the series?

1. In Dog We Trust

After a bad divorce and a brief prison term for computer hacking, 42-year-old Steve Levitan has returned to his home town of Stewart's Crossing and taken a part-time job as an adjunct professor of English at his alma mater, Eastern College. While walking around his gated community, he becomes friendly with his next-door neighbor, Caroline Kelly, and her golden retriever, Rochester.

When Caroline is shot and killed while walking Rochester, Steve becomes the dog's temporary guardian. Together, these two unlikely sleuths work to uncover the mystery behind Caroline's death.

2. The Kingdom of Dog.

When his mentor, Joe Dagorian, director of admissions at prestigious Eastern College, is murdered during a fund-raising event, Steve Levitan feels obliged to investigate. He and his golden retriever, Rochester, go nose to the ground to dig up clues, including a bloody knife and some curious photographs. But will Steve's curiosity and Rochester's savvy save them when the killer comes calling?

Second in Neil S. Plakcy's Golden Retriever Mysteries, The Kingdom of Dog is funny and charming-- and who can resist a gregarious golden character like Rochester?

3. Dog Helps Those.

It's almost time for graduation, and Eastern College is in trouble. A prominent alumna is dead, and a faulty computer program is jeopardizing student records and financial aid. It's up to Steve and Rochester to dig into the situation and retrieve the culprits!

Dog Have Mercy

Rita Gaines wasn't a nice person—but she did love her dogs, and most of her clients respected her financial acumen and her talent in training dogs for agility trials. When she's found dead, there's a long line of potential suspects from Wall Street whiz kids to doting doggie daddies-- including one of Steve's former students.

Felae is an art prodigy now studying with Steve's girlfriend, Lili, chair of Eastern's Fine Arts department, and Rita hated his controversial senior project. When she tried to have his scholarship cancelled, he threatened to kill her. But is he the villain behind her death?

4. Dog Bless You.

Autumn has come to Bucks County, and Steve Levitan has a new job: develop a conference center for Eastern College at Friar Lake, a few miles from campus. But on his first visit to the property, his golden retriever Rochester makes a disturbing discovery, a human hand rising from the dirt at the lake's shore.

Whose hand is it? Why was the body buried there? The answers will take Steve, his photographer girlfriend Lili, and the ever-faithful Rochester to a drop-in center for recovering drug addicts on the Lower East Side, a decaying church in Philadelphia's Germantown, and finally to a confrontation with a desperate killer.

5. Whom Dog Hath Joined.

Reformed computer hacker Steve Levitan still gets a thrill from snooping into places online where he shouldn't be. When his golden retriever Rochester discovers a human bone at the Friends Meeting during the Harvest Days festival, these two unlikely sleuths are plunged into another investigation.

They will uncover uncomfortable secrets about their small town's past as they dig deep into the Vietnam War era, when local Quakers helped draft resisters move through Stewart's Crossing on their way to Canada. Does that bone Rochester found belong to one of those young men fleeing conscription? Or to someone who knew the secrets that lurked behind those whitewashed walls?

Neil S. Plakcy

Steve's got other problems, too. His girlfriend Lili wants to move in with him, and his matchmaking efforts among his friends all seem to be going haywire.

Whether the death was due to natural causes, or murder, someone in the present wants to keep those secrets hidden. And Steve and Rochester may end up in the crosshairs of a very antique

ABOUT THE AUTHOR

Neil Plakcy's golden retriever mysteries have been inspired by his own goldens, Samwise, Brody and Griffin. A native of Bucks County, PA, where the books are set, Neil is a graduate of the University of Pennsylvania, Columbia University and Florida International University, where he received his MFA in creative writing.

He has written and edited many other books; details can be found at his website, http://www.mahubooks.com. Neil, his partner, Brody and Griffin live in South Florida, where Neil is writing and the dogs are undoubtedly getting into mischief.